# SKINNER'S HORSE

BY THE SAME AUTHOR

*(as Philip Woodruff)*

Call the Next Witness
The Wild Sweet Witch
The Island of Chamba
Whatever Dies
The Sword of Northumbria
Hernshaw Castle
Colonel of Dragoons
The Men Who Ruled India:
*Volume I,* The Founders
*Volume II,* The Guardians

*(as Philip Mason)*

An Essay on Racial Tension
Christianity and Race
The Birth of a Dilemma: The Conquest and Settlement of Rhodesia
Year of Decision: Rhodesia and Nyasaland, 1960
Common Sense About Race
Prospero's Magic: Thoughts on Class and Race
Patterns of Dominance
Race Relations
Man, Race and Darwin *(editor)*
India and Ceylon: Unity and Diversity *(editor)*
A Matter of Honour
Kipling: The Glass, the Shadow and the Fire
The Dove in Harness
A Shaft of Sunlight

PHILIP MASON

# SKINNER'S HORSE

HARPER & ROW, PUBLISHERS
NEW YORK
Cambridge
Hagerstown
Philadelphia
San Francisco

London
Mexico City
São Paulo
Sydney
1817

**FOR GEORGE**

This work was first published in England under the title *Skinner of Skinner's Horse*.

 For information address Harper & Row, Publishers, Inc., 10 East 53rd Street, New York, N.Y. 10022.

FIRST U.S. EDITION

---

Library of Congress Cataloging in Publication Data

Mason, Philip.
Skinner's Horse.
First published in 1979 under title: Skinner of Skinner's Horse.
1. Skinner, James, 1778-1841—Fiction. I. Title.
PZ3.M38577Sk [PR6025.A7926] 823'.9'14 79-1803
ISBN 0-06-013036-9

---

80 81 82 83 84 10 9 8 7 6 5 4 3 2 1

# Contents

# PART ONE
# COUNTRY-BORN

## 1 The Dagger

THAT day in 1790, when he was twelve years old, was the last of James Skinner's childhood. It was a day he never forgot but could hardly bear to remember. For a long time his thoughts would come back to it and then shy away like a frightened horse. Then he would find he was remembering, dwelling on every detail with a sick fascinated horror.

His father was a captain in the service of the East India Company and the regiment had been stationed in Bengal, first at Barrackpur and then at Calcutta, for as long as James could remember. His had been a happy childhood till that day. He had watched the soldiers drilling in their red coats under the English flag, tall handsome brown men who teased him and laughed at him when they came off duty, but did everything he wanted them to do because he was their captain's son. He had listened to their stories and to the stories his mother told him about her own people, the Rajputs, the princes and warriors of the North. She had told him a Rajput must never fear death; she had filled him with stories of last stands against fearful odds and of desperate charges. He was proud that his mother was a Rajput. Out there in the sunshine, away from his mother, playing with other boys or simply dreaming, he would picture himself, as boys will, leading a charge or storming a fort, and then suddenly he would be a child and one of the overwhelming woes of childhood would engulf him and he would run to his mother for comfort. That was how it had been in his childhood, which came to an end on that day.

It was the middle of the forenoon and already it was hot. He was happy but he was tired and thirsty. He came in from the burning sunshine and went through the curtains into his mother's part of the house, sure that he would find comfort there, rest and certainty and love, all he asked for, all he always did find. It was cool in the women's quarters; the light was muted; it was as though dusk was falling. There was a scent of sandalwood and jasmine. His mother gave him a drink of cool buttermilk; the mild sourish taste slaked his parched throat. He sat down by his mother, whose hand gently ruffled his head. He was the centre of her interest as soon as he came. She was beautiful, fine of feature, with a proud nose and great wide eyes, still slim after bearing six children, not yet thirty.

She asked James if she should tell him a story and he said that was just what he wanted. Should she tell him a story of the *jauhar*, she asked, that last desperate defiance of death, when there is no hope left, when the Rajput warriors put on saffron robes and ride out for a last charge to certain death and the women throw themselves living on the funeral pyre? No, not that, he said, and she began to tell him a tale he knew well, but loved to hear again, of a Rajput prince who fought till all his men were killed and then broke from his enemies and rode for home. But the gate of his castle was barred and from the battlements he heard his wife's voice. She knew her husband was dead; he would never have left the battle defeated and alive. That must be a ghost she heard at the gate. She had lighted the pyre and was about to throw herself into the flames to die with her husband. So the prince turned wearily back to meet his enemies and die.

James listened enthralled. Then, suddenly, his father burst through the curtains. He was still in his regimentals; that in itself was startling. Usually, when he came into the women's side of the house he would have changed into soft, white Indian clothes, cool and loose. Now he stood there, stiff and angular in scarlet serge and gold lace and tight breeches. He had something to say. He wanted to be out with it and be done with it. He could not wait. In the half-light, he looked harsh and forbidding. It was not his nature to be harsh but he took refuge in harshness to get his way. He was a little afraid of the fierceness he knew he would find in his wife.

'I've made up my mind,' he said. 'There must be no more talk. Everything is arranged. Tomorrow the girls will go to school. They must learn to read and write and behave like English ladies.'

His mother began to speak in a hard strained voice, like the scrape of a man burnishing a sword. 'You've made up your mind? You want to take everything from me? You mean to take my daughters away and hawk them round the world and sell them to the highest bidder like harlots in the bazaar? Am I not a Rajput? Am I not of a noble family? Is there nothing to be left me of my honour? Do you not know that to a Rajput honour is more than life? I shall kill myself, I tell you. You shall not do it. I had sooner die. I shall kill myself.'

Her voice rose as she whipped up her anger and gave it rein. He tried to reason with her, his homely Scottish voice growing more tender as he spoke. Jeanie, he called her, perhaps to bring her closer to his own remote childhood. But his Hindi came slowly and sounded Scottish, prosaic, legal.

'Will you no' be sensible, Jeanie? Will you no' look at what cannot be avoided?'

James heard no more. One of his mother's maids caught him by the arm and led him out. He went with her in a kind of daze. He heard his mother's voice go on and on; wild words about death and honour reached him, fragments screamed at the top of her voice; he heard his father shout back at her, trying to make himself heard. Then his father came out, sweating, out of breath, his face red. He stood on the veranda, mopping his brow. He saw the boy.

'Och, Jamie,' he said in English, half to his son, half to himself. 'Your mother – women are the devil. I love your mother, Jamie, but can she no' *see*? It stares her in the face but she won't *see*. What's to become of your sisters if they don't marry Englishmen? Where's the sense of talking about Rajputs? No Rajput will marry my daughters. No Rajput would eat in their presence or in mine. No Englishman will marry them either unless they can read and write. They'll be safe at school. The missionary ladies will look after them. When they know how to behave like ladies we'll find husbands for them fast enough.'

He looked again at the boy. 'I'm not being unkind,' he said. 'She'll get over it. She'll come round. She's in a rage now but she's been in rages before. Your mother's a grand woman, Jamie, there's no one like her. If only she'd *see* that this makes sense and nothing else does.' He paused, sighed, looked at his son uncertainly, then walked away along the veranda to his own part of the bungalow.

James Skinner sat there on the veranda thinking of his mother. He understood her feelings better than his father did. He had heard so many of her stories about Rajput pride; he was half a Rajput himself. *She* would have behaved like the princess in the story. She would have thrown herself among the blazing flames. She put courage and honour before everything. And at that moment there came a scream from the women behind the curtain. He ran in, and there was a crowd of women bending over her; one had turned away and was weeping silently. One was still screaming, gazing, her hands to her mouth. James pushed through them and saw his mother. She lay on the floor, crumpled; there was a little blood coming from her mouth and a pool of blood beside her.

'What has she done? What has she done?' he heard someone cry. 'She used the steel,' he heard another woman say. 'She drove the dagger to her heart. She was a Rajput. She knew she must die.'

Then a second time they led him away.

That was the end of his childhood. After that, there was no hand to ruffle his hair; no kind and beautiful face; no voice to tell him stories; no sweet-smelling dusk where he could escape from pain and mockery. He was on his own now.

## 2 Bondage

MANY years later, when James Skinner came to write an account of his life, he said very little about his mother's death. 'My poor mother,' he says, 'put herself to death.' She was afraid that 'the Rajput honour would be destroyed' because her daughters were 'removed from the care of their female relatives'. That is all.

What it meant to him at the time can only be imagined by picturing the scene, pondering on it, remembering how later he spoke always with such reverence of Rajput honour, surely thinking then of his mother, perhaps thinking too of that other Hindu girl whom later he saved from being burned alive with the corpse of her husband. Surely in that moment of shock and conflict when he saw his mother bleeding on the ground lies the key to much of his own readiness to throw away his life? Surely he saw her again in his dreams, young and happy and loving? And then the dream would turn to horror as his father burst in, stiff, angular, scarlet. Once again, he would be taken away from her cool sweet-smelling presence, helpless, only a boy in the hands of grown people, leaving her – *his* mother – alone with that spiky menacing figure. And then the dream would change and he would see her again. Crumpled, dead, stiffening, cooling, in a pool of her warm, vivid blood.

In his waking moments, he shrank from that horror. He records the bare fact. 'My poor mother put herself to death. . . .' Nor does he say anything, in his memoirs, about the five years that followed his mother's death, except that for the last two he had been at a boarding-school. No doubt that too was a time he did not care to think about. One side of his life had been wrenched away. The household went on; servants prepared food; there were women in the women's quarters and he was cared for. But there was no one now to share his thoughts with, no one to whom every concern of his was important.

His school he mentions only once, when he says, after a

battle between the two great Maratha chiefs, Scindia and Holkar, that among the dead were no less than sixteen of his schoolfellows, officers killed on one side or the other. It must have been a school intended mainly for the sons of officers of the East India Company's army and most of them had Indian mothers. A voyage to England at that time usually took nine months or a year, sometimes eighteen months; an English wife was still something of a rarity and the time had not yet come when children born in India were sent 'home' as a matter of course. 'Country-born' was the name used for these children of Indian mothers.

It was a time when 'the great English schools', as the phrase went, were brutal and often cruel. They were meant to prepare a boy for life in a harsh world, to make him 'manly', which meant that he should be self-reliant and should endure pain with courage. No doubt James's school was modelled on 'the great English schools' and added to his character an outer mask of withdrawn stoic self-sufficiency. But while at Westminster high standards of scholarship might sometimes be set off against the brutality, at an imitation Westminster in Calcutta, one can be more confident of the brutality than of the scholarship. Skinner's Persian, however, was good, both spoken and written, and he was master of the mathematics that an officer needs.

It is only a guess that at school he felt himself separated from his schoolfellows; he does not say so. But his brother Robert was too young to be altogether a companion and a quick, sensitive and intelligent boy does often have such a feeling. James Skinner was marked by his mother's death, still more by what she had taught him. No one else of his age had had a mother like his, a Rajput of a landowning family. No one else had had a mother so beautiful, so fierce and so high-spirited, so proud of the traditions of her people. That she – who had borne children to an outcast infidel – should have resented for her daughters what she had accepted for herself did not strike James as inconsistent. He thought with his emotions. Something of her lived on in him and set him apart.

When he first saw her, Hercules Skinner, James's father, had looked at the girl who was to be his wife only with desire for her beauty. She had come into his hands as a captive in war, when she was a girl of fifteen. James wrote later that this happened in the course of the operations against Raja Chait Singh of Benares, but that expedition took place when James was already three years old. Perhaps that was what his father told him or allowed him to suppose; it was all James knew – she never spoke of it. However it came about, she was suddenly the prisoner of a strange barbarian conqueror – red-faced, blue-eyed, like a creature from hell. She stood before him, trembling with fear and passion, like a wild hawk, ready to strike. She was still a child in all but body. But he pitied her; he was tender and kind; he waked her as a hawk is waked, he mastered her, he tamed her a little; he came to love her and even to fear her a little. She bore him six children.

Hercules Skinner had of course been right when he told her that there was no future for his daughters unless they married Englishmen – a phrase in which, in the usage of the day, he would have included himself, a Scot. No Rajput would take in marriage a child of mixed breeding. But she would not listen to reason. Five years later he must have thought his wife had come alive again as he put to James arguments that to him seemed just as unassailably sensible and met the same perversely emotional response.

'But, Jamie, can you no' see,' he said, 'that you're neither English nor Rajput and I must do the best I can for you? Can ye no' *see*? If you were English, I could get you a commission in the Company's service. You might be a country cadet, as I was myself, commissioned out here. But there's a rule against that now; you know it well. Your mother was a native of India and they'll not commission you. It's the law. If you were a Rajput, I could take you as a recruit and you could rise to be a subedar. But you're not a Rajput either. You're country-born. There's no place now in the army for one of your birth. I'm to blame. I know it. I know it well. I blame myself severely.'

'But, Father, I *want* to be a soldier, I want it more than anything. Can I not serve a native prince?'

'Ah, you've been hearing tales of the fortunes these adventurers make. But for one that makes a fortune there's a score that are killed before they're thirty. And what would you do when there was war with the British? It'll come in the end, sooner or later. This prince of yours couldn't trust you then. You'd be clapped in gaol or have your head cut off or worse. No, I've found you a safe line of life that will bring you a comfortable living when you're old – and I can't do more than that for you. You're apprenticed to a printer and you'll start tomorrow. In seven years you'll be out of your indentures and earning good money.'

'But, Father, I *must* be a soldier,' James cried in despair. 'Let me go North and try to get employment, under de Boigne, like my schoolfellows.'

But Hercules Skinner was as obstinate as his wife and son. He had no influence, he said; he could do nothing for his son in the North. Anyhow, he was marching with the regiment next morning for Cawnpore. It was too late to make changes now. He had made an arrangement that was in his son's best interests and with a friend of his, a fellow countryman, and James must do as he was told. They parted sulkily and angrily and James was still sulky and angry next day when he went into bondage to the printer.

## 3 Escape

THE printer was a stout pursy little man from Dundee. His printing-works and his bungalow stood side by side in a compound – two acres of open ground on the edge of the city; there was a low mud wall round the compound and behind the bungalow and the printing-works a little village of servants' quarters. James Skinner was to eat at the printer's table and sleep in his bungalow but his new master did not look at him with a friendly eye.

'Ye'll learn this trade from the bottom up,' he said. 'First, ye'll spread ink on these blocks of type, as these native boys are doing. You must learn to get it even or it's no good. Ye'll keep on till the work's finished, all night if need be.'

James was at it till two in the morning and it was the same the next day and the day after. He sat gloomy and silent at meals in the printer's house. During the third day he made up his mind to run away. It had been in his mind, as a possibility, half an intention, from the moment he went. He was a strong boy of seventeen and he was sure they would take him on a ship.

There was nothing difficult about the escape. Doors and windows are never shut in India and the *chaukidar* – the night-watchman – knew him. Instead of walking from the printing-works to the bungalow, when he finished at night, he just walked out of the compound and in a hundred yards he was lost in the bazaar – a rabbit warren of little shops and lanes and warehouses. He went on and on till he was far from the printer's compound. He found a doorway closed by a big wooden gate. It looked deserted, and he slept there on the ground with his back to the gate. No one took any notice of him.

He had nothing in his pocket but four *annas*, which would buy him two days' food, and one battered old spoon. Apart from that, he had only the shirt and trousers he was wearing. The spoon was one of his earliest memories. It had been a plaything – the only toy he possessed. Indeed, it had been the only possession that was really his own, for clothes to a child seem part of his skin. The spoon had come to be more than a toy. When he was very small, he would talk to it, tell it secrets and ask it questions. It would tell him the future and make comments on grown people that he would not have put into words on his own authority. Sometimes he would tell his mother what the spoon had said to him. Later, his mother had taught him to use his spoon for his rice. He was an Englishman, she had told him, and must eat rice with his spoon and not with his fingers. He was a Rajput, too, she always added, and must never forget that a Rajput was a warrior and a prince. So the spoon came to stand for his double heritage as well as for his own separate identity as a person in his own right, a person who could own something that was his and no one else's. And since his mother's death it had been doubly precious. It was the one link with her.

His clothes showed he was not a native Indian. But in complexion he was as brown as his mother. Hindi, the language of Northern India, was the tongue of his mother and his mother's personal servants and of the Indian soldiers in his father's regiment. It was the language that came first to his lips. But he had picked up Bengali from the lower servants, the sweepers and gardeners and grooms and washermen, and he spoke it well enough. He begged a twig of *neem*, chewed it into a toothbrush and cleaned his teeth. He spent one of his *annas* on a double handful of cooked rice, served on a banana leaf, and a couple of *chapatis*. There was a man unloading bags of rice from bullock-carts at the shop where he bought this food. He helped this man to unload and by working with him all day earned the price of his supper.

Of course he didn't mean to do this sort of thing for ever. He was going to run away to sea – but he did not go down to the waterfront yet. The sea meant nothing to him. For the moment this life was better than smearing ink on blocks of type. And something might turn up. A shred of irrational hope numbed his will. He found a carpenter grumbling angrily because the boy who worked his drill had run away. He offered to help and bargained for two *annas* a day. He held a bow, a bent stick with enough spring in it to hold tight a string wound twice round the drill. The carpenter held the wood with his feet and guided the drill to the point where he wanted a hole. It was James Skinner's task to push the bow backwards and forwards, briskly but steadily, when the carpenter gave him the word. It needed some skill but he learnt quickly.

He was improving rapidly at this when he heard a voice that seemed familiar. Someone was speaking to the carpenter sharply, in a tone that was haughty and bullying.

'Son of an owl! Child of a pig! What are you doing! Where is the chair you were to mend for us?'

'Great king! Maharaj! Forgive! All my work has gone wrong. The boy ran away; I have only this *kirani* to help me and he knows nothing.'

James did not like to be called a *kirani*, which means a native Christian or an Anglo-Indian clerk; it is not a polite word. He looked up in protest.

'I am not a *kirani*,' he was beginning – when he saw the face of the man who had just come. They stared at each other in astonishment. The other man spoke first. His manner had changed altogether.

'Jamie Sahib! Chota Sahib! Why are you not at home? What is this you are doing?'

It was Nagendra Singh, one of his mother's old servants, a Rajput from Upper India. He had known James since he was a baby and called him Chota Sahib, the little Sahib. Nagendra Singh had left the service of Hercules Skinner when James's sister Margaret married Mr Templeton; he had gone with her to the new master.

James answered him rather sullenly. 'My father' – he used a polite formal term, *mera walid*, to show he meant no disrespect – 'my honoured father put me to work with a white man' – and this time he used a word which means a white man without education or good manners – 'who made me smear ink on bits of metal. It was not work for a Rajput nor for an Englishman. So I ran away.'

'And is this work for a Rajput or for an Englishman? This man is a carpenter, a village servant. *I* couldn't take a drink of water from him. No Rajput could. And you're *working* for him! Listen, Jamie Sahib, you must come with me. Captain Burn Sahib is coming soon. He is your father's friend, he held you in his arms when you were a baby, when you were given a name; he has always loved you. He will think of a way to make you a soldier – as a Rajput should be, as an

Englishman should be. Carpenters and printers! These are not people for your mother's son. Come with me, Jamie Sahib. I served your mother and her father. I know what is right for you.'

James turned back to the drill. He wasn't going to be ordered about. But he was a boy of sense; he stopped to think. He saw that what Nagendra Singh said was reasonable. He got slowly to his feet. He felt in his pocket. He had just two *annas* left and those he gave to the carpenter; it was a proper gesture for a Rajput, the gesture of a prince. He went with Nagendra Singh.

## 4 The River

HIS sister Margaret ran to meet him with a cry of joy. She was fairer than James, no darker than an Italian. There was a sing-song note in her English, a little like the Welsh, a touch of sharpness on sounds the English blur; but except for that the missionaries had made her just like any of the middle-class English ladies in Calcutta. She had heard nothing of James escaping from the printer. But she was a little scared of what her husband might say.

Mr Templeton was a lawyer and had no sympathy with anyone who wanted to be a soldier. He made that very clear. There was no certainty of advancement in the army unless you had influence and, even if you had, there were obvious risks to health and life. To be a printer was not very genteel but it was safe and lucrative; it was mere idleness for James to run away from the career his father had chosen for him. That was the burden of the scolding he administered. Behind what he said was the feeling that this had all been arranged and to change it meant trouble – unpaid work and expense and an unsettled problem. However, he was fond of his wife in a dusty respectable way and to please her he agreed that James should stay till his godfather Captain Burn arrived.

Meanwhile, he should earn his keep as a lawyer's clerk by copying legal documents.

James knew that his father respected Captain Burn and looked up to him. It was not only that he was senior to his father in the regiment; he had been on the staff, he knew people in a wider world than the regimental. He had money of his own. He was sure of promotion; he would go far. James of course was a little in awe of him, but he had always been aware of his goodwill and he was the one source from which some good might come. James was suddenly full of hope.

Captain Burn came to dinner with Mr Templeton a day or two after he reached Calcutta. After dinner, he carried James away from the drawing room into the lawyer's study. James went with an apprehension which he hid beneath a silence that might have been thought sulky, but when alone with this easy, genial, smiling gentleman he quickly felt at ease; here was someone who understood him, someone who was ready to like him.

'You see, I want to be a soldier, sir,' he said – in English not quite so fluent as his Hindi, and a little more Welsh in intonation than his sister's. 'My father is a soldier and my mother's people are soldiers. We are Rajputs, you know. I am born to be a soldier. I ought to make a good soldier.'

'Yes, there's something in that and it's a noble profession and a proper one for a young man of spirit. But there are difficulties, James, as you know.'

'In the Company's service, yes – I know, sir. But could I not serve a prince? If I served him truly I might rise to high rank.'

'Well – I *have* met de Boigne. He's made a fine army for the Maharaja Scindia. I could give you a letter to him and I think he might take to you. His officers are a terrible lot – French deserters, Irish adventurers, Alsatian butchers. Not bad soldiers, some of them – in fact most of them good soldiers – but some of them ruffians. He'd be glad of you. The men are good stuff – just like our own sepoys. You'd see plenty of service and you'd get command very quickly, years and years before you would with us. But – how can I make you see the risks you'd be running?'

'There must always be risks,' said James.

'Ah, but I don't mean fair risk by sword or bullet. As you say, that's part of a soldier's life. No, I mean that you may wake up one morning and find you're in disgrace, not because of anything you've done, but because of a change at court – a new favourite perhaps – and the man you've been serving with absolute fidelity is out of a job and lucky if he hasn't had his ears cut off and been hanged into the bargain.'

'But I'd risk that!' said James eagerly.

'Of course you would, because you can't really have any understanding of what I mean. The question is whether I ought to let you run the risk.' He paused and looked long at James. He liked him; he felt drawn to the boy and he shared altogether his feeling that to be a printer or even a lawyer in Calcutta was no life for a man. He made up his mind.

'A boy like you shouldn't be wasted copying old papers. Come – give me your hand – I'll help you if only your father agrees. We'll go to Cawnpore together and see what he says.'

So it was settled and a few weeks later they started up the River Ganges together in a budgerow, a kind of house-boat or barge. Another boat followed with the servants and the kitchen stuff. Sometimes the budgerow sailed before the wind; sometimes, in a reach where the wind would not carry them, it was rowed or it was towed by bullocks on the bank; some time after midday and well before evening it was tied up and they would land to stretch their legs and walk through the fields – bright and fresh with young crops – in the hope of a brace or two of partridges or some snipe for their supper.

One day was strangely like another yet each was different. Sometimes there would be water everywhere, the river itself two miles across and lagoons of shallow water shining among the sand dunes, millions of birds wading and floating among the water-lilies and the lotus, a glare and glitter of bright light on smooth water and white sand. Sometimes the banks would close in and they would float in a narrow channel between islands. In that flat green country, the water changed its course every year after the rains, dividing and coming together so that it made a network, as fine as Honiton lace. A boat nosing its way up the river without a guide would have been lost in a maze of winding channels. Even the *serang*, who had lived all his life on the river, had to learn afresh every season where the banks might lie and where the boat might run aground; a man stood always in the bows with a lead, calling the depth in a monotonous sing-song. 'Two fathoms! Two fathoms and a quarter! No bottom!'

Burn sat under an awning in the stern and spent much of the day reading; James gazed and gazed. The little pied kingfisher hovered with quickly beating wings or plunged like a stone to come up with a fish; the Ganges tern flashed and swooped in graceful flight; herons, plovers and duck of every kind stalked on the sandbanks or waded in shallow water or sprang suddenly into the air with cries that were harsh, melodious or piping. Time had no meaning any longer; there was only the brown water sliding past the boat, the wake eddying in dimpled modulation, the creak of mast and boom, the waterfowl, the gliding banks with great black water-buffaloes and white cattle-egrets sitting on their backs, women with water pots staring at this apparition and calling to each other, now and then a log on a sandbank turning suddenly into a crocodile and plunging beneath the surface. There was no other way of life, only the river and the barge, light flashing on ripples, blinding sun and the smell of river water and the shifting shade of the sail.

Imperceptible as their progress seemed, they were moving in time as well as in space. They crept across the face of India; the earth tilted; the season drew on. You could not say that one day was longer than another but after a week you were aware of a change. Early February is still the cold weather, late March is the beginning of the hot. They moved in time at the pace of a celestial snail, on the river at the pace of an ox, but the day grew longer and the sun fiercer, the air sharper and drier, and the cool of the evening came more suddenly. They had left Bengal behind.

He was drugged by the sun, hypnotized by ripple and eddy and running water. But there were times when James withdrew from this timeless contemplation of the river and talked to his godfather about India as it was in 1795. He was very ignorant. No one at school had taught him anything about the times he lived in. They had taught him something about Alexander the Great, nothing of Clive. He knew that the British were rulers of Bengal and Bihar – two great provinces – but how or why he could not say. They were foreigners to him, though he was also somehow one of them. They were foreign to the land he knew. He knew that they had some footing away in the South and the West, in Madras and Bombay – but these places were far from Bengal and in his ears sounded almost as strange as England. He had heard of the Mughal Emperor at Delhi but had no idea of whether he still had powerful armies nor of whether his edicts still ran in broad territories or in none at all. He knew that there were powerful Maratha princes – Scindia, Holkar and the Peshwa – but whether they were allies or enemies to each other and how they stood in relation to the Emperor – these were matters about which he had never been told and about which he had not concerned himself. All he did know for certain was that somewhere near Delhi there was an army under General de Boigne where country-born boys from his own school could be commissioned. Knowing so little, he was reluctant to expose the depth of his ignorance. He would try sometimes to persuade Captain Burn to talk and to pick up what he could of the background. But he was shy of direct questioning.

During the six weeks of their journey, James came to know his godfather well. He was tolerant in his judgments about people and the way they behaved – not expecting too much, slow to condemn. But he insisted on exact obedience from his servants and in return looked after them carefully. He was interested in all he could learn of the people of India and their ways. James now felt confident that his father would agree to anything Captain Burn proposed. He tried to sound him about the life that lay before him and he talked himself, telling the captain much that he had heard from his father's sepoys and recounting the stories his mother had told him. Captain Burn was interested in it all. No doubt as they talked he was aware that James wanted to learn without asking and with an amused irony answered that desire by telling without teaching.

One way and another, James learned a great deal. He came, for instance, to understand how quickly the Marathas had degenerated. A peasant people, hardy, brave, unhampered by the scruples of chivalry and honour that were everything to the Rajputs, the cavalry hordes of the Marathas had swept across India a century ago. They had had no guns, no infantry; they could not undertake a siege. But they moved with unheard-of speed – sleeping with the bridle on the arm, living on a handful of parched gram and giving their horses not much more – fighting at first simply to throw off the rule of the Mughal Emperor, later for plunder rather than conquest. Their terms for peace were simple: a quarter of his revenue to the Marathas every year and any prince might be their vassal.

All that had changed. With wealth and conquest had come luxury. Now – in 1795 – their armies moved ponderously with long trains of elephants, with women and merchants and bullock-carts and great tents with silk hangings. Once they had been one people with one military commander who was their leader in everything. That was Sivaji. But in three generations the descendants of Sivaji had been reduced to a purely ritual supremacy. They counted for nothing now. The five great officers of state under Sivaji had made themselves hereditary rulers, independent chiefs loosely linked in a confederacy of which the Peshwa – the descendant of Sivaji's prime minister – was nominally the head. But the convention was observed only when it suited the others. Of the other four, Scindia and Holkar were usually at daggers drawn with each other and often with the Peshwa. Sometimes they were openly at war with each other. Of the five great Maratha States, two do not come into the story of James Skinner. Scindia was the most powerful of the five at this stage, because he had a force of disciplined infantry under de Boigne.

'But mark my words, Jamie,' said Captain Burn, 'it's a double-edged weapon, this famous army of de Boigne's. Scindia can use it to beat any other native prince – and so far it's a strength. But against us – it's a weakness. It's playing our game – and at our own game of course we can beat them. We'd have had the devil of a job to beat the old Maratha cavalry. No army of ours could have caught them. But de Boigne knows that. I'm not sure his master does.'

One evening when the boat tied up they walked to a stretch of water where they were told the wild duck came flighting in at dusk. They were a little too early and sat talking.

'Tell me more, sir, about General de Boigne,' James asked, for once breaking through his shyness.

'De Boigne?' said Burn thoughtfully. 'He's rather a great man, I think. A born soldier. He comes from Savoy, near Switzerland. He had a commission in the Irish Brigade in the French army once – but he left because there seemed no likelihood of promotion. He's not a French subject. Fought for the Russians against the Turks. He was taken prisoner, I believe, but got away somehow. Adventurous life. Then he was in our service, on the Madras side. I did hear there was some trouble about a brother officer's wife but I don't know. Shouldn't repeat it really. I dare say slow promotion was the trouble once again. Anyhow, he resigned. Then he turned up in the North, took service with Scindia – and now – well, he's master of Hindostan. He's organized this disciplined army, trained like ours, drilled like ours. Their confidence is tremendous. They've won battle after battle. De Boigne is really the ruler of Northern India. His territory's as big as the British.'

'It's very puzzling,' said James. 'I thought the Emperor – '

'Ah, the Emperor. The last of the Mughals. Well, you see, James, nothing in India is quite what it seems. The last Mughal Emperor – Shah Alam, the King of the World – you're right, he's ruler of everything – in name. But only in name. We rule in his name. We do everything in the Emperor's name. We are his deputies for Bengal and Bihar – but he knows very well he can't move a man or a horse in our ground. And in the North too it's much the same. There the Marathas have the power, just as we have here. The Emperor has made the Peshwa his deputy for everything – all the way from Bombay to the Himalayas. The Peshwa's *supposed* to be the Emperor's man. The Peshwa is *supposed* to be the head of the Marathas. Scindia is *supposed* to be the Peshwa's man. But in fact the Emperor knows he has no strength at all – the Peshwa knows that he can't do anything in the North without Scindia – and Scindia knows that his strength depends on de Boigne.'

'Because de Boigne is a better soldier than anyone else?'

'Because he's – reliable. He *is* a good soldier too. He's a good trainer. He has his men so trained that they know just what to do. As though by instinct – in the middle of battle. And his men are faithful – absolutely. Most battles in India are won because somebody changes sides. Not de Boigne's troops. They've never lost a gun. Nor a colour. For one thing – but that's not the whole story – his are about the only troops in India, except ours, who get their pay regularly. Most of the soldiers in India are a year in arrears – some of them two years. There's always something else for a prince to spend money on. Anything else comes first – and the soldier comes last! Who can blame them for changing sides?'

'Our sepoys used often to say that only the Company's men got their pay regularly.'

'De Boigne's too. He has forty thousand men now, in four brigades – and he insisted that he must be practically a prince – have territory allotted – before he'd raise a man. He collects the revenue from half a dozen districts and he makes his troops the first charge on that money. He sees that those districts are peaceful too. He gives a pension to a wounded man – pensions to widows and old soldiers. Oh, he's a great man – practically a prince, and one of the most powerful in India. A fine man to serve under. And one thing – he made it a condition when he joined Scindia that he'd never fight against the British. He knows very well that we have training and discipline and regular pay just as much as he has – and better officers and more of them too. Sometimes he has only two to a battalion. Come on, those duck'll soon be here. We must get to our hides.'

The duck came whirring in through the green dusk over still, golden water, a myriad swerving as one living creature, swerving again, quicker than the twinkling of an eye, quickening the heart with their swiftness. The guns spurted fire. Men splashed through the shallows to pick the birds up.

James and Captain Burn walked back to the boat in the half dark. There was a sharpness in the air; it was colder than James had ever known before. The air had cooled so quickly after the heat of noon that it pressed down on the earth and spread the scents of the day in overlapping layers. They passed through the raw smell of mud and marsh to the smell of dust and the smell of fields lately irrigated and then, as they came near a village, to a rapid succession of intoxicating scents, the warm rich scent of cattle and buffaloes, the sharp acrid tang of the smoke from dung fires, and that strange earthy smell like the heart of a freshly cut raw potato that comes from dew forming on thatch. It was as though in a few hundred yards they had walked through two thousand years of Indian life.

As they walked, Burn talked of de Boigne's first victory. There had been a charge of Rajput horsemen – they were Rahtors, the proudest of all the Rajput clans – starting at a walk, quickening to a canter and a gallop, ten thousand men vowed to conquer or die, charging at full gallop de Boigne's two battalions of infantry, never doubting they would sweep them away. Then the ranks of the infantry divided and showed the guns. The guns poured charge after charge of grape into the oncoming horse till the plain was covered with dying men and screaming horses. Volley after volley of musketry followed; again and again the Rajput horse formed up and charged – again and again – up to the muzzles of the guns and to death.

'Desperate courage, they showed,' said Burn. 'But it took another kind of courage to stand and face them. Cold, disciplined courage.'

James asked shyly if he might tell a story his mother had told him about that other kind of courage, cold, passive courage. He did not often talk about his mother. Captain Burn encouraged him to tell it.

'There was a fortress in the Jodhpur country which the Mughals had taken from us Rajputs.' He paused at that 'us', but Captain Burn smiled and told him to go on. 'They must have taken it by surprise, because it was one of those places on top of a rock which no one can get into by direct assault if the garrison keep a good watch.'

'I've seen many such. India is full of them.'

'The Rajputs – they too were Rahtors of Jodhpur – came back to take it again,' James went on. 'They had no heavy guns. It might take months to starve the Muslims out – and there were our own townspeople inside. There was no hope of getting in except by some trick. They knew the Mughals were short of forage for their horses. So they ordered forty bullock-carts of forage – for themselves, of course – ' he paused and looked to see that Burn understood him – 'from a village some way off, to come by night, by a route carefully settled in advance. But, somehow – it was very careless – ' and again he cocked an eye at Burn – 'someone told someone in the town that these loads of hay were coming, and the route they were coming by. So the Mughal commander sent out a squadron of horse who captured those carts. They brought them into the fortress in triumph.' He paused and tried to picture all that had happened.

'You will have guessed,' he said. 'Before those carts started, the Rajput chief had sent for forty men. There was to be a man in each cart. He made them swear; there was not to be a sound! Whatever happened, not a sound nor a sign that a man was there. They all swore. They swore on the heads of their sons.

'Well, when the carts got to the gate of the fortress, the guards were pleased and laughing and careless. It was dark and there were torches. Everyone was laughing. They made jokes about how easy it had been and how they would have plenty of fodder for their horses now. They stood a long time, laughing and careless. Then some officer said: "All right. Pass them in. But just to make sure, run a spear into every load."

'So, one by one, each cart came to the gate and someone ran a spear into the load. There was never a sound – not a cry, not the faintest murmur. So he waved it on and the next took its place and he ran the spear into the load and again there wasn't a sound and he waved it on. All the forty carts went in; they were to stand in the market place till next morning.

'But at two in the morning, a little after moonrise, came the signal that had been agreed – the cry of an owl three times repeated. Some of those loads of hay began to stir. Out came the warriors. But less than twenty; the others were dead or dying from the spear thrusts. But no one had uttered a sound and some of them had staunched their wounds with hay so that no blood should drip. The twenty who had survived were enough. They killed the guards and the fort was taken.'

'That took some doing,' said Burn. 'You'll make a fine officer, James. There's nothing Indian soldiers won't do for a man who understands them, a man they trust.'

It was in such talk that they passed the time till they reached Cawnpore.

PART TWO

# SOLDIER OF FORTUNE

## 5 General de Boigne

IN temperament, James Skinner was nearer to his mother than to his father; India too was much closer to him than England. He had seen and smelt India, heard the cries of the Indian night, the sounds of the Indian day. England was a place remote and dim which he had never seen, of which he had only the haziest idea. He was supposed to be a Christian but neither the Age of Reason nor the unimaginative Protestantism of the eighteenth century had much appeal for a boy who was both sensitive and spirited. India's consciousness of eternity on the other hand he absorbed from his mother, from the servants who looked after him, from the soldiers who surrounded him. The difference between creeds seemed to him chiefly a matter of what you might eat and drink; Muslim, Hindu and Christian alike accepted some degree of supernatural order and looked on death as a gateway rather than an end. And this he took without question. Death was always near. He saw it every day, the long white bundle carried shoulder-high to the burning *ghat* or the grave.

Since he felt deeply but did not brood on abstractions, James did not question his father's authority. This was a matter in which there was no conflict between the traditions on which he drew. Neither a Hindu nor a Muslim boy of good family would sit in his father's presence. An English son knew that his father might beggar him if he chose and his consent must be obtained to marriage or to the choice of a profession. So there was no doubt that Hercules Skinner must be consulted. But, as James had guessed, his father raised no objection to Captain Burn's proposal. He gave his son a sword, a horse and a bag of rupees.

James did not stay long in Cawnpore. He did not feel at ease with his father; he had dreamt too often of that day when his childhood ended. Besides he was burning to get on and to begin his real business in life. Captain Burn gave him a letter to General de Boigne and with that in his pocket he rode away to the north-west to make his fortune.

Nagendra Singh came with him. He had not found Mr Templeton a sympathetic master and Margaret had agreed to let him go. He was still at heart the servant of James's old Rajput grandfather – dead ten years ago – and James, he felt, was his responsibility. For James, it meant buying a pony but a few rupees was enough for that and some kind of personal attendant there had to be. It was a fortnight's journey and James, though he felt himself a Rajput, was outside the network of caste; there was no one from whom he could claim hospitality. It was easy enough, in early April, to sleep on the ground in a grove near a village but he must not be a tramp or a vagabond; someone must fetch milk and firewood, someone must explain who he was.

The sugar-cane had been cut two months ago; the barley and the wheat were not long harvested. In the villages, the bullocks were still treading out the last of the grain, walking round and round in the threshing floors, or men were pouring the heavy grain from a height on to a sheet, letting the wind blow through it and winnow away the light chaff. The fields were bare and baked, waiting for the rains and the next sowing; only in the sandy country near the river, wherever a weighted pole could be used to swing up baskets of water, the Muraos were at work on their pumpkins, gourds and melons, watering them by day, and at night anxiously guarding them against wild pig and black buck.

He learnt a little, he laid a foundation. He learnt something of the crops and the life of the village people, the network of caste and kin, the loyalties that held the priest and the barber, the carpenter and the washerman, to their patrons, the ties that bound tenant to landowner, servant and fellow-clansman to landlord. These were the kind of ties by which Nagendra Singh was bound to himself. But he of course was an anomaly; he was country-born, he was outside this network. One day, he told himself, he would have a place in it, when he had made his fortune and had won an estate of his own. He learnt too – talking to the villagers, listening to Nagendra Singh asking them questions – something of what they suffered from war, from bad government, and from the lack of government, when robber bands took the place of marauding armies. Peace and a strong prince who would put down crime – that, he began to see, was what they needed.

They had no difficulty in finding their way. Everyone had heard of de Boigne's great fortified camp at Ko'el near Aligarh. It lay in the middle of the vast property allotted to de Boigne for the upkeep of his army, most of it in the Doab, the fertile land between the Ganges and the Jumna, south and east of Delhi. At the gate, the letter from Captain Burn was a passport. Two soldiers were ordered to take him to the general's tent.

Everywhere he looked, he saw intense but orderly activity. He saw squads of men in red tunics with black facings and accoutrements, drilling and marching; he heard orders shouted at them, the rattle of muskets presented and shouldered and grounded; further away he could see squadrons of cavalry in long green coats, wheeling and turning in formation; in another direction, blue-coated gunners serving their guns with exact precision – every move designed to speed up the pace of re-loading and firing. He had seen these things before, in the Company's lines near Calcutta – but here it struck him there was an extra edge to the bustle. They were doing everything against time – to please one presiding genius.

His escort brought him to a tent much larger than any of the others. There was a flagstaff before it, flying the white cross of Savoy. Sentries challenged, in English. A junior officer came out; an Indian, a jemadar, a Muslim, James judged, by the tie of his turban. He spoke to James and looked at the letter. 'Wait,' he said and took it inside. He was back in ten minutes and beckoned James to enter – the palm of his hand turned downward, as Indians always beckon. James went through the light curtains of split cane that made the front of the great marquee. After the bright sun outside, it seemed dark but his eyes soon grew used to the subdued light. There was a tall man sitting at a table; junior officers, risaldars and jemadars, were bringing him papers. He read each quickly and either signed it or asked a question and sent it away. He was very quick and absolutely concentrated. He took no notice at all of James. James waited, keeping quite still. It needs courage to keep still, he thought, remembering the Rajputs in the bundles of hay. I will keep still but I will stand up to him and answer him boldly – boldly, truthfully and with respect.

At last the man at the table looked up and put out his hand. The jemadar commanding the guard gave him the letter James had brought. He took it but did not open it at once, first giving a long steady look to James, who stood up straight and gazed back at him. Then he read the letter. He looked up again, nodded to the jemadar and told him to go back to his guard, dismissed with a gesture the men behind him who were still waiting with papers.

'Sit down, Mr Skinner,' he said, speaking in English, though with a slight accent unfamiliar to James. 'You are a friend of Captain Burn. I have a regard for Captain Burn. You want to be a soldier?'

'Yes, sir. I want to be a soldier.' James repeated once more his old saying that his father was a Scot and his mother a Rajput and both peoples made good soldiers.

'And you speak Hindi?'

'More easily than English or Persian,' said James with a smile.

'And what do you think of your mother's people?'

'I am proud to have some share in a people of such courage and – ' he paused, hunting for words ' – such pride – and sometimes so – noble.'

'Yes. I like that. Your father is in the Company's service. But the British won't have you as a soldier?'

'No. I am country-born.' He gave the words a touch of scorn. '*They* say I am neither English nor Rajput. But *I* say I am both.'

'And so – your father suggested you should come to me?'

'No, sir. He was against it at first. He apprenticed me to a printer. But I did not like that. I ran away. My father agreed only when Captain Burn took my side.'

'So you come to me because the British will not have you?'

'Not entirely. I suppose I should not have come if the British would have commissioned me. But I think also that I should have a better chance with you of seeing service and getting responsible command.'

'That is true. But suppose there is war between Scindia, whom I serve, and the British?'

'I have thought of that, sir, because my father's sepoys used to say that it will come, sooner or later. My father, too; that was why he did not want me to come. I should not like to fight against my father nor against Captain Burn. If it did come, I cannot be sure – but I think it must be right for – for a soldier of fortune – to fight for his employer, whoever the enemy may be. Like the Swiss. I have heard of the Swiss, guarding the King of France. I hope it won't come.'

'Not so long as I have any influence.' He stood up and James rose too, thinking he was to be dismissed. But de Boigne came round the table towards him and continued the conversation. He was very tall, nearly a foot taller than James, a strikingly handsome man, though his face was worn with fatigue and haggard with malaria. So far, he had been the General, interviewing a young man who wanted a commission; now he seemed to lay aside the formality of office and speak as an older friend to a younger. The sudden relaxation was very engaging; James felt as though he had been chosen for this great man's special confidence.

'You know, I suppose,' de Boigne continued, taking a turn to and fro in the vast tent and then sitting down again, 'that the Maharaja Scindia whom I served so long died a year ago. He was a brave and vigorous prince who knew how to reward good service. His nephew, who is the Maharaja Scindia now, is – what shall I say? – less experienced. Just as ambitious but less – reliable. I think he trusts me – but I have no *time* to build up his confidence. I must go to Europe, Mr Skinner. I must have some rest. I have not been well. I have bouts of fever. It is the curse of this country. And I have become very tired. I have been raising new battalions, training them and fighting battles – all the year round – for ten years, without rest, in this climate. Let me tell you something. Trust, Mr Skinner, trust, is the secret of success in this profession of ours. A soldier of fortune, I think you said. The men must trust their officer; they must know that he will look after them, that he will never desert them, that he will never ask them to do anything he would not do himself. But there must also be trust between the officer and his employer. That was the secret – that was how Madhoji Scindia – the old Scindia – and I made ourselves the masters of Hindostan. The old *patel*, he used to call himself. It means a village headman, you know, Mr Skinner, in the Maratha language. That was his name for himself. The old *patel*. He was a prince whom a soldier of fortune could trust. He trusted me and I trusted him. But now he is dead; there are difficult times coming and – and, Mr Skinner, I am tired.'

He went back to his seat at the table.

'Mr Skinner,' he continued, more formally now, 'I think if you are lucky you will do well with us. There is always the question of luck. You are sure you want to join us? My officers are all soldiers or I would not keep them, but some of them are scoundrels, ruffians. You are not. You are sure you want to join us?'

'Quite sure, sir.'

'Very well.' He called one of his Indian officers. 'Jemadar Arjan Singh will make out a commission for you as ensign on one hundred and fifty rupees a month. He will bring it to me to sign. You will draw pay from today. You will go to the Second Brigade at Muttra under Colonel Sutherland. Goodbye, Mr Skinner. I am confident I shall hear of you before long.'

James never saw de Boigne again. But he did not forget his words.

# 6 Harji Scindia

In James Skinner's account of his own doings he says very little about his first months as a commissioned officer. He served in a battalion under a Hanoverian, Captain Pohlman, who had once been a sergeant in a corps of Hanoverians in British pay in Madras, a man reported to be of cheerful disposition and a good soldier. But Skinner says nothing of the training he received. It must be assumed that he quickly mastered the drill and words of command, which were all in English and with which he had been familiar as long as he could remember. At any rate, he went, in the course of those first few months, with a Maratha army into Bundelkhand, south and east from de Boigne's headquarters, where he took part in several small sieges and what he calls 'two field battles'. Of these experiences, he says only that they increased his eagerness for a soldier's life.

Even in those early days, he seems to have paid the closest attention to the comfort of the men in the ranks. Right through his career the men who served under him showed a remarkable devotion, a complete personal commitment to him as a leader. Such devotion was not won simply by 'looking after the men' in a cold professional spirit, merely seeing that they were well fed, well clothed, promptly paid and given adequate rest. That may represent no more than the concern a farmer feels for a herd of dairy cattle. What won the hearts of Skinner's men was something beyond that, a lively interest in their homes and families, their life outside the ranks. He says little enough about this in his memoirs because he took it for granted, but it impressed everyone who met him; and since he won his men's confidence from the start, they must have felt his interest as soon as he joined.

What he does say of his early days is that he practised hard with his weapons and that he made friends with some of the Maratha chiefs. One of these friendships became important for him. One day in the autumn of 1795, he was at this practice with his weapons in a grove of mango trees near his battalion's camp. He made a point of it every day; as soon as parade was over and his formal duties finished, he would move away by himself and go through the *kasrat*, an ancient Indian exercise for the muscles of the legs and back; draw the steel bow to strengthen his grip and the muscles of his forearms; practise with sword and spear and shoot arrows at a target. He had not forgotten de Boigne's words. He must be able to do anything his men could do – and do it better.

He had the spear in his hand and was lunging at an imaginary enemy and recovering when a friendly voice said:

'No, no, not like that!'

He had been so absorbed that he had not noticed the arrival of a Maratha chief, with a hawk on his wrist, accompanied by two or three mounted orderlies. The chief gave the hawk and his reins to an orderly, put his hands on the saddle-bow and vaulted from his horse.

'You see, you must be able to throw the spear as well as to lunge and parry as you do with a sword. Look – this is the grip; you must hold it like this. Now, you take your spear and I will lunge at you – and then – as we are playing – I shall throw it at you – but to miss, you understand! Here, Mannu, give me a spear.'

Soon they were fencing with the spear, lunging and parrying and nearly hitting, laughing with pleasure. Suddenly the chief disengaged, danced back and threw his spear so that it whistled by James's cheek.

'You must learn to do that! It may save your life one day.

You are a new ensign in the Second Brigade? Have you seen any service yet?'

'Nothing serious. I have been for a few months in Bundelkhand, bringing refractory rajas to heel. We took some little forts and I was in a few skirmishes. Enough to increase my appetite. I'm determined to be as good a man-at-arms as any of my men.'

'Have you learnt to parry a spear-thrust from behind? Look?'

He sprang on to his horse again, cantered to the other end of the grove, turned and galloped back, and as he passed James, disengaged one foot from the stirrup, swung his leg over his horse, and parried an imaginary thrust from behind.

'Let me show you,' said James. 'I must borrow your horse.'

They were about the same age and they were friends from the start, without thought of rank. They sat talking, after the exercise.

'There will be war soon,' said the Maratha. 'And it will not be a good war.'

'What do you mean, not a good war?'

'I mean it will be a war among ourselves, between Marathas, and not even a war between two great Maratha princes. Oh, we have had wars enough between Scindia an Holkar. We are never on the same side as Holkar unless there are Muslims to fight. Wars of course are always bad – except for us soldiers, *if* we happen to survive and *if* we contrive to be on the winning side. Wars are always about the same things – women, gold, land – you know the old saying. But it is better to fight Muslims than one's fellow Hindus. And better to fight Holkar's men than vassals of Scindia. Civil war is the worst. And this will be a civil war among Scindia's own followers.'

'Tell me,' said James. 'I am only a soldier. I do as I am ordered by the commanding general. But I should like to know more.'

'When my uncle died,' began the Maratha, ' – I am Harji Scindia, by the way, a second cousin – when the

Maharaja my uncle died, he left three wives. I am told the youngest is very pretty. Of course, if we Marathas were grand people like Rajputs, they would have thrown themselves alive into the flames.'

'My mother was a Rajputni,' James broke in. He did not want his new friend to say anything that might lead to a quarrel. 'She killed herself to avoid dishonour.'

Harji bowed. 'We Marathas are more commonplace,' he said. 'Well, of course it was my cousin's duty, when he succeeded my uncle, to make a proper establishment for his aunts – to give them landed property and a fortress of their own to live in. And he did not. He kept them in his own camp and paid less and less attention to them. At least – to the two eldest aunts. *They* say – the two eldest I mean – *they* say that he paid far too much attention to the youngest and prettiest. And that of course is a dreadful scandal – even with prosaic people such as we Marathas are. My uncle had accepted him as heir and was on the point of adopting him when he died. So you see he was almost a son. She is not only his aunt but practically his mother. It is – oh, shameful beyond saying. They *may* have invented this affair – the two elder aunts – to get sympathy for themselves. In that at least they have succeeded. They have a strong party now. They have had all kinds of adventures and escapes – carried off by one party and rescued by another. Now they are with Holkar – who is always Scindia's enemy – and the Peshwa has joined them and many of our own chiefs.'

'So the Peshwa and Holkar are friends?' said James making a note of it, only half as a question.

'Oh, they can never be friends. That would degrade the word friend beyond hope of recovery. The Peshwa had Holkar's younger brother trampled to death by elephants and watched the sight from a balcony. Holkar does not forget that. But for the moment they are joined together. They are agreed on one thing only – jealousy of Scindia and the empire that de Boigne's brigades have won him in the North. You have a great deal to learn about Maratha politics my friend.'

'Well, I have nothing to do but obey orders. Scindia can rely on de Boigne's brigades.'

'I fear Scindia may have not much else to rely on. And now that de Boigne has gone to Europe – I wonder how long he will have that.'

'But General Perron is carrying on just as de Boigne did.'

'So far. But he is not de Boigne. And it will take a very wise man and a very strong man to keep his feet in our politics in the next few years. There are very strong currents. Well, we shall soon be fighting – and then you will be glad to use your spear as I showed you. God be your protector, as our dear Muslim friends say.'

He vaulted on to his horse and rode away, smiling, carefree, sparkling.

## 7 The Gun in the Pass

WAR came, as Harji had predicted, a civil war, the War of the Aunts, a war between Scindia and his own vassals, a war in which men were killed, women raped, villages laid waste. It was a war in which the open cause of dispute was that Scindia had failed to make proper provision for his uncle's widows. But the varying course of Scindia's affections added a sharper bitterness to the conflict. Nothing was now heard of the pretty aunt, her place having been taken by a still more dazzling beauty whose father, Sarji Rao Ghatke, had become Scindia's principal minister. Behind the stated purpose of those who supported the Aunts lay a determination to remove Ghatke from office; he was 'respectable neither by birth nor character' says the chronicler – a considerable understatement, for his actions show him cruel, revengeful and avaricious. No one has ever had a good word to say for Ghatke. Since Maratha armies invariably lived on the countryside, the War of the Aunts was a more than usually wasteful and horrible way of settling a political dispute. Yet even in such a war, there may be justice on one side rather than on the other, and in this war, if there was justice anywhere, it was not with Scindia.

Scindia, however, had the support of the four 'brigades' of de Boigne's army, now commanded by General Perron. The 'brigades' were more like what today would be called divisions, numbering nearly ten thousand men each; each brigade included ten battalions of infantry – each battalion equipped with four six-pounder guns – and one regiment of ten squadrons of cavalry. These were much the best disciplined troops on either side. The rest of Scindia's army was 'feudal', in the sense that each body of troops owed some kind of personal allegiance to its commander, who in his turn was one of Scindia's vassals. But Scindia's faithful vassals disliked the infamous Ghatke almost as much as their opponents did; what most of them hoped for was an outcome in which Ghatke would be dismissed but they themselves remain in favour because they had been faithful. But it was a matter of nice calculation whether a moment might not come when it would be better to go over to the powerful forces on the side of the Aunts.

With none of this, however, did James Skinner concern himself. He was a soldier, not a politician. This was his first real war and he was about to take part in his first large-scale battle. Scindia's general was one Ambaji Englia, not usually a very dashing commander. He had pushed forward towards his opponent an advanced force of fourteen battalions of organized infantry – two of them de Boigne's, and twelve feudal in allegiance and less disciplined – together with another ten or twelve thousand men, mostly cavalry, who were not organized on European lines at all. This advanced force was meant to find out the enemy's intentions but had rashly allowed itself to be manoeuvred into a position from which the sole line of retreat was by a narrow pass through steep and rocky hills. Now they faced an enemy force of much the same strength as their own, with fifteen battalions of organized infantry, drawn up for battle and clearly preparing to attack.

On this decisive day, when he was to encounter treachery and to be faced by what appeared certain annihilation, James Skinner, aged just twenty, found himself in command of a battalion, one of the two of de Boigne's disciplined battalions in the advanced force. The other was commanded by Captain Butterfield, who was in general charge of both battalions. The two young officers met briefly, about three in the afternoon. They could see the line of enemy infantry drawn up to face them, with clouds of horse on both sides.

'I've got bad news,' said James at once. 'One of my men has just told me. He has a cousin in one of the battalions on our left, I'm not sure which. But he has sent word. All those twelve battalions on our left will go over to the enemy once battle is joined. Their leaders have been exchanging messages with the enemy.'

'It doesn't surprise me in the least,' said Butterfield gloomily. 'Though, mark you, it may not be true. If it is, we must fall back by wings, half a battalion at a time, keeping that river on our right. And of course it will fall to us to cover the retreat of the rest of the advanced force through the pass. It always does fall on us.'

James had often been under musket-fire before. Now for the first time cannon were being aimed at him and round-shot were falling among his men, causing frightful mutilation. But they held their ground, under three hours of cannonade. Then came the first charge of cavalry and again they were as steady as men could be, firing and loading as coolly as though they were on parade. That first charge of cavalry withered away. Then came the news they had feared and half expected. The battalions on the left were marching away. Only the two battalions raised by de Boigne stood firm – but now they were hopelessly outnumbered. Again the orders came which they expected; they were to fall back towards the pass.

They moved back, half a battalion at a time. Four companies would fall back while twelve faced the enemy and kept up a steady fire of musketry and cannon. They had four six-pounders with each battalion and the gunners were loading them with grape and firing with the practised mechanical speed they had learnt on the parade ground, the infantry following each round of grape with volleys of musketry and closing in on the guns if the cavalry got too close. They were losing men, but they kept their ranks so closely, they loaded and fired with such exact precision, that the enemy never pressed home a charge. They had lost one man in three by the time they reached the entrance to the pass. It was beginning to be dark.

'As I expected, we are the rearguard of the advanced force,' Butterfield told James Skinner. 'And you, with two companies and one six-pounder, are the rearguard of our two battalions. Once the advanced force has filed into the pass, I shall follow with my battalion and six companies of yours, all but the two companies you keep. You will follow into the pass and fall back as you can. But you *must* hold them in the pass till dawn. You've done well today. Good luck!'

'I shall need it.'

They held a line defending the mouth of the pass till the column of march was formed and the cavalry of the advanced force were on their way. Butterfield took his men into the pass and Skinner with his two companies fell back till he held the entrance of the pass only. The attacks had died away; no charge was pushed home now, but there were skirmishers in sight and feints were made, picquets pushed forward to see whether they were on the alert. The enemy were still in touch, ready to come on as soon as James fell back. It was darker still in the pass; the moon had not yet risen. The sides were steep and the way grew more narrow. They moved back by companies, one defending as the other moved, the enemy following up, cautiously, as they fell back.

It was slow work. There were wounded men; they were all deadly tired; the ground was rough, strewn with boulders and sometimes steep. The gun carriage had been damaged. But they kept going. Some time after midnight, when the waning moon had risen, they knew they were not far from the top of the pass. James was with the defending company. The subedar commanding the leading company came scrambling back down the pass; his name was Shadul Khan.

'The gun-carriage is broken. The wheel that was hit in the cannonade has given way.'

James went up the pass to where the gun lay. The carriage was quite beyond repair. They brought back one of the ammunition tumbrils and emptied it. Somehow, heaving and straining, they got the gun off the wrecked carriage and on to the ammunition tumbril. They put the two teams of bullocks together and began to drag the gun towards the crest of the pass. But the ground was steeper here and they could move it only foot by foot, with men helping the bullocks. It was desperately slow. Foot by foot, they heaved and struggled.

It was hours and hours since the battle had begun. Bellies were empty, mouths dry; they were exhausted. They struggled on in the half dark.

There was a burst of firing down the pass. The enemy had moved up and were pushing the defending company, sounding them to find out where they were placed, getting ready for a full-scale attack. The defending company could delay them, but not for long. There was a clear choice. They must either leave the gun or both companies must stand and fight round it. Few of them would survive such a stand.

It was for James to decide. He was the only commissioned officer. He knew what he meant to do. He was not going back without that gun. But he wanted his men with him, altogether with him.

'Shadul Khan!' he said, 'Get the men together round me. Quickly, quickly. I want to ask them a question.'

They scrambled towards him, fierce tired faces gleaming in the pallid half light.

'Men – what shall we do? Leave the gun or stand and fight?'

'Stand and fight!' they cried. Someone added: 'De Boigne's battalions have never lost a gun!'

'Right!' said James, 'we stand and fight! Messenger! Go back to the other company. Tell Subedar Amrit Singh to get his men up here by half companies at a time. Quickly, quickly.

'Now – ' he turned to the men round the gun. 'Load that

gun with grape and point it down the pass. Lay it on that point fifty yards away where the track winds round that big rock. Do you see it? Subedar Shadul Khan, do you stay here to check the laying of the gun. You are in command here. Jemadar Dhalip Singh, take up a position on the left where your fire commands the same point. Jemadar Habib Khan, take your men up there and place them so that they can bring all the fire they can on the head of the enemy's column. Then wait in silence for my order. Absolute silence!'

There was only just time. The other company scrambled back; they took up their positions. The enemy were coming on confidently now; they were making too much noise themselves to hear the movements of James's men.

The two companies waited, hearts thudding, drawing their breath long and deep, shuddering. There was just enough light from the moon to see the rock at the corner. The enemy drew nearer; they could hear the scuffle and stumble of armed men moving in poor light over broken ground. They drew nearer still; they could see a movement by the big rock.

'Wait!' James said to himself. 'Wait!'

They came on. He could see them more clearly now. Wait. A few more steps. Wait. Wait.

'Fire!' he yelled.

Flame belched from the gun, spurted from the muskets on the hill-side.

The head of the column was wiped out; it collapsed.

'Come on!' he shouted. 'Sword in hand.'

They charged with sword and bayonet. They drove back every enemy who was still on his feet. But not too far – only far enough to crumple the head of the column, to make sure that the survivors were running to save themselves.

'Back to the gun!' he yelled.

Then they were back in their positions, waiting again. But the enemy did not return and by dawn they were over the head of the pass and the going was easier. Soon they were out of the pass. They brought their gun home to the main army.

James hardly dared to believe that he was after all still alive. He had made up his mind that they could none of them live. It would all come to an end, there in the dark, in the narrow pass. But – somehow – there it was! He was alive!

## 8 The Ambush

A DAY or two later there came to James Skinner's tent a *chobdar*, a mace-bearer, splendidly dressed, with a sash embroidered in gold and silver worn across his breast, and a great silver mace which he carried over his shoulder and held before him as he delivered his message. He brought an invitation to James to attend the Maratha Commander-in-Chief, Ambaji Englia.

The Commander-in-Chief held his court in an enormous marquee; the whole of one side was open to the air. He sat on a gilt throne on a raised dais. General Perron, as commander of de Boigne's brigades, sat on his right; clustered about him were a group of the great Maratha nobles, brilliant in silks and jewels. Among them James recognized his friend Harji Scindia. On either side of the marquee, leading up to the dais, sat two converging rows of lesser nobles and officers. The *chobdar* announced: 'Ensign James Skinner, Sahib Bahadur!' James walked forward as steadily as he could, as though on parade. The Commander-in-Chief gave an order to a herald, who read out in the most flowery of Persian an account of the retreat in the pass. The Commander-in-Chief clapped his hands and an attendant came forward with a robe of honour, a splendid garment of gold brocade which he put on James's shoulders. James then bowed deeply to Ambaji Englia. The herald gave him the Persian scroll; General Perron announced that he was promoted from Ensign to Lieutenant. He was presented with *pan* and scent was poured on his hands. Then he was led to a place among the ranks of officers.

When this assembly broke up and he was walking back to his tent, he heard a voice calling his name. He turned and saw a tall man with very bright blue eyes in a fair tanned face.

'Mr Skinner! Don't be in such a hurry! You've done well. I congratulate you, me boy. You'll go far if you keep on as you've begun. George Thomas is me name, by the way.' He spoke in English, though with a strong Irish brogue which James had never heard before.

'Colonel Thomas!' he said with pleasure. 'But of course I have heard your name! Who has not heard of Jaj Jang – George Jung – George the Warlike?'

'Och, I've had some luck,' said Thomas, 'mainly by always taking the bold course and attacking.'

'I didn't know you were here.'

'Sure, I came only yesterday. I brought six battalions to see if I could be any help.'

'Then you're Scindia's man now?'

'No I'm not then. I'm not anyone's man now but me own. I served the Begam Somru and then I served Appa Khande Rao for I don't know how many years and I was as faithful to him as night is to day or death to birth, though he did try to murder me twice. But he's dead now and I'm in business on me own. I've a snug little property to the north-west of Delhi – the size of an Irish county or maybe two – and I make my own cannon there and mint me own rupees. There's the sinews of war for you, guns and rupees! My own rupees, mark you! With the Emperor's titles in Persian and me own monogram of the letter T in a wreath of shamrock! That's not bad for a village lad from Tipperary that never had any schooling!'

'And now has a name that's worth six battalions by itself!' said James, who at once felt a liking for George Thomas, as everyone did. 'But – if you're not Scindia's man – ?'

'I'm me own man, as I said, a prince in me own right, but a soldier of fortune none the less and for the moment Scindia's my client. He's hired me to settle this bother with his aunts. But now, Mr Skinner, I was thinking a day might come when you might want a little more independence yourself?'

James shook his head. 'No, I'm just a soldier, in de Boigne's brigades.'

'Well, you never know how things may turn out. If the luck changes – and I'm still in business – you might do worse than come and see me. You're a soldier of fortune like myself – and I'd sooner have you by my side than a good many I can think of!'

George Thomas was an adventurer to whom every young officer looked with envy and admiration. It was thought, though no one was quite sure, that he had deserted from the Royal Navy in Madras. When he appeared in the North, he already had some experience as a soldier; he took service with the Begam Somru, the widow of the infamous Alsatian butcher nicknamed Sombre or Somru, who had slaughtered the English captives at Patna long ago. There was a territory north of Delhi, of which the Emperor had made a grant to her husband; he had had to fight to get possession of it and fight afterwards to keep it. Somehow the Begam had managed to hold on to it after his death – and there she ruled, virtually independent, with her own army, skilfully keeping her footing in the shifting tides of war and diplomacy, contriving to end every war on the winning side.

She had a liking for vigorous and handsome young men and at first George Thomas was a great success at her court. He won her battles, he came back from the wars her acknowledged favourite. One day, as he left her bed for an expedition to defend her western borders, she gave him one of her youngest and prettiest slave-girls to take with him as a wife, a permanent companion. She could not always be with him herself, she said – and his energies obviously needed an outlet. Perhaps it gave her satisfaction to think of him with another; perhaps she was already planning to be rid of him; perhaps it was a passing whim – teasing mockery, no more. At any rate, he took the slave-girl. In the end he was supplanted, by a Frenchman called Le Vassoult, who joined in a conspiracy with everyone else who was near the Begam –

all jealous of George Thomas – to persuade her that he was plotting to make himself master of her principality. He heard of the plot and escaped; he was lucky to get away with his life. But some years later, when she was in prison and her life in danger, it was to him that – with characteristic effrontery – she sent a secret message asking for help. And it was with a chivalry no less characteristic that he responded, coming to her rescue and restoring her to her throne and marching off again, free as air.

Now he was, as he said, in business on his own. His life was soon to impinge on James Skinner's again but before that James, who had already begun to be heard of among the Marathas, was to find his career in de Boigne's brigades hanging in the balance.

The incident occurred a few months after the meeting with Thomas. The War of the Aunts was still in progress but it was not being waged with great determination. The two Commanders-in-Chief were both nobles of Scindia's and though each hoped for the destruction of the other, neither would risk his own. And each hated Ghatke. A river lay between the two armies and was regarded by both as a boundary, which each talked of crossing. Meanwhile, the armies supplied themselves by plundering the neighbouring villages, who paid for the war by the loss of all they had.

That morning, James Skinner was exercising his horse not far from the boundary river, practising with his weapons, wearing a metal helmet and chain mail on shoulders, thighs and breast, as he would have done in battle. As he swung and turned his horse, leaning down now and then to decapitate with his sword a young plant of the tamarisk, he became aware of a body of horse approaching from the direction of Scindia's camp. He rode to meet them and found they were led by Harji Scindia.

'Ah, Lieutenant Skinner!' he said. 'Practising your horsemanship as usual. That is good. Would you like to come with us?'

'Where are you going?' James asked.

'The Commander-in-Chief has ordered me to look into a

report he has received about a ford of the river. He wants to know if this ford would be a place where a considerable body of men could cross at night. He says that if he could get such a body across by night, he could order a general attack.' He spoke with some formality of tone and looked at James with a slight air of questioning mockery.

'Then he really wants to attack the enemy?'

'Ah, you are making progress. You begin to learn. That is the question I asked myself too. But, like you, I am a soldier; I must do as I am told. But one is permitted to ask questions of oneself, if not of one's commanders.'

'But – why else? Why else should he send you?'

'Oh, perhaps to make *me* think he means to attack. Or perhaps to make the enemy think he means to attack. Or perhaps – ' He left the sentence unfinished.

'Or perhaps?'

'Well, in my position one has always to consider whether it is a compliment to be chosen for some special service. It may give one the chance of glory – or on the other hand disgrace – or perhaps death. I have plenty of enemies, you know. Our Commander-in-Chief does not exactly love me. Nor do my two dear aunts. I do not think I should be very well treated if I fell into their hands. And there are people in our camp who would not be sorry if I did. Partly it is because I am close to Scindia by blood. Partly it is because I talk too much. Oh, far too much. But I am learning to be careful that I do not talk to everyone as I do to you, my friend.'

'You have guides who know this ford?'

'Two. There they are. Supplied by the Commander-in-Chief. Each guarded by one of my own personal men – with a drawn sword in his hand. And each of them mounted on a very bad horse – the worst we could find.'

They rode in silence for a few hundred yards. It was sandy country where nothing much grew but *jhao* – tamarisk scrub. There were sandy dunes and flatter places where the ground was harder. The track wound between the dunes.

'Did you see that?' James asked suddenly.

'No. Where?'

'Up there to the left. There was someone in the *jhao*. He ran back over the brow of the hill. I saw the *jhao* shake and I saw a flash as though he had got on a horse which reared and showed his helmet.'

'A wandering robber, no doubt,' said Harji grimly, pulling up. He considered for a moment, then made up his mind. 'Well, I am not going back just because you have seen a man in the *jhao*. What sort of report should I make? But this is not your quarrel, my friend. You go back. I have five hundred chosen men.'

'Leave a friend in danger! What sort of figure should I cut before my men? Of course I am coming.'

Harji told his men to be ready for an attack.

'And we might as well be beforehand with them,' he said. 'We will be first at the rendezvous. Come on!' He broke into a canter.

The track wound down a slight slope towards the river, between two bluffs. As they cantered into more open ground they could see horsemen coming out from the *jhao* on either side of them, massing on the level ground by the river. They were outnumbered by at least two to one.

'Kill the guides!' shouted Harji. 'It is a trap! God is my defender. God will avenge me. Charge to the left!'

His men yelled back. They were men of his own household.

'We will die for you!' they yelled. They shouted his name.

'Harji for ever! Victory to Harji,' they cried. 'Harji! Harji!'

They charged to the left, drove the enemy back in confusion, pulled up, turned, made another charge to the right. They were much better disciplined than most Maratha horse and did not lose themselves in mad pursuit. They delivered the charge, reined up, disengaged, came back and gathered about Harji near the point where they had come out into the open.

'Madhu Ram and his men – stand fast and front the enemy,' Harji shouted. 'Beni Ram's men – get back two hundred yards towards the camp and stand again.'

After those first two charges, they had a little respite. If they had come out of the *jhao* five minutes later, the enemy would have been united and they would have been caught in column before they could form line. Now they had the chance to make an orderly retreat and this they began to do, with skirmishing parties out, covering their rear, the main body moving at a walk and at any moment ready to face about and stand. But during this movement the enemy commander got his men together.

'They are going to charge again,' said Harji. 'It is Bala Rao commanding them. I know him. Call in the skirmishing parties. Face about and receive them.'

Now came the most formidable charge yet. Bala Rao had got his men in good order again after that first repulse and now he had them in a compact mass. Both sides had lost men but the enemy were still at least twice Harji's strength. They came on like a whirlwind and though Harji's band stood firm many of them were swept back by sheer weight of numbers. In the mix-up that followed things began to go badly. James felt several sword cuts from which his chain mail saved him; he saw his mare bleeding. He saw blows falling on Harji though he too was saved by his armour. He saw one man drive a spear at Harji which glanced from his shoulder but pierced the upper part of his left arm. James cut that man down before he could close and use his dagger. He managed to get close to Harji's shoulder.

'Our men are beginning to break,' he said, 'We can't hold them much longer. Look – do you see there? Bala Rao, with a mass of troopers, charging what's left of our line, making for us. If we can meet them and kill him, we have a chance. It's our only chance.'

Harji managed to make his voice heard.

'To me!' he yelled. 'To Harji! A charge at that ruffian Bala Rao! Let us kill him or die like soldiers. To me! To Harji! Charge!'

Some fifty men answered his call and with a great surge, men and horses dripping blood and sweat, they fought their way to Harji and threw themselves into an effort which they knew was the last they could make. One last charge against Bala Rao's charge!

'Harji! Harji!' they shouted.

A desperate push of tired horses trying to gallop, men spurring and hewing. Somehow the two chiefs came together and James saw Harji stand in his stirrups and bring down a tremendous slash on Bala Rao's neck, saw Bala Rao topple and sway and fall, down, down, into the bloody rubble beneath the horses' feet. And he heard someone shout:

'Bala Rao is down!'

And the crowd began to thin and the pressure to drop and the enemy were beginning to fall back. They could draw breath again, long deep shuddering breaths; those with authority could begin to get the men together and again move back towards the camp. They had lost nearly half of those who had ridden out.

When they drew near to the camp, James turned his weary mare – bleeding from a dozen cuts – and made Harji a formal salute before moving away to his own tent. But Harji would have none of it and insisted that he must first come to his tent. It was not much smaller than the Commander-in-Chief's. Servants appeared in crowds to lead away the limping horses, to bring cool drinks and sponges and bandages for the warriors.

When they had rested a little, Harji rose and embraced him.

'My friend,' he said, 'those others who fought with me today are my kinsmen, my clansmen, my servants. They did their duty. They did it nobly. But you did far more than your duty. You fought by my side as a friend and as a friend I wish to give you presents.'

He took a pair of golden bangles, studded with diamonds, which a servant brought him, and put them on James's wrists. And then he gave him a sword, a shield, a splendid horse.

James thanked him with a warmth that was deeply felt.

'I am a poor soldier,' he said, 'and I am Scindia's man but I am yours too, as much as Scindia's, and always shall be.'

'I shall never forget you,' said Harji.

'I shall never forget you!' said James.

'We are brothers!' said Harji.

Hardly had James reached his own tent before orders reached him to report to Colonel Sutherland, his commanding officer. Sutherland, as James was aware, had been cashiered from the Black Watch, but he knew his work as a soldier. He spoke with a Scottish intonation that reminded James of his father. He had already heard the whole story of the day's doings.

'What do you mean,' he asked severely, 'by going on an expedition of danger without orders? You are under my command and it was a most insubordinate act to go off on this irresponsible adventure with a Maratha chief.'

'Well, at first,' said James, 'it did not appear to be a dangerous adventure but merely a reconnaissance ordered by the Commander-in-Chief. When it became dangerous, I thought it my duty to give what help I could to a near relation of our employer.'

'You have no business to get mixed up in the intrigues of Maratha politics. You have nothing to do but obey my orders. I shall have to report this matter to General Perron and ask that his severe displeasure shall be recorded in your service book. Unless of course – ' he paused.

'Unless?' James repeated, a little puzzled, hardly daring to believe what he feared.

'I understand you received a present of a valuable horse. That makes the whole affair more serious. If that were transferred to – someone else, I might overlook the matter.'

James looked at him steadily. His temper rose but he kept it under control. 'I also received a pair of gold bangles with diamonds on them,' he said. 'Those I am ready to hand over if you wish. But not the sword, the horse or the shield, which were the present of a brave man to a friend. I am ready to wait General Perron's decision.'

Two days later, James received by the hand of an orderly a summons to attend General Perron in his tent. His heart sank. As he went to the tent he saw Colonel Sutherland approaching from another angle.

'That settles it,' he thought. 'If he calls us together, he must have decided against me. If he was on my side, he would have seen Sutherland alone.'

They arrived before the tent at the same time; James of course saluted and made way for his superior. Sutherland went in without taking notice of him. They did not have long to wait in the anteroom. A young French officer called them both in together.

'Colonel Sutherland! Lieutenant Skinner! Will you please to step this way?'

Perron had no manners and his English was poor. The dislike of the English which he was later to show so openly had been hidden in de Boigne's day. It began to show from this stage onwards.

'Good morning, Lieutenant Skinner,' he began, taking no notice of Sutherland, 'I 'ave to give you congratulations once more. I am tell you 'ave distinguish yourself once again, this time in defence of Maharaj Harji Scindia. I 'ave write you a letter to praise you, by order of the Commander-in-Chief. Here it is.'

'Thank you, sir.'

James took the letter and stood still; he expected to be told to go, but Perron gave him no order but turned to Sutherland.

'Colonel Sutherland, you are dismiss,' he said. 'You 'ave plot against me since the day General de Boigne is left. Oh, I know very well. Now you try to thieve present from own officer – present from Maharaja Scindia's cousin. Thieve from own officer cause very bad feeling. Ruin General de Boigne's brigades. You take all pay due and go.'

Sutherland was black with anger. He began to speak but James heard no more; he saluted and went. Two days later he met Harji.

'I don't understand,' he said. 'Why did the Commander-in-Chief congratulate me? I thought it was he – '

'Hush!' said Harji. 'Hush! Hush! Hush! It *was* he – of course it was. But I pretended I did not know. I went straight to his presence and in open durbar I said I had been betrayed by someone – I did not know who. And I demanded recognition of what you had done. He dared not say no. He had to show that it was no doing of his. So he sent strong instructions to Perron. And I told Perron about Sutherland. Perron was delighted; it was the chance he wanted. Sutherland tried to get Perron's place when de Boigne went – so you see . . . James, you have been useful to Perron this time. But trust him like you trust a snake.'

James began to understand something of what his godfather had feared on his behalf.

## 9 The Fish of Honour

THE War of the Aunts came suddenly to an end. An Afghan army invaded India and threatened Delhi and the Emperor. It was enough to make the Marathas hastily patch up their quarrels; Scindia made a proper arrangement for his aunts and the rebel Commander-in-Chief, Lakwa Dada, became Scindia's Commander-in-Chief. Outwardly all was forgiven.

But there was a rising in Kabul and the Afghans hurried home to attend to their own affairs. James Skinner and the rest of de Boigne's brigades came back to the country south of Delhi. He was still only twenty, but he was beginning to be known. He had twice come to the notice of the Commander-in-Chief. The men he commanded, and others too, began to call him Sikandar Sahib, Sikandar* being their name for Alexander the Great and not too far distant from their pronunciation of Skinner. But it was after the Battle of Malpura that he became a legend. It was a very severe battle in which many lives were lost and he and his battalion distinguished themselves. But on this occasion it was not valour that won him fame but a stroke of luck that set everyone laughing. On that same day, while the men were still

* To rhyme with thunder.

laughing, fate struck him a heavy blow, the most painful since his mother's death.

There is no need to dwell on that day's fighting or on the futility of the war to which it was a climax. The Maharaja of Jaipur had consented to pay tribute to Scindia as the Emperor's Deputy and overlord of Hindostan. Now – in January 1798 – he refused to pay the tribute. An army of fifty thousand men was sent against him and of this de Boigne's Second Brigade formed a part. It was now under Pohlman the Hanoverian instead of Sutherland. Jaipur put a force of similar numbers into the field. After some manoeuvring, the two forces met at Malpura, in a battle very costly to both sides, a battle which ended the war. It was made more bitter by the memory of a previous occasion when Madhoji Scindia, the old *patel*, the uncle of the present Maharaja and of Harji, had been forced to fly, narrowly escaping with his life and leaving his turban on the field. It was a memory felt by the Marathas to be a deep disgrace.

Now for the first time, James saw the famous charge of Rahtor cavalry. To the end of his life, he told the tale; how ten thousand Rajputs of the Rahtor clan charged the Chevalier Dudrenec's brigade of eight thousand infantry, quickening from a walk to a trot and then to a canter and a full gallop, charging home against cannon blasting them with grape, against volleys of musketry and a line of glittering bayonets. Thousands fell; it seemed impossible that they could go on. But they went on, riding over their own dead. He saw Dudrenec's brigade ground to powder, destroyed, ridden over – and saw the Rahtors go straight on to attack and scatter and pursue the Maratha horse a thousand yards in the rear. When at last they came back, the Rahtors thought the battle was theirs; they rode in small groups, careless and at ease, laughing at their victory. They saw the colours of their allies flying and did not know they had all been captured. While they had been chasing the Maratha horse, the battle had been won by de Boigne's infantry brigades in the centre. The Rahtors were taken unawares and mown down by disciplined fire.

It was a terrible battle. In the Maratha camp, it was known that the Maharaja of Jaipur had fled defeated from the field – but not whether he had halted and reformed at his camp or abandoned the field altogether. James was sent with some three hundred horsemen to find out. He moved forward cautiously at first but with increasing confidence; there was no opposition. Not a shot was fired. He had left the battlefield and its ghastly sights behind; he was nearing the enemy's camp. Here and there a wounded man, flying from the battle, had stumbled and fallen – but there were no picquets, no scouts, no sign of resistance. He reached the camp and with constant halts to look about him threaded his way between the outer tents. Dogs nosing for scraps, abandoned gear, crows in the horse-lines, scattered bedding, not a man in sight. He came to the Maharaja's great tent.

James pulled aside the curtains and peered warily in. He was still caked in sweat, dust and blood. His eyes searched the space within. It was more magnificent than anything he had ever seen. But no one, not a soul, was there; it was deserted, strewn with signs of abandoned wealth and sovereignty – jewelled peacock fans, maces, standards.

Stiffly he walked in, drawn sword in one hand, loaded pistol in the other. Still not a soul. He went forward to the throne, looked behind it; nothing. The two troopers with him were round-eyed with astonishment. He turned to them.

'They've gone!' he said. 'We must get back quickly and report. We may take a few things, though; we needn't leave all the loot for those who come after us. But we must be quick.'

He picked up a box that lay on a rich Persian carpet near the throne, a box that had been flung down half-opened. It held precious objects used by the Maharaja in his private worship, jugs and spoons and cups of gold and two small golden figures with diamond eyes. James took as many of these things as he could carry or thrust inside the breast of his tunic.

'Come on!' he said to the troopers, 'we must get back and report.'

But as he turned to go his eye was caught by something which seemed more curious than valuable, a brass fish, suspended behind the throne, with two yak's tails hanging from the mouth like moustaches. He seized it and once outside the tent hung it carelessly from his saddle, concealing the precious objects in a cavity within the pommel.

He rode back to the Maratha camp and made for the Commander-in-Chief's tent. But as soon as he entered the camp he heard cries of astonishment and sudden laughter. Men stared at him with open mouths, then waved, pointed, laughed. He could not understand it but he would not stop to enquire. He had to get his news to the Commander-in-Chief.

He found the General in front of his tent. By his side was Major Pohlman – James's battalion commander when he first joined – now in command of the Second Brigade. James gave them his message without dismounting. The enemy had entirely deserted their camp. But they were smiling as he spoke and in ribald laughter when he finished.

'Please dismount, Captain Skinner,' said the Maratha Commander-in-Chief.

James was afraid that if he parted from his horse, someone else might get possession of those gold figures hidden in the saddle. He said: 'Forgive me, Maharaj, but I have had several narrow escapes and some minor wounds. I am in need of rest.'

'Well, you shall have rest – but I want to thank you. You see, I think – I rather think – that you have struck a great blow today and avenged the honour of the old *patel* – Madhoji Scindia – whom we all served once.'

Lakwa Dada rose and walked towards James, who was still sitting his horse, altogether bewildered. 'What is this that you have, hanging from your saddle?' He put his hand on the brass fish and looked at James with a curious smile.

'I have no idea. I found it hanging by the Maharaja's throne. I did not think it was of value.'

'It is the Fish of Honour – the greatest reward the Mughal Emperor could bestow on a vassal. It was given to this Maharaja's father – with whom our old master had a debt of long standing – which now you have paid. Will you give me that fish?'

'Of course – on one condition! That you ask for nothing else!'

'To that I willingly agree.'

So James handed over the fish and, since his own orderly had now come, at last dismounted and gave him his horse, whispering orders that he should be very careful of what was hidden in the saddle. The Commander-in-Chief embraced him, gave him a robe of honour and a magnificent palanquin and at last allowed him to go. That was how James Skinner became really famous – as the man who had captured the Fish of Honour without even knowing what it was.

He escaped to his tent, followed by laughter, but it was kindly laughter; everyone was pleased with him. He was wounded and deadly tired but elated; he longed for rest but his mind was full of pleasure at what had happened and yet obsessed by the thought of what he must do before he could rest; Shadul Khan, he had to see Shadul Khan about the men, and he must see the Marwari banker who was with the camp and hand over to him those precious things he had taken from the Maharaja's tent. Then he could rest. Shadul Khan had been left in command with orders to see that the men were comfortable and to report. He was there at the tent, almost as soon as James; he made his report, about their comrades killed in action, men they had both known; about the wounded and who was still missing; about the condition of those who were still capable of marching and the arrangements for their comfort. He finished his report; all had been done that could be done. James gave him the jewels and gold and told him to take all this to the banker. But Shadul Khan did not go. He stood there silent.

'What is it, Shadul Khan?' James asked.

'Sahib, there is bad news, news that will grieve you.'

'Tell me. Tell me, quickly.'

'Sahib, it is Maharaj Harji Scindia.'

'Oh, not Harji. Not Harji.'

'Yes, Sahib. There is no doubt. He was killed by the

Rahtors in their charge after they overran Dudrenec's brigade.'

James sat down.

'Not Harji,' he said again.

'Do not grieve, Sahib,' said Shadul Khan very gently. 'God will send other friends.'

'But not Harji.'

He sat still.

'Kindness, Shadul Khan,' James said dully, which means 'Thank you'. And he added: 'Permission', which means leave to depart. Shadul Khan left him. He sat still with his head between his hands for a long time, till Nagendra Singh came and gently persuaded him to bath and eat and sleep.

After that battle, the Maharaja of Jaipur agreed to pay his tribute and all was as it had been before.

## 10 The Raja of Uniyara

Not long after the death of Harji, Robert Skinner, James's younger brother, arrived. He was full of excitement, delighted that he had been commissioned, delighted that he had been posted to the battalion James commanded. James took him by the hand and presented him to the officers of the battalion, fierce grizzled old men, twice the age of these two boys, men with their great beards brushed upward and outward like tigers' whiskers.

'This is my brother!' he said. 'Protect him! Be to him a shield. Teach him, as you taught me. Teach him as a father teaches a son. And he will become a father to you – as I have become your father and you my children.'

They laid their hands on breast and forehead.

'On our heads be it!' they said.

Of course James was glad to have his brother with him. He remembered what Shadul Khan had said: 'God will send other friends.' But not like Harji, he answered once again.

Robert was seventeen to James's twenty-two; he could be talked to, he could be trusted; he was a friend and a brother. But Harji had surprised him at every meeting; he had always a new thought, a new way of looking at things – at life, at politics or at war. James was aware too that Shadul Khan, who had been virtually his second-in-command, had, as he would have put it himself, taken one pace to the rear. Robert could never take Shadul Khan's place – how could he ever have that knowledge of what the men were feeling? But Robert must be there whenever he and Shadul talked and his presence dropped the lightest of filmy veils between them. Shadul expected him to be closer to Robert than he was.

James was very much alone. He was young and vigorous, with death always near him and the possibility of death always in his thoughts. The stimulus of constant danger, constant exertion, heightened the demands of his body. It cried out for women. He satisfied it but not as yet with any woman with whom he felt more than physical attraction and passing satisfaction. How could he feel at one with a woman who had no understanding of the pleasure he took in command, in power, in being the father and the leader of his men? If he could have met a woman like her – his mother – who understood the pride and valour of men!

Robert's coming was followed by a round of petty duties. Not merely training of the men, though that was always a duty not to be neglected and an interest that never failed, but skirmishes, little sieges, tasks that turned sometimes on getting a refractory chief to pay his tribute, sometimes on bringing to book a brigand who, after a few successes, had begun to fancy himself as a prince. Robert was wounded in one of these encounters and had gone to headquarters to recover when something happened that James felt later had been of critical importance in his life. It loomed so large in his memories that he may perhaps have attributed to those crucial hours – hours when he lay half-conscious on the battlefield, dying, as he thought – decisions, trends of thought, resolutions, on which he had long been pondering but which seemed to crystallize only then.

The battalion was sent on an expedition in which, even more than in the War of the Aunts, the outcome was a matter of indifference and, if right lay anywhere, it was with the other side. There was a quarrel between two Rajas, the ruler of Karaoli and the ruler of Uniyara. The cause of the quarrel was of no importance. It concerned nobody else. But one of the two, the Raja of Karaoli, asked General Perron if he might hire one battalion of de Boigne's famous infantry. A price was agreed, and James Skinner was sent with his battalion. He was the only commissioned officer.

After some manoeuvring, there came a day when the two little armies were occupying positions fairly close to each other. It seemed likely that there would be a battle very soon. Shadul Khan, together with Amrit Singh – who had also been with James in the affair of the gun in the pass – came to him one evening.

'Sahib,' Shadul Khan began, 'from what I hear, the Raja we are fighting against is a better man than ours.'

'I had begun to think the same,' James replied with a smile.

'The man who has hired us does not come into camp with his army, like a man of courage. And he does not give their pay to these other battalions that he has scraped up from God knows where. They are all in arrears, a year behind at least. He is a mean man and I think he is a coward. His own villagers haven't a good word for him.'

'And this is what you all think?' He turned to Amrit Singh.

'We do.'

'You may be right,' said James thoughtfully, 'and I fear you are. None the less, we are soldiers; we are Scindia's men and we are under General Perron's orders. We have been ordered to fight for the Raja of Karaoli against the Raja of Uniyara. All we have to do is to obey orders and keep bright the honour of our battalion and of our corps and do our duty as soldiers.'

'Indeed, Sahib, that is true. But it is permitted to consider what may arise in the hazard of battle?'

'Certainly. And that too is something you have talked over with your brothers?'

'With the officers, yes.'

'Tell me what you think.'

'Sahib, we think that if battle is joined tomorrow these five battalions on our right will go over to the enemy and all the horse – and we shall be left alone to face six times our number of infantry and all the other Raja's horse.'

'And then what do you think we should do?'

'It will depend how hard they press us and on the time of day. We could fall back on that deserted village; there is cover behind those mud walls. But not for long. Their guns are well served.'

'And then?'

'There are those ravines two miles further to our rear. There we could take up a position in which we could stand. The question is whether we can reach them.'

'By the courage of men and with the help of God, subedar, we shall. All is in God's hands. I agree that your plan is the only one possible and if it comes to the worst, that is what we shall do.'

Perhaps with a corner of the mind they had hoped he would think of some way they might change sides without loss of honour. But he had given a firm lead and they took it.

'By the courage of men and with the help of God . . .' Those words, '*Himmat-i-mardan wa madad-i-khuda*', were to become the motto of Skinner's Horse and are so to this day. But next day, 31 January 1800, it seemed as though God's help was not forthcoming. Towards evening, the worst *had* come to the worst. James Skinner's battalion alone had stood firm; all the rest of the Raja of Karaoli's army had deserted or fled. The one battalion had fallen back on the village and had then tried to make a further retreat to the ravines. But they were surrounded. The enemy were attacking them from every side. It was clear there was no hope of reaching the ravines. The Raja of Uniyara himself had led one charge and was mustering his men for another.

James Skinner spoke to his men.

'Death is something every man must face,' he said. 'It is no use trying to escape from death. It comes to all. The question is whether you die facing it or run away. Shall we die like soldiers – or like cowards?'

'Like soldiers!' they roared.

So it was decided.

'It all ends here,' he thought – as he had thought in the pass.

He led them in a charge against the enemy and they captured two guns.

'Form a square!' he shouted and for a wild moment he thought that there might after all be some hope. But there was another charge and there were enemy inside the square. He saw a horseman gallop towards him and as he galloped he put a matchlock to his shoulder and aimed it. James remembered no more of that battle.

When he came to himself, the sun was rising. He had been stripped of weapons and uniform; he must have been left for dead. He was cold and trembling; he was parched with thirst and very weak. He found he could move his arms. He explored his body; there was a wound in the groin, throbbing, caked with blood; that must have been the matchlock bullet. There were clouds of flies already. Crows – he could hear the sound of crows, quarrelling over food, pecking at the dead. And vultures, he could hear vultures too. He was surrounded by death. He was still trembling; the thirst was growing more intense; so was the pain in his groin. Two centres of torture but pain in the whole body.

As the sun rose higher, it began to scorch his exposed skin. He raised his head; there was a bush which gave a little shade and he tried to drag himself towards it with his arms. Then for the first time he was aware of Subedar Amrit Singh lying within a few feet of him. He was not dead. His eyes were open and there was recognition in them.

'Leg,' he said, 'leg gone. Leg not there.' He was not pleading or asking for anything. Each word he said seemed a discovery. 'Water. Water. Captain Sahib.'

James could just drag himself inch by inch to the shade.

He could do nothing for Amrit Singh. He heard him say: 'Not much longer.' That was all. The day dragged on. As thirst grew worse there were long spells when he was unconscious. There were times too when he was only a tiny speck – of what? a speck of self – floating in a bowl of luminous haze. And then again all would go. On and on the day dragged. Night fell and he was cold again and trembling. Now there were jackals instead of vultures and crows, tearing at the dead, crunching and tearing and snarling. One came and sniffed at his face; he could smell its rank breath. He made a movement; there was a stone; his hand had closed on it before; it was a weapon of a kind. He jerked it at the jackal, which slunk away. But he knew it would soon be back. He sank back into the haze.

When morning came they were both alive. Again Amrit Singh said: 'Not much longer.' Then as the sun rose higher, James was for the first time aware of a living, moving, human being. There was an old woman moving among the dead and a man with her. He managed to utter a faint cry.

'*Aré*,' he called. '*Aré, bahin.* Oh, sister.'

She began to move towards him and then it struck him that perhaps she had some sinister purpose, that she had come with a knife to mutilate the dead and dying with some horrible rite of witchcraft in view. But no, she had a goglet of water, she had a basket of bread. She poured water for him. He made a channel for it with his hands as a Hindu does. It was like water on burning sand; it was soaked in a minute into his parched flesh. She gave him more. She offered him bread. 'For the love of God,' she said. It was coarse bread, made from *jawar*, the millet that grows in the rains, the coarsest and poorest food of the Indian peasant. He could not eat at first but she soaked it in water and he took a little; it made him feel better. She gave him more water. He pointed to Amrit Singh, but the subedar made a faint gesture of refusal. He was the highest of high-caste Rajputs; she was a Chamar – a skinner of dead cattle, a worker in leather. He could barely whisper but he said:

'Two or three more hours' pain. Better than die polluted.'

She smiled in pity, made a gesture of resignation and acceptance, offered water again to James. He remembered what he had said about the courage of men and the help of God. He thanked God that he was alive. He thanked the old woman. He asked her name and village.

'If I live,' he said, 'I shall remember you.'

She went on to other wounded. The water and bread had given him strength but she had brought more than that, she had brought hope. He began to think that he would live. And that afternoon there came a chief, one of the nobles of the Uniyara Raja, with an escort of horsemen, with carts for the wounded and gravediggers for the dead. They wrapped James in a sheet and laid him in a cart and took him to a tent where there lay many of his men, more than three hundred he learnt later.

'Ah,' they cried in joy, propping themselves up as they lay on the ground, 'here is our dear Captain.'

They gave water to Amrit Singh. There were *vaids*, Indian doctors of an ancient school of learning that goes back more than two thousand years. They cleaned James's wound and took out the matchlock slug, putting healing herbs over the place and securing it with soft comforting bandages. Then orderlies lifted the *charpai* – a low flat wooden bed with neither head nor foot, strung with broad webbing – and carried him to the Raja's tent near by. James had been told not to sit up; he made a gesture of respect by putting the tips of his fingers together. The Raja stood up to greet him and then brought a little round stool of rushes, a *morha*, the humblest and simplest piece of furniture there is, and sat on it by the bedside.

'That was a gallant fight,' he said. 'You fought like a Rajput. Tell me who you are and why you fought against me with such valour.'

James told him who he was and that his mother was a Rajputni. As to why he fought:

'I am a soldier,' he said. 'Now your prisoner. As a soldier, it is my duty to fight as well as I can, just as I am ordered. I do not ask questions. I do as I am told.'

The Raja, who was about his own age, looked at him with pleasure. 'We will talk more later,' he said. 'Now you must rest.' The orderlies carried him back to the hospital tent. The chief *vaid* came to him with a preparation of opium.

'When you have drunk this,' he said, 'you will sleep and the pain will go and you will wake refreshed.'

But before James could drink it, a *chobdar* came from the Raja. He ushered in a great tray covered with cooked food and a bag of silver rupees.

James said: 'Count out a hundred rupees to the *chobdar*. Divide the rest between my men. Divide the food among the wounded who can eat. Give my salaams to the Raja. One thing before I sleep, *vaid-ji*. Amrit Singh, Subedar Amrit Singh, will he live?'

'There is hope,' he was told.

'And Shadul Khan?'

'He lives.'

He drank the opium and in a few minutes he was asleep. He slept for more than twelve hours.

Next day, the Raja came to see James and sat by his bedside. He begged him to move to a smaller tent near by where he would be quieter. But James said he would stay with his men and see them through their sufferings.

'Well, indeed, they deserve your care, for they stood by you gallantly. Of all those you had with you, hardly twenty were left alive and unwounded.'

'You asked me why *I* fought,' James said. 'Let me ask you something. Why do *men* fight? As I lay on the battlefield, thinking I should die, I was on the point of making a vow that I would never fight again. But I did not quite make that vow. I was too tired. I think I became unconscious before I made it.'

'It is strange you should ask me that question,' said the Raja, 'because yesterday, when you told me you thought it was your duty as a soldier simply to fight as you were ordered, I remembered our holy book, the *Gita* of the Lord Krishna. You do not know that holy book, Captain Skinner?'

'No.'

'Nevertheless, you have learnt some of its lessons. The first lesson is that you must do whatever it is that is laid down for you to do. Perhaps you learnt it without knowing it from your mother, who was a Rajput lady, I am sure of good family. It is written in our holy book: "Valour, glory, firmness, skill, generosity, steadiness in battle, and ability to rule – these constitute the duty of a soldier – they flow from his own nature." And when the Lord Krishna speaks of a soldier, he means of course a born soldier, a Rajput, a soldier by nature. And again he says: "Blessed are the soldiers who find their opportunity. . . . If killed, they shall attain Heaven; if victorious, they shall enjoy the kingdom of earth. Therefore, arise – and fight!" So you see, if you are indeed a soldier by nature, as I think you are, being in part a Rajput, it is your duty to fight and I am glad you did not make that vow.'

'I believe you are right.'

'We are all of us – each of us – part of something much larger, part of something eternal, Captain Skinner. It is man's great task in life to find his true self and know what it is that he has to do. It is easier for a Rajput. He knows his task. He must rule or obey, according to his station. And he must fight.'

'And you think it is my task and my nature to fight? I shall remember what you have said. I shall think about it. But it seems to me very strange that I am still alive and I begin to wonder what it is to be alive. I never wondered about that when I was well. I was always too busy. How near I was to death! How thin the veil! I did not think I should come back. I am glad I did not make that vow. But I think I will make a vow – but another vow. If I live to a good age and am in comfort and have money, I will build a church for the worship of my father's God, and a temple for my mother's gods, and a mosque for the God of the men who follow Mohammad and have fought by my side. I swear it.'

James had many more talks with the Raja. But that was the most important. The Raja was kind to him and to all his men. He was a true Rajput, brave, generous and chivalrous.

To James he gave a robe of honour, a shield and a horse. To every man of the wounded he gave a present of money. He sent them all back to General Perron.

Subedar Amrit Singh lived, though he lost his leg. Shadul Khan lived.

## 11 The Lord of the World

When James had fully recovered from his wound, he was made commander of two battalions who acted as a special bodyguard to General Perron. Robert Skinner, now also recovered from his wound, was ordered away to service not far from Uniyara and before he left he came to say goodbye to his brother in his tent.

James felt, in those months after his recovery, as though he had been born again. Something hard and external had fallen away from him, something within had renewed the springs of his being. He felt a new warmth and pleasure when Robert came to see him. His reserve had dropped away; now he could tell Robert everything.

He began to tell him as much as he could put in words of what had happened at Uniyara, of the old woman who had brought him water when he thought he would die and of his talk with the Raja.

'Since you are going to those parts, will you find that old woman for me? Here is her name and village and a thousand rupees. Give her the money and tell her I look on her as a mother.'

'A mother!' said Robert fiercely. 'A Chamar! A leather worker! It is an insult to our mother!'

'No, no,' said James, with a smile, 'you must not look on it like that. She gave me water and food – for the love of God; she gave me life and hope and I said I should never forget her. Since she gave me life, she is my mother. But, Robert, I am sorry you are going away just now. There is a great deal

I want to talk to you about. The Marathas are more divided than ever. I miss Harji sadly. He was a brave and honest man; he knew what was going on and told me a great deal. Well, he had a soldier's death, in battle.'

'Maratha quarrels are not our business. You've often told me that all we have to do is to obey orders.'

'But it is as well to know the dangers. You remember the ambush I told you about, when I was with Harji? He and I obeyed orders, but we knew there was treachery – and it was a good thing we did know and that we didn't walk into that trap unsuspecting. Just step outside and take a turn round the tent, will you?'

Robert came back. 'No one listening,' he said. 'I don't understand what's happening at all. Perron seems to be hated by everyone who dares to speak. And what is George Thomas doing here?'

James told him, as far as he could, what had brought Thomas to Aligarh. The War of the Aunts had been patched up – but Scindia was still enamoured of Ghatke's daughter. And the horrible Ghatke still had influence. He waited for the right moment and then seized several of those chiefs who had supported the Aunts. He had them executed by means that were cruel and spectacular, tying some to rockets that were discharged into the air and causing others to be beaten to death with wooden tent mallets. After this, no one felt safe and there were few of his vassals on whom Scindia could rely with any certainty. He was therefore more than usually vulnerable to attack from Holkar and even from his nominal overlord the Peshwa. He dared not leave his capital at Ujjain in the South, where he had one of de Boigne's brigades, Perron having three in the North. Scindia called on Perron for support, asking him to send another brigade south. But Perron only made excuses – belated and unconvincing excuses.

He had several good reasons for keeping three brigades in Hindostan. All four brigades depended for their pay on the lands in the Doab allotted first to de Boigne, and now to himself. These must be protected and kept in order.

Apart from that, possession of the Emperor's person in Delhi was essential; so long as he held the Emperor, everyone believed he was master. The Emperor was the Lord of the World. And west and by north from Delhi lay George Thomas, a dashing ambitious soldier of fortune, with a force nearly equal to one of Perron's three brigades. If Perron's back were turned he might seize Delhi and the Emperor. It would then be easy for him to ally himself with the Sikh princes and make himself master of Hindostan.

That was a reasonable fear and one that Perron could legitimately plead to Scindia. He had another motive which he kept to himself. He was a Frenchman and, what is more, a revolutionary citizen-patriot who meant one day to retire to France. He had sent an envoy to Buonaparte; he asked for a French landing in Western India and for a party of French officers to take over command of de Boigne's brigades. Meanwhile, he promoted such French officers as he had. A French empire in India – with Perron as Governor-General! It was essential to these hopes that he should have as many as possible of the disciplined brigade troops concentrated under his own hand. So he would send nothing to Scindia in the South.

Thomas could not be ignored. Perhaps he could be absorbed. He had been offered an appointment under Perron – but he had refused. He had a great dislike for the French, going back perhaps to the days when a Frenchman had succeeded him in the favours of the Begam Somru. Scindia had then decided to offer him an independent command, directly under himself.

Scindia did not yet realize the full extent of Perron's ambitions and he entrusted the negotiations to Perron – whose aims of course were very different from his master's. Perron saw at once that if he could trap Thomas into marching south to help Scindia he would have solved two of his problems at the same time. But if Thomas refused – well, he would be no worse off than he was now.

That was the reason why George Thomas was in Aligarh, and just as James finished explaining as much as he knew of the situation to Robert, the conference between Perron and Thomas was coming to an end. Thomas had listened to Perron's proposals with growing impatience. Surely there must be something more coming! But no, Perron had finished. That was his offer! Thomas sprang to his feet.

'And is that all you have to say? I'm to give up my property in Haryana – which I've built up myself and which gives me guns and money – and I'm to take an allowance instead? How would I know whether I'd get the money on pay day? They'd keep my troops waiting whenever it pleased them and soon my men would be no more reliable than the Marathas. Why would I give up my property for that? And I'm to march away to the South to get Scindia out of the scrape he's got himself into and which *you* won't help him out of? Leaving you to look after the Emperor in Delhi – and add my property to your own – and make yourself Maharaja of Hindostan no doubt. And then what? Bring in the French, eh? I don't trust you! Damned French upstart! Do you take me for a fool? Amn't I a prince already in my own right and an officer of the Emperor with a licence to mint my own rupees and found my own cannon? Why should I give that up just to pull the chestnuts out of the fire for you? You go to the South and help Scindia yourself if it's so important. I'll stay here, thank you very much. There's a kingdom to be made from all these Sikh chiefs, a kingdom of the Punjab – and let me tell you I'm the boy to make it. And it won't be at the feet of Buonaparte that I'll lay it when I have it! King George is the boy for me. Tell Scindia he's got to make me a very much better offer than that if he wants me as an ally.'

Perron's English might be poor but the meaning of his reply was perfectly clear. He would tell the Maharaja that his offer had been insolently refused. And that left the Maharaja no alternative but to crush Thomas on the field of battle. Thomas stamped out of the tent. Perron turned to an aide-de-camp to whom he spoke in French: 'Just as I expected!' he said. 'Far too hot-headed.'

Meanwhile, the Skinner brothers had said goodbye.

Robert went off on an expedition into Rajputana; James, a few days later, went with Perron to Delhi. Perron wanted to make sure of his grip on the Emperor.

Six battalions, with guns and cavalry, camped outside Delhi, near the tomb of the Emperor Humayon. Perron sent an officer to the Qilladar, the Governor of the Fort, a Maratha, ordering him to present himself before General Perron, Scindia's Deputy for Hindostan and his superior officer. The Qilladar sent a contemptuous answer; 'Come and get me!' he said in effect. Perron and his men marched into the city, unopposed. But the gates of the Red Fort were shut against them. They began to bombard a stretch of wall that was in poor condition.

On the third day a *chobdar* came out of the Fort followed by a Muslim, who appeared to be a noble of high rank. He was brought to Perron, who saluted him.

'On behalf of the Emperor, the King of Kings, the Lord of the World,' he said. Perron bowed in reply, made a salaam, and said: 'I await the Emperor's commands.' Perron's Persian was poor. He spoke through an interpreter.

'The King of Kings, the Lord of the World, is surprised,' the herald continued, 'that the Imperial Palace should be rudely assaulted by one whom he believed the faithful servant of his own faithful servant, the Maharaja Scindia.'

Perron's reply was that the Emperor's humble servant sought the inestimable boon of an audience with His Majesty. He had begged only to be allowed to enter the Fort and had been denied entry by an insolent and insubordinate Qilladar, who would be punished for the affront he had put upon His Majesty and His Majesty's humble guest and servant.

After further compliments, it was agreed that the Qilladar should be allowed to leave without being made a prisoner and that Perron and his men might enter the Fort and seek audience of His Majesty. After his rash defiance, the Qilladar must have had second thoughts and he had taken fright when he saw that Perron meant business. He had used the prestige of the Emperor to surrender the Fort and escape punishment.

They marched in by the great gate that faces the Jama

Masjid – the Mosque of Assembly – and the Qilladar left unobtrusively by the River Gate. Perron deputed officers to take charge immediately of every administrative department of the Fort and of the City. One appointment only remained unfilled – that of Qilladar or Governor of the Fort. Everyone knew Perron had decided that this should be Captain Drugeon, a French officer. But the Emperor's approval was necessary. The Imperial Chamberlain was asked if an audience might be granted next day and gracious approval was accorded.

Next day, Perron took with him a dozen officers and a score of troopers. They were escorted by the imperial *chobdars* to the *Diwan-i-Khas*, the Hall of Private Audience. James saw stained uniforms, frayed brocade and rusty weapons. Courteous manners, profound salaams. A host of servants, servants at every door they passed, but all shabby and haggard. Cobwebs in the doorways, grass between the stones of the pavement. Then the Hall of Private Audience, where in faded splendour were gathered the last shabby courtiers and their old, blind and shabby Emperor. James raised his eyes, and found inscribed high on the wall the famous Persian verse of which he had heard so often:

> Agar firdaus ba-ru-i-zamīn ast
> Istīn ast, istīn ast, istīn ast.
>
> If there is a paradise on the face of the earth,
> It is here, it is here, it is here.

A herald stepped forward, the same noble who had accompanied the *chobdar* to make terms.

'On behalf of the Emperor, the King of Kings, the Lord of the World – welcome!'

Perron was the son of a French peasant, short, round-faced, ruddy; one hand had been blown off. He was surrounded by a glittering escort, the European officers in uniforms of bright colours, scarlet, blue, green and white, sparkling with gold lace and burnished steel; the Maratha nobles in subtler shades of silk brocade, orange and pink and pale blue, mulberry, peach and damson, starred with jewels, but with armour and headpieces of shining steel. The Emperor's retinue in tarnished *sherwanis* of sad colours – grey, mauve, cinnamon – looked poor and hungry by contrast.

First came acts of homage and the presentation of *nazrana*, ceremonial gifts. Perron and each of his officers in turn came forward and did obeisance, then presented to the Emperor costly presents on a silk cushion. The presents were taken away by the Emperor's servants.

At last, Perron spoke and his interpreter said for him in Persian: 'The humble slave of Imperial Magnificence seeks a boon.'

The Emperor Shah Alam, King of the World, spoke: 'Does the cat seek a boon of the mouse whom he keeps in a cage?'

Perron was silent for a moment at this. It seemed almost that he was abashed. But he quickly recovered. 'Imperial Magnificence is pleased to mock a humble servant.'

'If there is mockery in what passes between us, I do not think it is only I who mock. Tell me without concealment what you want.'

'I seek leave to introduce to the King of Kings Captain Drugeon, who is here by my side, and I beg that Imperial Magnificence may be pleased to appoint him Governor and Constable of the Fort and Palace of Delhi.'

The Emperor's thin blind fingers tormented his beard. 'I am an old man now,' he said, 'and I do not expect much pleasure on earth. All I ask for myself is peace, to be left alone before my death so that I may pray to God and sometimes write a little poetry. I should have liked to give up the throne to one of my sons. But it suited you better to keep me. You ask me to agree to a change of gaoler. No, you need say nothing about that word, which I choose because I have no time left for pretence. The Governor of the Fort has been my gaoler a long time now. One of my gaolers blinded me because he could not find any treasure in the Fort. There was nothing very surprising in that, because I had never been able to find any myself. Since then I have had gaolers who have not practised bodily cruelty but they have robbed me. There is an allowance – an allowance that would not be ungenerous if it reached me. Let me remind myself. I think that among those of my faithful servants who are my masters it is the Peshwa who is my deputy as ruler of this vast Empire? And *his* deputy I think is the Maharaja Scindia? And *his* deputy as ruler of Hindostan I think is the noble General Perron who stands before me? What escapes my memory is which of these faithful servants of mine it is who pays the allowance of which my last gaoler kept at least half?'

'It is the Maharaja Scindia who pays the allowance.' Perron was rather surly, a peasant with the whiphand who is being played off the stage by a man with style. 'As for that Qilladar, I have suspected him for some time. That was why I came to Delhi. He will be punished.'

'He has already been pardoned,' said the Emperor, scattering the dust of the Qilladar on the pavement with those slender eloquent fingers. 'What I have to ask of you, General Perron, is that the allowance shall be fully paid in future. How shall we make sure of that?'

'Captain Drugeon, if Your Majesty is pleased to appoint him, will see to that.'

'Let me take Captain Drugeon by the hand. I cannot see you, Captain Drugeon, to read your face. A dry warm hand. It is easy to rob an old blind man who has many mouths to feed. Would you do that, Captain Drugeon?'

'Your Majesty – '

'A foolish question, for you can hardly be expected to say yes. Will you follow the custom of this country and say: "On my head be it!"?'

'On my head be it,' said Captain Drugeon.

'On your head and on your son's head,' said the Emperor, 'though I do not think Europeans mind very much what happens to their sons. God will remember you if you remember that promise, Captain Drugeon.' He paused. 'There are many mouths to feed, and it is not fitting to greet me with titles of honour when my children are hungry and my servants in rags. You will require the Imperial seal on the warrant of appointment. My Chamberlain will affix it as soon as he has received the arrears of my allowance. I shall trust Captain Drugeon. Let *pan* and scent be brought. You have leave to depart.'

## 12 One Irish Sword

PERRON had decided on the destruction of George Thomas. That was his next move. For this purpose, he detached the Third Brigade, including James Skinner and the two battalions which had been acting as his personal bodyguard. In command of the whole force was Major Bourquien, formerly a cook and said to have been better as a cook than as a soldier. He was a connexion of Perron's by marriage but another motive for giving him this appointment – quite unjustifiable on military grounds – may have been to humiliate both Thomas and some of the fine officers of British parentage in the Third Brigade. Once again, James Skinner found himself committed to fighting on the wrong side in a futile quarrel.

Bourquien's force advanced from Delhi towards Hansi, Thomas's capital – a considerable fortress where he had established his celebrated mint and his cannon foundry. Some way short of Hansi, at a place called Georgegarh, they were confronted by a force skilfully drawn up in a strong defensive position. Having some advantage in numbers, Bourquien's men attacked. It was a very severe battle. The troops on both sides were experienced, well trained and, up to battalion level, well led. But, perhaps because no one felt much confidence in Bourquien, the advantage lay with Thomas. His men had stood firm all day against repeated attacks and only nightfall prevented him from turning the defence into an attack and driving Bourquien from the field.

On that night of December 1802, James Skinner came to the mess tent of the officers of the Third Brigade. He was covered with blood and dust and very tired. He had been fighting all day; he had come to the mess as he was, unwashed, thinking of the dead and of the futility of the quarrel in which they had died, hoping for news of other battalions. The lamps had been lighted but there was no one in the tent. He sat down in a camp chair of wood and canvas; a servant brought him brandy and water. He sat with his hand over his eyes. He had not waited long when Carnegie and Stewart came. Carnegie was a Scot; Stewart, like James, was country-born. They had been commanding battalions at the other end of the line.

'I am truly glad to see you both,' said James, looking up for a moment only. 'After such a day. We have had very heavy losses. The most severe battle I have ever been in. So many killed in a quarrel between Perron and Thomas! And nothing gained either way. What is the news with you?' He broke off.

'Don't you know? You can't know. James – I'm sorry – your brother – '

'Robert? Killed?'

'Hit, they said, and feared killed, just as dusk was falling. It was a jemadar of the Second Battalion told me and the subedar confirmed it.'

'I must go and look for him. Perron and Thomas! Curse them both!'

James hurried out. There was a waning half moon, just risen, and he knew where the Second Battalion had been posted. But he had not much hope of finding his brother among so many dead and wounded. There had been a long cannonade; each side in turn had advanced against a steady fire of grape and musketry. Each in turn had been driven back with dreadful losses; the ground was strewn with corpses and with the torn bodies of men in stupor or coma. He wandered among the dead, calling out in case Robert was lying conscious and in pain, turning over any body that looked as though it might have been an officer's. But he could find no sign of Robert and at last, sick at heart and yet half-hoping for the unbelievable, he turned back towards the mess tent.

As he walked in at one door, Robert walked in at the other. 'Robert!'

'James!'

'I thought you were dead!'

'*I* thought *you* were dead!'

'I've been looking for you – out there!'

'And *I've* been looking for *you*!'

They embraced. Everyone brought them drinks. A cannon-ball had fallen close to Robert at the end of the day and he had been knocked down by the body of a man killed near him and half-buried in debris. How the story about James had arisen they could not be sure, but he had had narrow escapes enough. Soon they had forgotten that and soon all the men in the tent were talking about the prospects for the next day. They were all high in praise of Thomas.

Carnegie looked behind him before he said: 'Half our trouble is Bourquien. He never came near us all through the battle. Did you see him?'

'None of *us* saw him. I believe he skulked here all day. Men won't fight if their commander skulks.'

'What can you expect? He was only a cook.'

At that moment Bourquien entered the tent.

'Good evening, Major Bourquien,' said Carnegie and the others said in chorus:

'Good evening, Major Bourquien.'

Next day a flag of truce was sent out and till midday both sides were engaged in bringing in the wounded and burying the dead. After that, Perron's Third Brigade were on the alert, anxiously expecting an attack which they were doubtful whether they could beat off. But it did not come. Day after day passed and there was no move from Thomas. Reinforcements were on the way – another brigade – and soon Thomas's chance would have gone for ever. No one could guess what kept him quiet, he who had been so famous for taking the offensive.

It was James who got the first news, from Subedar Shadul Khan. 'On that day when we fought the battle, Sahib, Captain Hopkins was killed. He was a very close friend of George Jang Sahib' – that is Warlike George, or Thomas – 'and his heart was very sad and he began to drink. And he has been drinking ever since. He drinks every night till he is unconscious and then he starts again in the morning. His heart was bound to Captain Hopkins. His star has deserted him. All his men believed in his star. They would have fought to the death for him when his star was bright. But now they say his star has faded. They're beginning to leave him.'

The reinforcements arrived. The trickle of deserters from Thomas continued. Suddenly Thomas shook off his lethargy and began to act. But fifteen days had passed and it was too late. He was surrounded now by thirty thousand men. He tried to break out with his whole army but every attempt was beaten back. At last he gave up hope of extricating his army and, late one night, with three hundred chosen horsemen, he broke through the lines of his enemies and galloped for Hansi, the fort that had been his capital. In the course of the next few days, those who were left surrendered. The reinforcements marched away. The job was done; Thomas, besieged in Hansi, was no longer a power. It was just a matter of finishing him off. In the officers' mess, Bourquien was triumphant. He made a proclamation that deserters would be favourably received; he had copies of the proclamation wrapped round arrows and shot into the town; he sent letters to Thomas's Indian officers by the same means. Some of Thomas's men in the town replied, offering to rise against him, to capture him and to hand him over.

'Aha!' said Bourquien in his broken English. 'Not long now! That rascal Englishman. Damn fellow. I going to have him by neck. I throw him in prison and he try bread and water in place of brandy.'

'But sir,' said James Skinner, 'as between soldiers of fortune – it has not been the custom to proceed harshly with a beaten enemy – '

Bourquien interrupted him rudely. 'English customs!

What they matter? Damn English. Soon I get him by neck. Do as I like!'

'Let me order you another bottle, sir,' said Carnegie.

'A glass of wine with you, Major Bourquien,' said Stewart.

And one and all they began to ply him with wine, standing up to drink his health, till he was more cheerful. Then Carnegie came back to the question of Thomas. 'It will be more to your credit, sir, if Mr Thomas surrenders personally to you, than if he is captured by a pack of rascally sepoys who have turned traitor. It is your reputation that is important. And since he can no longer have any hope of success, he *will* surrender if we go to him on your behalf and offer him honourable terms. It will be your name that will triumph. And everyone will be impressed by your success and your generosity. He has a considerable military reputation.'

'No, no, I catch him, I put him in prison,' cried Bourquien, but they did not give up. James Skinner and Stewart repeated Carnegie's point in different words, and at last, having drunk a great deal, and being very merry, Bourquien called out: 'Well, gentlemen, you do as you wish. I give power. Though I not see why you love him. He be one damn Englishman, and Englishmen treat their children very bad.' He looked round with a sneer at his officers, who were nearly all country-born like the Skinners and debarred from the Company's service.

Next day Captain Carnegie went to the fort with a flag of truce. He found Thomas moody and unhappy, sitting despondently with his head in his hands. 'General Thomas,' he said, 'I have come to save you from dishonour.'

Thomas brightened up at that and came to meet him.

'And what is it you've come to tell me now?' he asked.

'I come on behalf of all the English officers – country-born and European – in Major Bourquien's brigade. I suppose you know that Major Bourquien has been corresponding with your troops?'

'Sure I know it well and I know that some of them have said they'll make me a prisoner and hand me over. Let them try!'

'But forgive my saying that your position is hopeless. The town is closely invested, there's treachery inside the fort, you're overwhelmingly outnumbered, and after your run of bad luck there's no chance of anyone coming to your help. We – the English officers – have prevailed on Major Bourquien to let us come and offer you terms. We would not like to see you captured by treachery.'

'Ah, 'tis noble of you. What are your terms?'

'Simple enough. You must hand over the fort. You may go free yourself, with all your private property – cash, jewels, furniture – and one of our battalions will escort you to the British frontier. Your men may march out with their private arms. Cannon, muskets – all the weapons *you* supplied – must be left in the fort.'

'How soon?'

'In two days. Meanwhile – cease fire on both sides.'

Thomas took two long strides forward and two back.

'I agree. Give me your hand.'

They shook hands.

'General,' said Carnegie, 'we were all sorry to hear about Hopkins. If you had had one or two more officers like Hopkins you'd have won that battle at Georgegarh.'

'He was my friend. The closest I ever had. Always to be trusted. It hit me harder than I could have believed.' Thomas made a large despairing gesture that swept away the memory and buried it. 'What must I do now?'

'You must sign this agreement. Then we hope you will do us the honour of dining with us.'

It was actually two days later, on 21 December 1802, that Thomas arrived at the mess tent of Major Bourquien's brigade with two officers and an escort of fifty troopers. As he came into the tent, it was clear that he was brooding on his misfortunes. The officers crowded round him, shook him by the hand and said how pleased they were at the privilege of meeting so renowned a soldier. He began to cheer up. He recognized Robert Skinner whom he had met a few days before in a hand-to-hand encounter on the ramparts.

'Ah, Lieutenant Skinner!' he cried. 'Let me embrace you!

That was a good cut you had at me the other day and 'twas only my armour that saved me. See, here's the tail-end of the cut on my belt.'

And with Bourquien he put on a special kind of superficial joviality with an edge of malice beneath it, the joviality that hated rivals put on when they meet on ground where they cannot harm each other.

'Ah, Major Bourquien, 'tis a pleasure to meet you and the greater pleasure because it's the first time I've set eyes on you. 'Tis generous of you to ask me to dinner. There'll be fine French cooking, that I know – with your experience – and it's the best of French wines I'm expecting. It's not long now till Christmas and the season of goodwill, Major. But I'm thinking there's no more Christmas now in the beautiful land of France?'

When they sat down to dinner, everyone was eager that both Thomas and Bourquien should be mellowed by wine.

'A glass of wine with you, General Thomas!'

'A glass of wine with you, Major Bourquien.'

The private toasts went round and round the table. Then the general toasts began. Bourquien rose to propose: 'A health to Mr George Thomas.'

Thomas rose to his feet and proposed: 'A health to Major Bourquien.'

That was followed by: 'A health to General Perron!'

That was drunk amicably and Thomas seemed to be enjoying himself. The talk was general and the wine was passing freely.

Then, with a sly sidelong look, Bourquien rose to his feet and gave another toast. 'Success to General Perron's arms and policies and all he seeks to achieve!'

There was silence. For a moment no one moved. Then Carnegie, sitting on Thomas's left and seeing the look on his face, turned his glass over. He would not drink that toast in that company. One by one the others did the same; the refusal went round the table from man to man as the wine goes round, with the sun. It ended with James Skinner, on

Thomas's right. Bourquien looked round, the smile fading, hatred and distrust taking the place of triumph. But Thomas sat still. Then he covered his face with his hands and burst into tears. Then he dashed away the tears with the back of his hand and sprang to his feet, his hand on his sword.

' 'Tis not because of any jumped-up little French revolutionary cook that my fall has come. 'Tis my own bad luck and my own folly and failings. 'Tis my fault, me own fault, and no doing of yours or Perron's. I'm nothing now; all has failed. But if I'd had a bit of luck I'd have pulled it off and made the Punjab mine and planted the British flag on the banks of the Attock and laid it all at King George's feet. Still, there's one thing left to me. One Irish sword! And 'tis worth a hundred damned Frenchmen!'

And with those words he drew his sword and raised it high in the air and took a stride towards Bourquien, who gave a cry of fear and bolted through the door at the back of the tent by which the servants entered.

'Gone away!' screeched Thomas, putting a hand to his ear like a huntsman. 'Gone away! I've made the damned Frenchman run like a jackal. After him! Tally-ho! Forrard on! Who'll be the first to whip off the Frenchman's brush?'

James Skinner caught his sword-arm, Carnegie caught the other.

'Don't bother with him, General, he's not worth your trouble.'

'He was drunk, he didn't mean to insult you.'

'Put down your sword, General, and sit down. We'll make him come and apologize. He was drunk, he didn't mean to insult you.'

James said to Robert: 'Get the soldiers out of the tent. Go after Bourquien. Tell him Thomas was drunk and didn't mean to hurt him. Get him to come back and apologize.'

Robert and two others went after Bourquien and persuaded him to come timidly back. They clustered round him at one end of the table saying: 'He was drunk. He didn't mean to hurt you. Come back and apologize.'

And at the other end of the table James and Carnegie

were soothing Thomas – whose hand kept straying back to his hilt – and saying: 'He was drunk. He didn't mean to insult you. He'll come and apologize.'

And, sure enough, he did, cringing a little as he came.

'Ah, we'll forget it,' said Thomas. 'A glass of wine with you, Major.'

They sat there drinking while James went away to inspect the guards. Thomas, when he left the mess, would have to get back into Hansi, once his capital. But now all the gates were guarded by men of Perron's Third Brigade. James Skinner warned each guard not to challenge Thomas and his escort when they came back; he told them that George Jang Sahib had had a great deal to drink and they were to let him in without question. But by bad luck Thomas came to the one gate where James had not yet given his warning. Torches flaring on steel helmets, they rode up to the gate.

'Who goes there?' challenged the sentry.

'The Sahib Bahadur,' replied the jemadar commanding the escort. It was the name his men had always used of Thomas and until today this had been his own fort – the centre of his kingdom. None of them had thought of being challenged there. But of course this was Perron's sentry.

'I know nothing of any Sahib Bahadur. You must wait till I call an officer.'

Thomas gave a great cry of rage and despair.

'One month ago,' he cried to his troopers, 'would anyone have stopped the Sahib Bahadur at this gate?'

'No, Sahib, no,' they said, soothingly. 'Of course not.'

In a sudden access of rage, Thomas sprang from his horse, drew his sword and struck a blow at the sentry that cut off his hand. The man screamed, the guard turned out. They raised their muskets, took aim and awaited the order to fire. At this moment, James Skinner arrived, just too late to warn the sentry not to challenge, just in time to stop the guard from firing. Thomas was pacing angrily to and fro, the drawn sword in his hand. His own officers and troopers were trying to calm him. At last one pinioned him from behind and a few minutes later his palanquin came from inside the gate, he was bundled inside and taken home. The confused and dangerous scene subsided into the routine of mounting guard.

Next day, Thomas visited the sentry and gave him a substantial present. A week later he crossed the British frontier. He never reached Calcutta. He died before the year was out, but whether from drink or from a broken heart it would not be easy to say.

## PART THREE

# DISPLACED

## 13 War with the English

THE battlefield at Uniyara had been one crisis in James Skinner's life. Another was soon to occur, when war broke out between Scindia and the English, that war long ago foreseen as inevitable by his father's soldiers, when James was a boy in Calcutta. For James, the months between the destruction of George Thomas and the outbreak of war with the English was a time of unhappiness. The mood of release that had followed his escape from death passed and he became increasingly reserved. Everyone talked about the coming war but he did not join in the discussion. There was a conflict between the ideas he had talked about with the Raja of Uniyara and his growing understanding of the futility, as well as the danger, of his present employment. The Raja had spoken of a man fulfilling the function for which he was destined – and emotionally this idea of surrender to a force greater than himself appealed to James strongly. But he began to see why Captain Burn had hesitated before sending him to de Boigne and his reason asked whether it could be the destiny of James Skinner to fight for Karaoli against Uniyara, for Perron against Thomas, for Scindia against the independence of Jaipur. Must he be always on the wrong side?

A message reached him from his father, who was not in good health and wanted to see him. He took leave and went to see him at Burhanpur away in the South; he found him much altered. He had always felt a latent irritation in his father's presence; he was fair enough to see that what his father said was usually reasonable but none the less the irritation was there. Now, seeing his father so obviously far from well, guilt was added to irritation. He felt that he ought to have liked his father better; he felt sorry for him. He stayed two months but all the time wanted to be off. He was ill at ease with his father's brother officers, none of whom had his experience of war or of commanding men but who treated him with kind condescension.

After that he went to see his sister Margaret in Calcutta. Here too he did not mean to stay long; here too he was restless. Templeton grated on his soreness; Templeton was reasonable, like his father, but being reasonable was no help at all to James. A Hindu raja – a Rajput on both sides – might see his way clearly enough; so might an English lawyer, though to James it seemed a dull stuffy way. But James was neither fish nor flesh. In battle he never felt any doubts but on leave he was at odds with himself and sure only that he could not stand Templeton much longer. He began to think of going to Lucknow, the capital of the King of Oudh, in order to finish his leave away from both Templeton and his father. But another message came from his father and he went back to Burhanpur. He stayed a month; his father seemed to be worse and he thought he must be failing though he was still performing duty. He was ashamed to feel so relieved when he left. He never saw his father again; news of his death reached him a few months later.

One moment of high drama came before the declaration of war but it did nothing to resolve the conflict in James. On the contrary, it brought it into the open. After many requests which he had ignored, Perron received an order to report to Scindia in person, an order couched in such terms that to disobey it would have meant open rebellion. At last he marched for Ujjain, Scindia's capital in the South, taking with him the Second Brigade, with which both James and Robert were serving. It was on 20 March that Perron arrived in Ujjain, reported arrival and asked for an audience. It was not until the twenty-fifth that an audience was granted.

To keep a man of Perron's importance waiting so long was a deliberate affront – not surprising since Perron had kept the Maharaja Scindia waiting more than a year for troops that were supposed to be his own. But worse was to come. On the twenty-fifth, Perron and a dozen of his senior officers, including James, were kept waiting in an ante-room, while the Maharaja amused himself by flying kites. There is usually a strong wind at the end of March, a wind which villagers in peaceful times use for winnowing the chaff from the grain. It was a good wind for Scindia's kites. The kite which he managed himself was made up in the shape of a hawk. Another, doomed for destruction and made up as a partridge, was flown by a courtier. When it sank dying to the ground, another courtier flew another partridge. Perron and his men sat waiting. Now and then one of them would tip-toe out on to the veranda and for a few minutes morosely watch this idle sport.

It was some hours before Scindia tired of his pastime and entered his hall of audience. Perron and his officers were led before him and knelt to do homage and to present their *nazrana*. Scindia touched the presents coldly, with his eyes on the other end of the hall. He made a perfunctory enquiry after the General's health, to which Perron made the conventional reply that by the Maharaja's favour the mixture of elements in his person was excellent. Scindia announced that the General would be informed of the occasion when he would next be required in the Presence. Scent was poured, *pan* presented, and the interview was at an end. Displeasure had been publicly conveyed.

There followed another eight days of irritated waiting. Scindia made no outward sign but everyone knew that those about him, led by the horrible Ghatke, were plotting how best Perron might be ruined. On the seventh day, Perron summoned his battalion commanders.

He told them in his stumbling English that he had received an invitation to Scindia's durbar. He was to bring with him his commissioned officers – that would mean the thirty or so of the Second Brigade who were with him. But he had also received information – most secret, most reliable – that waiting in the durbar tent would be five hundred Afghans with orders to kill him and everyone with him. He had therefore decided to take *all* his officers – the subedars and jemadars as well as the captains and lieutenants. That would mean three hundred men instead of thirty. They would go in full dress uniform, which included two pistols each. And those pistols would be loaded. Six hundred shots. A sharp deterrent. Perron did not lack courage.

Next day, when they marched into the durbar tent, there, sure enough, were the five hundred Afghans lining the tent on Scindia's right. They looked very fierce; their moustaches bristled, their hands were on their swords. Scindia rose to receive Perron, who with his principal officers knelt before him. They presented their *nazrana*. But, as each man knelt, two stood by him, hand on pistol, watching Scindia. And the rest watched the Afghans. Then they fell back to positions lining the tent on the left side. There was taut silence.

Scindia said: 'General Perron, I thought I had invited only your European officers.'

Perron answered in Hindi: 'Maharaja, there are standing orders of your revered uncle that when the General of the Brigades is honoured by an invitation to full durbar he is to bring the subedars and jemadars, so that the hearts of these officers too may be cheered and their valour increased by the light of the Maharaja Scindia's presence. And these orders your Highness confirmed to me when I became General of Brigades.'

Scindia was taken aback. He turned to Ghatke who fawned by his side and whispered to him. On the other side of the tent, the Afghans twirled their moustaches and scowled and loosened their hilts from the scabbard. They thought they could make a meal of Perron's men and wanted to begin. Perron's European officers now smiled at them and outwardly appeared quite at their ease; they were confident they could stop a sudden rush and laughed at the discomfiture of their enemies.

Scindia, plainly disconcerted, went on whispering to

Ghatke. Then he turned to his other side, where there stood the soldierly figure of Gopal Rao, an old warrior who had long served Madhaji Scindia. He whispered to him and the old man shook his head and James thought he was warning him against some course proposed. Then there was more whispering with Ghatke and again Scindia turned to Gopal Rao and there was more head-shaking. At last Scindia appeared to make up his mind. He told the Afghans they had leave to depart, and they went, fiercely and sulkily, like dogs whipped off an adversary. When they had gone, he began a speech about the sterling services that the brigades had performed and how he esteemed them above all other forces that he possessed. Perron listened with propriety but one or two of his officers could hardly keep from laughing – the change of front had been so sudden. And it was whispered round that it had been Gopal Rao – Scindia's old trusted adviser – who had sent warning of the ambush. It was a piece of news that added cynical amusement to released nervous tension and made men more inclined to laugh.

When Scindia had ended his speech, he called for a robe of honour for General Perron, which was brought. It had been prepared for his murderer, and since the Afghan was a tall man and Perron short, it did not reduce the hilarity.

But Perron rose to his feet and coming before the Maharaja unbuckled his belt and laid it, with its sword and two pistols, at Scindia's feet. In spite of the ill-fitting robe, he achieved a certain dignity.

'I have grown old in the Maharaja Scindia's service,' he said, speaking in Hindi, 'and I have been honoured by his confidence. It is not fitting that I should be disgraced by knaves and bullies; I seek leave to depart. I ask for my discharge. I shall return to France. I am too old to continue in service when I have lost the confidence of my Prince. I must retire.'

Scindia rose and embraced Perron. He said that he regarded Perron as his uncle, using a word – *chacha* – that means father's brother and conveys warm respect and affection.

'What *can* have offended my dear uncle?' he went on. 'What *can* have led him to feel he has lost my confidence? It is more than I can understand. As for his resignation, I will not accept it.'

When the durbar ended, Perron had not withdrawn his resignation nor had Scindia accepted it. But Perron had not yet given up hope of a substantial French expedition which would make him Governor-General of India. It did not suit him to break with Scindia yet. He made Scindia a magnificent present and patched up the quarrel, but everyone knew that his influence with Scindia was gone.

Perron went back to the camp at Ko'el with the Second Brigade and resumed his old policy. He was gambling on the French expedition, already overdue. He promoted French officers to every important post, and when Scindia asked for reinforcements, made excuses and did not send them. He was trying to keep as many as possible of de Boigne's disciplined brigades under his own hand in the North. But in the South, quarrels between the Maratha princes came to a head and there was a great battle near Poona, in October 1802, in which Holkar defeated the combined armies of Scindia and the Peshwa. It was a hard-fought battle and nearly went the other way; Scindia would have been the victor if he had had one of the brigades Perron had refused to send. And, as it fell out, Scindia's defeat in this battle – the result of Perron's treachery – led to Perron's downfall and to all that he had hoped to avoid, the success of British arms, not French.

After the battle of Poona, Baji Rao, the Peshwa – the head of the Maratha confederacy – fled from his capital. He had nowhere to turn, no ally to help him. He begged the British for protection and they agreed to restore him – but at the price of his independence. On the last day of 1802 he signed the Treaty of Bassein, by which he accepted the presence of a British force in Poona and undertook not to have any dealings with the French.

Meanwhile, Perron, unaware of the Treaty of Bassein, gave up hope of the French expedition and resigned a second time. This time he meant it. He wrote to Lord Lake, the British Commander-in-Chief, asking for an escort to Calcutta, where he would embark for France with his immense possessions. Lord Wellesley, the Governor-General, agreed. He was well aware that Perron was putting French officers into posts of importance and that he had been in correspondence with Buonaparte. In fact, in Calcutta, in ordinary conversation, de Boigne's brigades were commonly spoken of as 'the French army of Hindostan'. Lord Wellesley was therefore relieved to hear that Perron had decided to retire; it looked as though he had given up hope of help from France for his project of a French kingdom in the middle of India.

But things changed suddenly. The news of the Treaty of Bassein took some time to reach Scindia and the other Maratha princes, but, when it did, they were for once agreed. The Treaty must be resisted; it was intolerable that they should give up their independence. Scindia begged Perron to stay on after all and fight the British in the war that everyone now regarded as inevitable. Perron agreed and drew up an extremely able plan for a war in which the combined forces of Scindia and Holkar would be deployed against Lord Lake. They could have put two hundred thousand men in the field, while he, in the war that followed, never had a field force of more than ten thousand and could not have increased its strength significantly without dangerously denuding his garrisons.

At this juncture, Lord Wellesley's information about Perron's activities was confirmed by the arrival in Pondicherry – in June 1803 – of three hundred French officers, meant for the 'French army of Hindostan'. They were taken prisoner by the British and interned. Lord Wellesley sent Scindia a peremptory demand that all French influences should be removed; Perron in particular must be dismissed. Scindia would perhaps not have minded losing Perron but to admit that Lord Wellesley had the right to dictate to him was to concede the whole point at issue. He refused. War was declared.

# 14 Neither Fish nor Flesh

EVERYONE had foreseen the war. But the actual shock of it took James and his friends aback. James had seen Scindia's treachery and his rapid change of front at the durbar – behaviour of the kind he most despised. Everyone at the durbar had lied. He knew that Gopal Rao had played Scindia false by sending word to Perron of the ambush; he detested Ghatke; he knew that Perron meant to use the war for his own ambition and throw off his allegiance to Scindia. But if every single leader was false, did that mean that James Skinner must be false too? Something in him revolted at the idea. A dogged obstinate fidelity surged up in him, something that he knew was against all reason. He would be faithful if he was the one loyal man.

Carnegie and Stewart were quite determined on the opposite course. Carnegie was the spokesman; he knew that Perron had always wanted a French empire, that he had withdrawn his resignation only because he saw the chance of making himself so powerful that he could overthrow Scindia. He had already shown his distrust of all but French officers; no one with British connexions had any hope of advancement – and indeed they might lose their lives. Carnegie put all this to James, who answered that he had eaten Scindia's salt for eight years and would not desert him now when he was most needed. And then he burst out:

'Think, Carnegie! The English wouldn't commission *us* – the country-born – because our mothers were Indian. They were unnatural parents to us – as Bourquien said, that day when we saved Thomas. They won't commission us now. We shall be junior to pink-and-white boys of eighteen straight from England, boys who've never heard a shot fired and who don't know the language or the country or the men.'

He was twenty-five. He had commanded a battalion for three years and at times had been in command of two or three battalions. He hated infidelity but that was not all. He could not bring himself to face the loss of power, the waste of experience, parting from his men. Could he advise Shadul Khan to come with him? It would go against all he had stood for. And he shrank from the ignorant contempt of British officers he could not respect.

'But, Sikandar,' said Carnegie, using the affectionate name the troops gave him, 'you haven't really any choice. Do you think Perron will trust you? "Damn English", he always called us all – country-born or European. Do you think Scindia will trust any of us? The least reverse and our heads would be off.'

'I agree with Carnegie,' said Stewart. 'I shall resign.'

'I shan't,' James repeated. 'I have no ties any longer with the English. My father is dead. I want to be faithful to the colours I've served with; I'd rather die, if I have to, like a soldier.'

He thought with a pang of his godfather. But he had lost touch with Burn.

'It isn't a soldier's death to be strangled in prison because you're not trusted,' said Carnegie.

Carnegie and Stewart had made up their minds and sent in their resignations. This was on 28 August 1803. On that very day, James Skinner, his brother Robert, and a number of others – all British or country-born and of English connexion – received notices of summary dismissal. They were paid up to date and told to be across the British frontier within three days.

'You see,' said Carnegie. 'It is just as I told you. You are not trusted.'

'Do you think the British will trust me?' said James. 'Would you trust a man who deserted his colours when a war began? I shall appeal to Scindia. I shall tell him I have served him since I was first commissioned and I am ready to go on serving him.'

'It is madness,' said Carnegie, 'you must come with us.'

'I shall go to Scindia,' James repeated. But Robert

Skinner – always impulsive and even more sensitive than James to the thought of a snub – decided he would take service with the wicked Begam Somru.

Next day James and four others started for Scindia's camp. But they did not get far. War had already broken out – though with Scindia only, since Holkar at the last minute had backed down – and Lord Lake, as brisk a soldier as ever marched, was already close. That very day he fought a battle near Aligarh and James, with the other four officers who were on their way to Scindia, heard the thunder of the guns. They found themselves, as the day wore on, on the route of the Maratha flight and, among the broken cavalry, by a strange chance, was Perron himself. James recognized him first and bringing his horse beside Perron's begged him to take them back, to let them rally the fleeing men and save something from the disgrace of defeat. But Perron would have nothing to do with him. He trusted no one of English origin – and in any case he had been defeated and all was lost.

'Go to the devil then!' said James angrily and he went back to his friends.

'We can still go to Scindia,' he said obstinately, knowing that he was being pig-headed.

'No, no,' said one of the others. 'It is too late. Scindia would never trust us now. Carnegie was right. We must go to the British and hope for the best.'

'We shall be snubbed and insulted,' said James. 'We are neither fish nor flesh. We belong nowhere and we shall have to start again, and be ordered about by the latest drawling baby from England.'

But, much as he disliked it, James Skinner was too sensible not to yield to the force of the situation. He gave in and joined Carnegie and Stewart. The seven of them went first to a fort near by that was in British hands. They heard the familiar challenge of the sentry.

'Who goes there?'

'A party of British officers who wish to speak with your commanding officer,' said Carnegie.

The sentry sent word to the officer commanding the guard. He was a young man named Clark.

'Officers of Perron's French army?' he said. 'Want to change sides, do you? Well, I've no authority to treat with turncoats. You'd better go on to the camp.'

'Can you spare us a guide or an escort?' Carnegie asked. 'We don't know the way and don't want to be fired at.'

'No, I can't,' said Clark. 'My instructions are to hold this fort and I've barely enough men for that if attacked. My orders don't provide for people like you at all.'

They went on their way, in the general direction where they believed Lord Lake's camp to lie. Skinner was silent; this was the kind of reception he had expected. Hope revived however when they met a senior officer with two orderlies, one Colonel Everard Brown, as they later discovered. It was he who first spoke to them, asking politely who they were and where they were going.

But though Colonel Brown was more courteous than Clark had been, he was not much more helpful. They must see the Commander-in-Chief himself, he told them. He could not spare them a guide nor go with them himself.

'I congratulate you, Carnegie,' said James Skinner, 'on the politeness and affability of your fellow-countrymen. Let us go to our tents.'

They had some light tents and had already fixed on a place where they could halt. James led the way there at once. He had had snubs enough.

Carnegie, however, was indomitable. He and one of the others decided to make one more effort to find Lord Lake that evening. This time they were successful. They rode on towards the British camp and on its outskirts met an officer who treated them quite differently. He was on Lord Lake's staff.

'Left the Marathas, have you? Very sensible. And want to see Lord Lake? Of course. I'll take you to him. But you look exhausted, both of you. Come to my tent first; it's just here. Let me give you a drink and something to eat. Tell me, by the way, have you met two young men called Skinner? I knew their father. He was in my regiment.'

'But James Skinner is one of our party!'

'Then we must get him at once. This is splendid news. The General will be very pleased. He has hoped some of you would come. Now, let me scribble James Skinner a line and send it at once by an orderly while you have your drink. Then we'll go and find them and take them to the General.'

James was still doubtful when Carnegie and Ferguson arrived with loud hurrahs. They were convinced that Lord Lake would treat them kindly; James was not. However, having gone so far, he saw that it would be folly to stop for fear of a snub. So the whole party rode into the camp and reached the Commander-in-Chief's tents just as dusk was falling. Their guide went in and almost at once Lord Lake himself came out to greet them. He was a man of rather less than the middle height, neatly and compactly built, open and honest of face, kind but firm, a man in whose presence insincerity would die on the tongue, brisk and forthright but a man who would take trouble to captivate.

'I'm delighted to see you,' he said. 'I've been hoping that some of you would join us because, frankly, there can no longer be any future for a British officer in Scindia's service. And I know something of the record of the battalions de Boigne formed. You have some fine soldiers among you and we need you. Now, let us leave till tomorrow the question of your future. We will discuss it after breakfast. What we are all in need of tonight is dinner. I know I am and I expect you are. I hope you will dine as my guests in the headquarters mess. Come and let me introduce you. Which of you is the senior? Captain Skinner? Ah, I have heard your name mentioned, Captain Skinner.'

The officers of General Lake's staff all knew that he had been hoping to welcome such a party as this. They had been chosen personally by Lord Lake and most of them combined good manners with a friendly disposition. They treated James with consideration; several of them had heard his name mentioned. It was not at all as he had expected and he enjoyed his evening. The General himself paid him marked attention.

Lake had seen service in Germany and the Lowlands, in America and in Ireland. He was a Guardsman who had everywhere been loved by those who served under him. He had the virtues which soldiers always admire – rapid decision, unflinching courage in battle, justice as a commander, immense energy, a readiness to attack, a habit of victory. He was direct, forthright and genial, a man of strong feelings. James took to him at once – but none the less it was with grave forebodings that he, as the senior officer, went for the first interview next morning after breakfast.

'Tell me, Captain Skinner,' the General began, 'why you left the Maratha service?'

'Not because I refused to fight against the British,' James said. 'No, I was dismissed. Carnegie and Stewart resigned because they wouldn't fight the British – and then I was dismissed. I wanted to stay. I didn't want to leave the colours under which I had fought for eight years. But Perron no longer trusted us. I appealed to him to take me back. But he would not have me. So I had no alternative.'

'You are very frank.'

'I am a soldier of fortune, sir. Not by my choice. I was forced to it by my father's countrymen. But that is what I am. And such a man is no use unless he is trusted. So I have to be frank. Trust is my livelihood.' He paused.

'My lord,' he continued, 'I thank you for the kindness with which you have received us. I am very grateful to you. But I think it is best I should say at once that I shall not be much use. I hope you will not ask me for information about Scindia's troops. And I hope you will understand that I cannot fight against Scindia. I have eaten his salt and he is my master. I speak only for myself.'

He spoke slowly and painfully; he wanted to help Lake, simply because he liked him, but he hated the position in which he found himself. Lake seemed to understand his feelings.

'Well, I am disappointed, Captain Skinner, because I had heard your name and I had formed a plan for you. I had meant to ask you to raise a regiment of light horse for us. We are badly in need of light irregular horse for scouting and information.'

'I am sorry, my lord, but I must decidedly say no, so long as it would mean drawing my sword against my old comrades in Scindia's service. There is nothing I would have liked better, but I must say no.'

'Well, I respect your motives. Would you write letters to officers in the brigades telling them that I should receive them kindly if they came over?'

James considered this.

'I am afraid I would rather not, my lord. It seems to me very like encouraging men to be traitors. I am not yet used to having become a traitor myself.'

He said that stiffly, with obvious pain. Then he went on: 'I must also point out that the messengers carrying such letters would almost certainly be put to death.'

'I see. You are not very accommodating. However, I don't suppose that all your companions will be quite so scrupulous. I don't want to lose you, Captain Skinner. I like your frankness. I can see a possibility – a situation which might occur. Suppose Scindia was virtually out of the war and we were fighting Holkar? Would that change your attitude?'

'Entirely, my lord. Holkar was always a possible enemy.'

'Then let us wait a little. I might be able to renew my offer of raising a corps of irregular horse; that is what I really want you to do. Meanwhile, there is territory that has come into our possession – de Boigne's old property, later Perron's, between the Ganges and the Jumna. That must be cleared of rascals of all kinds and reduced to order. Will you go with some of my troops with the local rank of Captain and be their political adviser? You won't be able to give them orders, but I shall tell their commander to listen to what you say.'

'I shall be very happy, my lord.'

'Good – but let us not forget – I have better things in view for you one day. You ought to have an independent command. Goodbye for the moment.'

'You have been very kind, my lord.'

## 15 The Thirteen Rajputs

A SMALL force of Indian soldiers in the scarlet tunics of the British East India Company were winding their way along a rough earthen track through the peaceful countryside of the Doab. The gleam of scarlet and sparkle of weapons shone through the cloud of dust that moved with them. There was hardly any wind and the dust hung suspended in the air for a few minutes when they had passed, drifting away imperceptibly and forming a fine silvery-dun coating on the vegetation of the nearer fields.

But except for this moving cloud, boring its way slowly across the landscape, the countryside was green. It was a patchwork quilt of little squares and rectangles, divided only by low baulks of dried mud about nine inches high. Wheat barley, still in the blade, a clear fresh green, was coming up in most of the fields; here and there were patches of the darker vetch-like gram with ferny foliage. Taller patches of pigeon-pea, like overgrown asparagus, and of red-stemmed sugar-cane, half-grown, made some variety, but the land was perfectly flat and the patchwork stretched as far as the eye could see, a calm ocean, in which at intervals of two or three miles a village rose out of the green, a dun-coloured island clustered about with groves of stately mango trees and orchards of guavas.

It was still 1803. James Skinner was still twenty-five. He had been in a dozen pitched battles, sieges and skirmishes innumerable. But while a few months ago he had been absolute master of a thousand men to whom he was virtually a king, now he could not give an order. He was a political adviser; he could make suggestions – if he was asked his views. That was all. It was his own doing but he did not like it any the better for that.

He was accompanying a detachment of half a battalion of Indian infantry, commanded by a captain of about his own age. But Captain Morton's experience was very different from James Skinner's. He was a tall fair man – amiable, undistinguished, unenterprising – and most of his nine years in India had been spent in regimental duty in cantonments. He was too much inclined, James thought, to listen to the advice of the three junior British officers who accompanied him and he did not consult the experienced subedars and jemadars under his command.

About the middle of the forenoon, this party observed a mud fort lying some quarter of a mile off their direct route. Its walls stood up from the plain like worn dried old bone. It was not in good repair. When they came abreast of it, Captain Morton ordered a halt and his officers gathered round him.

'A rubbishy little place,' he said, 'but I suppose it will be manned by some kind of rag, tag and bob-tail and we had better reduce it. What do you think, Skinner?'

'I expect there will be a dozen or so of Perron's old *sibandis* there,' he said. 'Armed, no doubt, but only with matchlocks and sabres; collectors of land revenue and police more than soldiers. But I expect they will be Rajputs and they might cause some trouble if you attacked the place head on. Let me go and speak to them, while you rest. If we offer them honourable terms, I expect I can get them out without firing a shot. Perron we know has deserted Scindia and is on his way to Calcutta. They've no master to serve any longer.'

'Terms!' said Lieutenant Baker contemptuously. 'Honourable terms! To a band of brigands! That's all they are. Of course they'll surrender at once if you say they can go with their lives.'

'If they really are Rajputs,' said James, 'as many such

men are, I would not be so sure. You might lose a number of lives if you went about it the wrong way.'

Baker's only answer was a contemptuous laugh.

Morton said: 'There can be no harm in Skinner's going to speak to them. Thank you for the offer.'

James rode over the open fields to the little fort. 'Aré, Qilladar!' he called out. This was a rather pretentious title for the commander of such a garrison in so small a mud fort.

The leader of the garrison appeared on the ramparts. He agreed that James might come closer and his companions joined him on the ramparts.

'Were you General Perron's men?' James asked. 'I see you are Rajputs.'

'Yes, we are General Perron's men,' they agreed.

'General Perron has gone away – gone to Europe. So you have no master any longer. All this country belongs to the English now. Will you give up the fort if we give you honourable terms?'

'What are the terms?' they asked.

'Very simple. You give up the fort and march out; you will be allowed to go to your homes.'

'We take our personal arms? Without them, we are disgraced. It is no disgrace to give up a fort – but our swords and matchlocks we must take. Without them, we are women.'

'That I understand. And I agree. That is what is meant by honourable terms.'

'And it is on your surety that we shall be allowed to go to our homes with our weapons?'

'It is. On my head be it.'

After some discussion, they opened the gates and filed out, thirteen Rajputs of the Chauhan clan, armed with sabre, matchlock and shield. James led them back to where Captain Morton and his party were resting.

'It is just as I thought,' he said, 'they were Perron's *sibandis*, and Rajputs by caste. When they learnt that Perron had left Hindostan, they agreed to an honourable surrender. They hand over the fort and we let them go to their villages with their personal weapons.'

'That seems all right,' said the easy-going Morton.

But Baker was of a different temperament. He was a short man, though neatly and sturdily built, dark of hair but with that pale complexion that does not tan easily; there were two dark moles on his face.

'With their arms!' he said. 'What kind of nonsense is this? They are lucky to get their lives. We should have marched up to that miserable little huddle of mud and thatch and demanded instant surrender. They would have given in at once, been disarmed and sent home. If they had defied us, we should have taken it at the first rush. Our orders are to pacify the country, not to leave bands of armed brigands roaming about. Tell them to down arms and get out quick if they don't want to be hanged.'

'Perhaps you're right,' said Morton.

'Of course I am,' said Baker. 'Tell them to down arms and be off.'

'I beg your pardon,' said James Skinner, 'but I cannot agree to what you propose and I cannot permit you to do it without the strongest possible protest. I fear you do not understand what is meant by "honourable terms". I have been in a score of sieges and it is always understood that "honourable terms" permit taking personal weapons. You told me I could make honourable terms and I made them. And I pledged myself. I said I was their surety. My personal honour is involved if I break my word. It becomes an affair of honour for me. These men are Rajputs and their honour is destroyed if they lay down their arms. They would not be able to go home without their swords. I do therefore very strongly advise that you let them go as I have agreed. They will go to their villages. They are not criminals.'

'This is a rigmarole of nonsense,' said Baker impatiently. 'Are we to pacify the country or are we not? Tell them to down arms and be off.'

Morton, rather uncomfortably, began to say:

'I really do think, Skinner, that since we are supposed to be pacifying the country – ' but James interrupted him.

'I am afraid there are only two courses open to you. You may act as I have suggested or, if you do not agree to the terms I arranged – *with* your authority please remember – you may go back to the situation as it was before I offered to act for you. So if you do not let them go, they must have safe-conduct back to their fort. Then you can start again – having rejected my advice.'

'You are only an adviser,' said Baker. 'We need not follow your advice.'

'You are, as you say, entitled to reject my advice. But when you authorize me to act for you, you are not entitled to repudiate the commitment I have made on your behalf. To do so is not only to dishonour me but to dishonour yourselves.'

'I see what you mean,' said Morton. 'No, Baker, that's enough. Take them back to the fort, Skinner, and we'll start again.'

'You will regret it,' said Skinner. 'There will be loss of life. I will first tell them what you want – so that you may see I am not exaggerating.'

He turned to the thirteen Rajputs.

'The English officers want you to lay down your arms,' he said.

'It was promised that we should not,' said their leaders. 'We will die before we agree to that. It is our manhood. Never. Never. Never. To anything else we will submit.'

'Take them back to the fort,' said Morton. 'We have wasted time enough. What can they do?'

'You will soon see. And you will regret it,' said James. Then, to the Rajputs:

'Come. All is as it was. Back to the fort.'

'Good,' said the leader of the Rajputs.

Skinner went with them till they reached the fort. At the gate, the leader turned to him and said:

'All right. Bring your army.'

As James rode back, he saw Baker with twenty men leave the party by the roadside and move towards the fort. James went to Morton and stood by his side. They saw Baker's party approach the ramparts without a shot being fired on either side. They marched straight on, making for a place near the gate where the wall had crumbled in the rains.

They halted.

'Will you surrender?' Baker shouted.

'Never!' came the answer.

Baker and his men began to advance.

Then from the ramparts came thirteen spurts of flame. Thirteen men of the attackers fell, dead or mortally wounded. Baker was among them. The eight men still standing began to run back.

Morton became active.

'B Company! Subedar Ram Kallan Singh! We are going to attack that fort. Form line.'

B Company moved off, Morton going with them. He was all right, James thought, when it came to action. James himself stayed where he was and watched. Once again, he saw thirteen shots fired at close range and again thirteen of the attackers down. Then the gates of the fort swung open – and stood open in menacing invitation. Bayonets fixed, the attackers rushed at the open gate. There was no more shooting; it was all hand-to-hand now. There was room for only three men abreast. A dozen or so of the leaders went inside without obstruction and then James heard a great shout:

'Har! Har! Mahadev! Har! Har! Mahadev!'

The Rajputs were on them with the sword. The attackers flinched back for a moment but recovered and went on, slowly now. Inch by inch the attacking party fought their way in. The Rajputs met them inside with their sabres but there were always more and fresh attackers. At last Morton came out; he was covered with blood, wounded and dazed. James spurred his horse and went to him.

'Are you all right?' he asked.

'It's only a scratch. Quickly patched. But a lot of dead.'

'Any of *them* living?'

'No, they wouldn't surrender. We had to finish them. All thirteen.'

'And you've lost at least forty,' said James. 'You needn't have lost a man.'

He went to look for Baker. He was quite dead, shot through the heart. James turned him over and looked at him.

'Obstinate, pig-headed fool!' he said.

## PART FOUR

# CAVALRY LEADER

## 16 We Want Sikandar

Not long after his first meeting with the Commander-in-Chief, James Skinner was in attendance on Lord Lake at the storming of Aligarh. This was an immensely strong fortress, but the Commandant, one of Perron's French officers, had omitted to breach the causeway leading across the moat, which was 'big enough to float a battleship'. Indeed, this officer wanted to surrender the fort, but the garrison rose in arms against him and put him in irons. His place was taken by a Rajput, a gallant and determined man, but by then it was too late to cut the causeway. A party from a British regiment, the 76th of the line – later, the Second Battalion The Duke of Wellington's Regiment – advanced over this causeway under heavy fire from the ramparts and blew in the outer gate at point-blank range with a twelve-pounder gun, later fighting their way through three more gates in the same way. When they were inside the first gate, Lord Lake galloped to the gate to give instructions to the commanding officer of the 76th. His eyes filled with tears as he looked at the dead on the causeway. 'Gallant fellows!' he said. 'They died like soldiers.'

Next day he sent for James.

'What did you think of the 76th?' Lord Lake began.

'They were superb;' Skinner replied. 'Bringing up that gun to the gate under such a fire as that was the height of courage.'

'I'm glad you think so. So do I. I suppose you know that

Captain Lucan was with them and that he helped beforehand with information about the fort. One of your former comrades, I think? An Irishman.'

James answered stiffly. 'I am afraid your Lordship is bound to look on Captain Lucan's conduct in a very different light from that in which I regard it. He was once an officer in the garrison of Aligarh. To me it is the act of a traitor to give away information about the fort. And, my lord – I make bold to say – that is what you would think if a British officer went over to the French and gave them secrets of a British fort.'

Lord Lake laughed. 'I dare say I should. None the less, I shall give Lucan a commission in the 76th and a reward. But I cannot yet do anything for you? I still want that regiment of irregular horse.'

'No, my lord. I will not fight against Scindia.'

'Very well – for the present. But things are moving fast and soon I hope that even you may feel that they have changed enough for you to agree. You know that Perron is on his way to France. Bourquien has proclaimed himself Perron's successor; he is in Delhi and has possession of the Emperor. But Bourquien isn't finding it a bed of roses. From what I hear, Delhi is all rumours. Nobody knew what Perron was up to or where Scindia was and they mutinied against Bourquien and shut him up in prison. Then they changed their minds, let him out and said they were sorry. Divided counsels! Nothing suits me better than divided counsels among the enemy! I'm on my way to Delhi to attack them and see whether I can get the better of Master Bourquien. I shan't expect you to help me now – but when I have Delhi and the Emperor I shall come to you again.'

It was only a week later that Lake attacked Bourquien's army outside Delhi, marching his infantry straight at a line of cannon and attacking with the bayonet. It was a battle that he won not by skilful manoeuvre but simply because there was determination and a single command on one side against jealousy and divided counsels on the other.

After that battle, Lake was the master of Hindostan. He

held Delhi and the Emperor. The day after the battle there rode into his camp eight squadrons of horse. They were Perron's cavalry, disciplined, trained men. They wore long green coats with scarlet turbans and sashes. They had not been in the recent action. They rode up to the camp in perfect order and halted when challenged by the guard. They wanted to see the General. They had arrived in column but now formed a line of squadrons, and stood, perfectly disciplined, motionless as though for a review.

Lord Lake was told and came himself to the guard. He rode out from the camp and called the eight risaldars to leave their squadrons and come to parley with him.

'Tell me,' he began, 'why you are here and what you want.'

'We are the cavalry of General de Boigne's Second Brigade,' said the senior risaldar. 'We have not been in action against the British. But we know that General Perron has run away. De Boigne's brigades are finished. We want to serve the British instead of Scindia. Only with the British shall we get regular pay and proper arrangements. We want to serve under an officer we know, an officer who will look after us. We have heard that Sikandar Sahib is with you. We want Sikandar Sahib to command us.'

'Do the men want this too, or only you officers?' asked Lord Lake.

'Everyone wants it, General Sahib. Every man of us.'

'Go to your squadrons. Ask them two questions. Tell them to shout so that I can hear. Do they want to join the British? Who do they want to command them?'

The risaldars galloped to their squadrons. They shouted the first question.

'Do you want to serve the British?'

'Yes, we do!' came the answer.

'Who do you want to command you?'

There was a great roar in reply.

'Sikandar Sahib,' they shouted. 'We want Sikandar. We want Sikandar.'

'Sikandar Sahib. Iskinner Sahib,' the risaldars told Lord Lake.

'You are sure you want Sikandar?' he asked.

'There is not a voice against,' they told him.

Next day Lord Lake saw Skinner once again.

'So you see how it is,' he said. 'Here is a corps ready-made. Nearly a thousand trained men organized in eight squadrons, asking for you as commander. *They* want you and *I* want you. It's exactly what I need. Not heavy cavalry to charge in line and sabre the gunners but light cavalry to skirmish with the enemy if need be but mainly to find out where he is. Why, at Delhi, we stumbled on Bourquien's army by accident. My men had been marching eight hours and were cooking a meal. We had no idea they were there. We ought to have had a screen of light cavalry out. But they must be disciplined, reliable men. That's why *you* must command them.

'However, there's your celebrated fidelity to Scindia – who wasn't very faithful to you, by the way. In the first place, I give you my personal word that I won't use you against Scindia. If you accept this command, your first task will be to keep the road open from Aligarh to Delhi and clear the country between the Ganges and the Jumna. There'll be gangs of armed deserters and fugitives over all the countryside for the next six months unless we act promptly and firmly. You'll be military police really, with full powers to pacify the country as you think proper. But I'm quite confident that after what has happened we shall have peace with Scindia before long. And then, against Holkar, you can take up your proper role.

'I should also tell you,' Lord Lake continued, 'that I'm making a proclamation offering terms to all British and country-born officers who served with Scindia. We will give them employment on the same pay as they had in de Boigne's brigades. But if they are found in arms against us in future, they will be punished. After what has happened, and after this proclamation, there won't be many of your old comrades left against us. Now, what do you say? Will you accept or would you like time to think it over?'

'My lord, you have been most patient with me. I accept.

And I can assure you I shall do my best to make my corps the best in India.'

'They shall be known as Skinner's Horse,' said Lord Lake.

The first weeks were very busy. James would have liked a few weeks at least in which he could get to know his men and give them the new training and equipment and above all the new spirit that they would need if they were to be the best corps in India. But the task for which they had to be used demanded that the squadrons should be constantly sent off independently on separate missions. How much better it would have been if he could have kept them all under his own eye!

It could not all be done at once. First of all, they must have a uniform of their own and he chose a colour altogether distinctive. The men should wear a long cavalry coat that was neither green, like that Perron's cavalry had worn, nor blue, as Thomas's had, nor red, as the Company's wore, but yellow. He had only one other commissioned officer, George Scott, country-born like himself; one of the two was usually out on patrol, but once when they were together at headquarters Scott asked him why he had chosen yellow. They were sitting together at night in James's tent. James stood up and took a turn across the tent. Then he sat down again and said:

'To most people I should simply answer that it is distinctive. I want my regiment to feel they are my own personal family, that they are different from all other regiments and in the end that they are better than all other regiments. But there was another idea in my mind and since we are together, you and I, in this enterprise, I think I should tell you.'

He paused and looked at Scott. He went on:

'I think you will understand. You know that my mother was a Rajput. She told me a great many Rajput legends. There is an old custom among the Rajputs that a prince who was riding out to a fight would sometimes vow that if he could not win he would die. He would not come back. And his followers would vow with him. They would put saffron on their faces and put over their armour a yellow cloak which they would tie with a yellow sash. These clothes were called the *Clothes of the Dead*. They were known as *Yellow Men* and they vowed they would not come back from battle alive unless they were victorious. Well, that thought was in my mind. A good soldier is vowed to death – and I want mine to be very good soldiers. But that is only for you.'

James fitted his men out with this new uniform squadron by squadron and whenever he could withdraw a squadron from active operations he set them to work in hard training, swinging their horses in small circles, making them gallop with the lance at tent-pegs hammered into the ground, making them practise with the sabre till they could slash through an iron cooking pot while at full gallop, making them fire a carbine at the gallop at an earthenware bottle hanging from a post. As well as this training of individual troopers there was squadron training. His squadrons must be able to wheel and deploy like flights of wild duck. They must be so disciplined that they would halt after a charge, reform and charge back. They must be a supple and responsive instrument in the hands of their commander. And, as if his tasks were not difficult enough already, another four squadrons were allotted to him within a fortnight of raising the regiment.

The headquarters of Skinner's Horse in this first stage of their existence were at Sikandra, between Aligarh and Etah. Here, whenever he was not out on tour with one of the squadrons, James Skinner would sit in his tent giving instructions to his risaldars; making arrangements for the purchase of warlike stores, food for men, forage for horses, tents, uniforms, horseshoes, saddles, bamboo shafts for lances; settling promotions; arranging transport and escorts for the silver rupees with which the men were paid. There was no adjutant, no quartermaster, only Scott and himself and one of them was always on patrol. He delegated all he could to his risaldars but he had to supervise everything.

Then he must see his *harkaras* – scouts, spies, informers, messengers – to get information about the movements of gangs of robbers or deserters, rumours of the movement of troops or of any activity by the larger landowners. If a squadron was just in from patrol he must hear the risaldar's report; if a squadron was just going out he must give the risaldar exact instructions. Quick rough justice was what they administered; robbers caught in the act or identified by those they had plundered would seldom deny the charge and were usually hanged at once from the nearest tree.

When he sent out a squadron he would show the risaldar the villages he had to patrol and he would say:

'In this piece of country, not an armed man must move without my knowing. I must have a man in every village who will send word here if the peace is broken. We are going to make so strong a peace that in every village an old woman can take a bag of silver in her hand and walk down the street without fear. If there is a gang of robbers, it must be destroyed, and every man killed or hanged.'

The men at headquarters must be inspected at their training; their sleeping quarters and their messing arrangements must be examined. For every squadron, at least once a month, James must hold a durbar, at which every trooper had the right to voice a complaint or make a suggestion. At one such durbar he presented to his assembled officers Shadul Khan, his old comrade, well known to many of them already, whom he appointed the risaldar of his own personal squadron. He would hear any complaints or requests; everyone in the regiment must have direct access to himself.

Sometimes a man had a regimental grievance. A comrade had been promoted over his head, perhaps. But this was rare; they were all picked men, good enough to be duffedars, so promotion usually went by seniority in the corps. Sometimes it was a matter so private that no one but the commandant and perhaps the risaldar must know, and in that case it would be something about a woman, an unfaithful wife, or the entanglement of a younger brother with some worthless girl. It might be enough to give him leave to settle that himself but to deal properly with such a case meant a long and patient hearing and sometimes it would be necessary to get help from a kinsman or a neighbour in the regiment. It would never be enough to give a perfunctory answer; the commandant could never say: 'That is *your* affair!' Nothing that was the affair of the soldier was not James Skinner's affair too; he demanded total allegiance, they demanded total protection.

More often than promotion or a woman, the complaint would be that enemies in the village had banded together and 'hemmed him in' – there is no exact translation. He would explain that they were 'constricting' him in his own affairs on every side, over the land, over grazing rights, over access to water. Just because he was away with the regiment, determined and malicious conspirators could do him much harm. It would be necessary to listen patiently, to determine what help could be raised, in this village and in others. The leader of the regiment was father and mother of his men; their troubles were his troubles.

When all minor business was finished, then would come the formal enrolment. Squadron by squadron, as the new uniforms appeared, the men would put on the yellow coats of Skinner's Horse, and swear allegiance to the colours of the regiment – the griffin's head and bloody hand which were the arms of the Scottish family of Skinner.

Picture such a durbar – an ancient custom of India, when a monarch, prince or chief meets his people and deals out personal justice. James would sit under a tree near his tent, on a chair; the risaldars and jemadars of all the squadrons would sit on the ground in two lines converging on his chair, their swords on their knees, their fierce whiskers bristling upwards and outwards. By now they were all in yellow. The troopers of the squadron to be sworn were still in green; they were standing at the base of the triangle of which James was the apex. He would make them a short speech.

'This yellow coat that you are going to put on is a robe of honour. You take off your old green coat and put on this coat and you become one of my family. You are my children now. Your good is my care. My good is your care. My honour is in your hands, yours in mine. Wherever this yellow coat is seen, there goes the good name of Skinner's Horse. When you put on this coat you are vowed to death; you have vowed to die sooner than be unfaithful to your colours. You are to remember the motto of our regiment: *Himmat-i-mardan wa madad-i-khuda* By the courage of men and the help of God. God does not help cowards. He does help the brave. Put on this coat. Swear you are faithful to your colours – faithful to death.'

He would have liked six months to fill them all with this spirit. But long before that, his regiment was put to its first test.

## 17 A Very Near Thing

FROM the day the first reports began to come in from his patrols, James had seen that some day he would have to come to terms with a certain Madhu Rao, who lived not many miles to the south of Sikandra in a fort called Malagarh. He was a Maratha chief whose grandfather had been a vassal of Scindia's grandfather. But in his own time he had contributed nothing to Scindia's armies. He had a small army of his own and used it for his own purposes, mainly collecting revenue and raiding his neighbours. Now – barely a month after the regiment was raised – he sent James a message haughtily demanding that he should at once leave the countryside.

James was actually discussing Madhu Rao with his risaldars when the message came.

'He must be brought to heel,' he had just said. 'And he shall be. But I must move carefully. He has guns and infantry and I have neither.'

It was at that moment that the *chobdar* from Madhu Rao was announced with his insolent message ordering Skinner's

Horse to leave the countryside. He was already moving towards them with horse, foot and guns.

'Go back to your master,' said James. 'Tell him it is he who must change his ways. He must surrender to Lord Lake and live peacefully instead of like a robber and a gangster. I give him one week in which to surrender.'

The moment the *chobdar* was out of earshot, James turned to Shadul Khan and told him to call a trooper ready to gallop at once on the road to Delhi. There was a line of messengers with fresh horses waiting; they would get the message to Delhi in less than twelve hours. He scribbled a note as quickly as he could to Colonel Ochterlony, whom Lake had left in command of Delhi and of all the outlying forces: 'I am going to fight a battle with Madhu Rao but I have only cavalry and he has guns and infantry. I know you can spare no infantry but can you let me have two six-pounders? In great haste.'

'Take this to Colonel Ochterlony. Gallop. Get it there as quickly as you can.'

Then to Shadul·Khan he said: 'Call in all patrols. Put out picquets towards Malagarh. But no offensive move till I have an answer to that letter.'

When the letter reached Ochterlony, he had just heard that Captain Birch, a country-born who had been one of Thomas's officers, had been defeated north of Delhi in an affair with a semi-independent chief, an affair very like this which James had on his hands. Birch had had two battalions of matchlock men and four guns. He had lost the guns. Ochterlony wrote to James: 'Since I have just lost four guns through the agency of one of your countrymen, I am not prepared to trust you with another. But you are in no case to retreat.'

James received this letter when the dusk had just fallen. Scott by now was at headquarters, all patrols having been called in. He threw the letter to Scott.

'Read that,' he said. 'Ill-natured, arrogant Scot! Throwing my birth in my teeth! What has Birch's being cut up to do with me? If it were not for Lord Lake – ' but that sentence he never finished. He paused and drew breath. 'I tell you, Scott, I am resolved. I shall die here rather than fall back a step. But if I do not die, he shall learn to address me in different language.'

This was the third time he had made such a resolve.

Another messenger arrived while they were still speaking. He brought a second challenge from Madhu Rao who again ordered James to be gone from the countryside. If he did not go, he would be driven out. Madhu Rao's forces were already moving towards him. Skinner again sent a contemptuous reply. He also sent out a small mounted party as scouts to give him warning if the enemy came too close.

They were back about four in the morning; the enemy had moved forward and were within two miles of the camp. By this time, Skinner's Horse numbered about 1,200 men, in twelve squadrons. James gave them orders to form up outside the camp and they stood in line, motionless, waiting for the dawn. When first light came, they began to see the dark lines of the enemy, about a mile and a half distant. They peered and strained their eyes but it was nearly half an hour before they were sure of what they saw. They were confronted by a battalion of infantry on rising ground ahead of them, with guns in the centre of their position and a body of horse in their rear. They showed no inclination to come closer.

Since they would not move, Skinner and his troopers advanced towards the enemy at a walk until the guns began to fire. Then they divided into two wings of about six hundred men each, Scott leading one and Skinner the other, and in two great hooks, like the claws of a scorpion, they charged the flanks of Madhu Rao's position. But the enemy were well disciplined and drilled and quickly turned their fire to the flanks. There were losses in both wings of the attack and neither charge was pushed home. Skinner's squadrons pulled up without orders and began to ride back. But in each wing the commander was aware in time of what was happening, turned too, rallied the men and kept them together. The two wings united. Skinner led another charge, this time at the centre of the enemy position. James himself rode straight at the infantry between the guns and rode through them. His horse was killed by a matchlock ball and came down. He felt the horse stagger and sprang clear. Shadul Khan was at his elbow. He reached down to catch his hand as he struggled to his feet.

'Up quickly, behind me,' he said, and James was up behind him. He became angrily aware that for a second time most of his men had turned back. The next minute they were riding back as fast as the horse would carry them to the starting point of the charge. Here Scott, wounded and covered with blood, was a second time rallying the troopers.

James mounted another charger. He called the men to him.

'I shall not live to command cowards!' James cried furiously. 'I am going to charge again. I am determined to die here if I cannot take those guns. Nothing shall turn me back and I mean to sweep this enemy away. Who rides with me? Who is a man and a soldier? Who will be my brother for life? We will leave the cowards behind. They shall have no part in the glory that will be ours. Come! My friends, my brothers, my regiment! It is death or victory! Come! Charge!'

On the words, he turned his horse and without looking to see if anyone followed charged the enemy's centre. But this time not a man held back. They strove to be first. They struck the infantry like an avalanche and scattered them in utter confusion. In fifteen minutes there was no remnant left of a formed body of troops. Those who were still on their feet were running.

James pulled up and told his trumpeter to recall his squadrons. He had lost two hundred men; Scott was badly hurt. But Madhu Rao no longer had an army that would take the field. They had captured his guns and colours and sent him scuttling back to his fort at Malagarh. James spoke to his men:

'That,' he said, 'is how Skinner's Horse will always fight and we shall be famous as the best corps in India.'

He went to Scott, with whom the *vaids* were already busy. He had no less than eleven sabre cuts and had lost a great deal of blood. There *was* hope – but – his life was in the hands of God. By which they meant that they had dressed his wounds and could do no more and that though he might live they did not really expect it. Care might save him, James thought, skilled and constant care, which he could not get in camp. He wrote at once to Ochterlony:

'I attacked Madhu Rao's force today, throwing my horse straight at his guns and infantry. We have cut him up and made him run to his fort. I have his guns and colours. I have lost two hundred men killed and wounded. Lieutenant Scott is badly hurt with eleven sabre cuts. Can you lay relays of bearers to meet him? I am sending him in a litter towards Delhi today but fresh men from your end would speed things up. Only skilled care can save him. I shall write a detailed account tomorrow.'

The letter would be in Delhi in twelve hours. Meanwhile he would start Scott on the journey. A wheeled vehicle would kill him; a team of skilled litter-bearers would hardly jolt him but there was no relay system of such men in readiness.

There was soon an answer from Ochterlony, in which he congratulated Skinner and Skinner's Horse on their victory in most warm and generous terms. Relays of bearers were on their way for Scott. Ochterlony published his congratulations too; like Lake, he was a frank, generous man who seldom hesitated and there was no meanness or sulkiness in his nature. He called James to Delhi for discussion and there greeted him in a manner which made them friends for life.

He came across the room to meet him and took him warmly by the hand.

'I do most heartily congratulate you on your victory,' he said. 'A triumph for Skinner's Horse and still more a personal triumph for you.'

'One is impossible without the other,' said James. 'It was a very near thing. Touch and go. At one moment, it looked as though we should be disgraced for ever.'

'I think that is often the case. One man's courage and energy gives life to everything. As yours did this time. And – Captain Skinner – I owe you an apology for the way I wrote about that gun. I couldn't spare a gun – and it would have been too late if I had – but I had no business to write as I did.'

'Think no more of it,' said James. 'I will not deny I was angry at the time – very angry. But it is done with now.'

They understood each other. They looked at each other with pleasure.

'Now, what are we to do about this Madhu Rao?' Ochterlony went on after a little. 'He's a kind of brigand king, levying tribute on all around. He can't be left.'

'No – but it won't be easy to get him out of Malagarh. It's quite a strong place; I've seen it from a distance and had some information from my *harkaras*. He still has some two thousand infantry, trained to some extent – quite good behind walls if not in the field. Guns? He still has some guns. I don't know exactly. Some horse. He won't venture out again – but I can't force a way in without infantry and without a battering train.'

'Well, you certainly can't have a battering train. I haven't got one. Nor infantry. I'm in a very critical position, Skinner, as I'm sure you understand. The Sikhs to my north-west are hopelessly divided but always formidable; there are various semi-independent chiefs within striking distance; the Rajputs can always put a dangerous force in the field. I think we shall soon have a settlement with Scindia but Holkar – Holkar's the big question mark. At any moment he might come into the war and if he did the best thing he could do – from his point of view – would be to pounce on Delhi. He can put a hundred thousand men in the field and he's a quick mover. You know the importance of Delhi. At the moment, I hold the Emperor, poor old boy. It's like chess; if Holkar moved towards Delhi, it would be check to us and to our king and Lord Lake would be forced to move – or be mated. I couldn't hold Delhi, with what I've got, for more than a few days against anyone. But I must be able to hold it long enough to give Lord Lake time to move. I can't spare you another man or a gun. I rely on you to hold the country south of Delhi. In the North, I rely on Colonel Burn at Saharanpur.'

'My godfather. I haven't seen him for eight years.'

'Well, you may see him sooner than you would like – for the Sikhs across the river are always threatening him and he's only got Birch and his matchlock men. I may have to move you up there to help him. Meanwhile – you must get your friend Madhu Rao out of Malagarh *without* a battering train. Would some money help? I don't need to tell you there are more ways of getting into a fort than banging your head against the walls.'

'How much?'

'Up to one hundred thousand rupees – £10,000.'

'Not even Madhu Rao can be bought for that.'

'But *someone* might be bought – for less than that.'

'I'll see what can be done. In any case, I can blockade him – for I don't think he'll stick his head out again. I may be able to make him hungry. Have you more recent news of Scott?'

'Steady improvement. They think he'll recover. Goodbye, Skinner. Good luck – and again, warm congratulations.'

## 18 On a Knife-Edge

ALL other patrol work had to be postponed. The task was to make an end of Madhu Rao's little kingdom as a centre for miscellaneous extortion and for raids on his neighbours. Skinner's Horse pitched camp about three miles from the town. Four squadrons had to be in the saddle night and day. Nothing must go into Malagarh and nothing must come out. Nothing, that is, such as food or stores or gunpowder. That a man should sometimes secretly go in, that a man should sometimes secretly come out – that was another matter and as long as James knew all about that man, it was all to the good. Madhu Rao contemptuously refused the offer of terms and at first sent his cavalry out of the town whenever there was a chance of their finding forage or provisions. But whenever they came out, they were attacked and chased back until cannon-shot caused their pursuers to draw up. James had given orders that his horsemen were not to expose themselves to fire from the fort. He was satisfied that the garrison was not getting any supplies worth mentioning.

This went on for a fortnight. It was hard on horses and men, hardest of all on the commander, who was usually out with the squadrons on duty and got very little sleep. But he kept time to see his *harkaras* every day. One of these men found a way of getting into the town secretly and came back with the information that all the fodder for the horses was stored in two stacks and that there was enough to last three months at least. The man was a Gujar, a people who are usually cowherds and sometimes nomadic, and he had caste-fellows inside the town employed near these stacks of fodder. He was confident he could set fire to them – if properly paid.

'How much?' asked James.

The Gujar drew a long breath. 'Five hundred rupees,' he said.

'Two hundred,' said James automatically.

'Four hundred,' said the Gujar.

'Two hundred and fifty,' said James.

'Three hundred and fifty,' said the Gujar.

They settled on three hundred as a reward with five rupees for expenses.

Three days later the Gujar was back. It was done, he said.

'How am I to be sure of that?' James asked.

'Watch,' said the Gujar. 'Tonight. There is a slow match laid to those stacks. They will burn tonight. There will be a big blaze.'

Sure enough, there were two big blazes that night. Both stacks went up. James paid down the three hundred rupees, with twenty-five extra for good measure. Three days later a man came at night to the sentries asking to see Sikandar Sahib. Madhu Rao's cavalry wished to surrender. James sent back a firm no. He would give honourable terms if the whole garrison surrendered. He would have no dealings with a part of it.

Another week went by, a week of constant patrolling, during which a few small parties and one or two individuals tried to escape but were all caught. Then a *chobdar* came out with an emissary prepared to treat on behalf of Madhu Rao. The terms were quickly agreed; the soldiers came out with their personal weapons and were marched under escort to Delhi, while Madhu Rao kept all his personal wealth and surrendered all claim to the town and surrounding countryside. He too was escorted to Delhi, where Ochterlony received him with courtesy and he was granted a generous pension.

James told Ochterlony how it had been done.

'So you see,' he concluded, 'out of one hundred thousand rupees, I have spent only three hundred and thirty.'

Ochterlony smiled at him.

'You have done well indeed,' he said. 'I shall publish my thanks and I expect the Commander-in-Chief will too. But everything still hangs on a hair. You must go on holding the country south of Delhi and Colonel Burn will hold the North but at any moment I may have to ask you to go to his help.'

James and his men went back to their patrolling, their training and occasionally to the subjugation of some minor chief, half brigand, who thought his mud fort impregnable. At last the expected summons came from the North. This was about three months later, in February 1804. Large bodies of Sikhs had assembled on the banks of the Jumna and were threatening to cross into the Saharanpur district. Skinner's Horse were told to join Captain Birch, who, with a battalion of matchlock men, had orders to guard a ford across the Jumna. They had a brief discussion.

'Do you know how many Sikhs there are over there?' James asked.

'Four or five thousand, I think,' said Birch. 'All horse. No trained infantry. But I think detachments come and go. Several chiefs have combined and sent forces. They send a few horsemen to cross the ford occasionally and our picquets fire at them and they move back. I think they're getting stronger day by day and building up their strength for a crossing.'

'No other fords?' James asked.

'None so good as this. But there *is* another, about eight miles downstream.'

'I don't suppose they know we're here yet. This very night, I'll go downstream, cross and surprise them. You keep up as much activity as you can. Move your picquets forward perhaps. At any rate, excite and interest them.'

Skinner's Horse snatched four hours' rest, then, keeping well back from the river, moved downstream to the crossing. They were all over by three in the morning. Then, cautiously, quietly, they moved upstream. Just at dawn, they swept down on the Sikh encampment. There were no sentries, no picquets. It had never entered their heads that anyone would cross the river and attack them. They were scattered after a brief resistance.

James and his regiment marched into Saharanpur to report their victory. Colonel Burn met them a mile from the town. He pulled up his horse by the side of the road in the shade of a mango tree. James left his men and rode to his godfather. He was very stiff and formal. He saluted.

'Sir, I have to report – ' he began; but Colonel Burn would have none of it.

'Let's not be so formal, James,' he said with a friendly smile. 'After eight years! It's too long since I saw you. I'm delighted – and I congratulate you from the bottom of my heart on a splendid victory.'

James relaxed a little. They shook hands.

'I needn't say how pleased I am to be under your command.'

'And I to have you. I want to hear the whole story – but not now, this evening, where I have maps and can understand just what happened. You'll dine with me of course and I'll hear of all your doings. But now, while they're here, fresh from their triumph, may I look at these men of yours, who already begin to be famous? I can see that you have them in fine fettle.'

That evening after dinner, when James had told him of how he had surprised the Sikhs and a good deal of what had gone before, Colonel Burn said:

'Well, James, you wanted to be a soldier.'

'Yes, sir, and I cannot thank you enough for sending me to General de Boigne. Few men of twenty-six have seen as much active service as I have. But – sir – I do not rise very fast in rank. I am still a local Captain – junior to the latest joined Cornet or Ensign in the Company's service though I command twelve hundred men.'

'True. But look at it the other way. If you had been commissioned in the Company's service, you would have had to wait till you were fifty before you had command of half as many. *And* tied down by rules and regulations so that you'd feel smothered. And probably deep in debt. You're much better off as you are.'

'I am sure you are right, sir, and I couldn't ask for a better occupation than I have now. I have so free a hand. And I have been publicly thanked by the Commander-in-Chief three times in six months. Still, I should like a proper commission and at least the permanent rank of Captain. I know I am neither fish nor flesh – but why should my birth make any difference? Do you think the Commander-in-Chief will be able to reward me one day with landed property?'

'I am sure he would like to, James.'

'It isn't something I brood about, day and night. Robert minds more than I do. Most of the time I have plenty to do and I get on with that and I don't worry. But there are moments. . . .' He paused, and went on impulsively: 'Colonel, I brought in Madhu Rao. My prisoner. I'd beaten him twice. And he was a villain – a *dacoit* – he'd oppressed all the villages round him – horribly. *He* signed a treaty; *he* was given a pension and a grant of land. As for me, I was thanked! All very well if you have a regular commission and expect a pension. But I haven't. The English are bad fathers to their children. It was a Frenchman said that to me – and, Colonel Burn, there are times when I think it's true!'

In the course of the next month, James persuaded several of the Sikh chiefs along the west of the Sutlej to cross the river for a peaceful visit to Colonel Burn. Here all of them signed treaties engaging to observe the peace.

The Saharanpur episode was in the February of 1804 and he was not back at Sikandra till late in the summer. Meanwhile, events had taken a turn which showed that not only Ochterlony at Delhi but all British forces in Hindostan were on a knife-edge. Scindia was out of the war but – just as Lord Lake had expected – Holkar was in with an army of a hundred thousand men. Holkar had placed far less reliance than Scindia on guns and infantry trained by Europeans. He had continued to prefer the old-fashioned Maratha armies of horse, moving swiftly, living off the country, avoiding pitched battles. He was a nimble harassing opponent.

This war with Holkar produced two moments of crisis for Skinner and Skinner's Horse. One almost ended James Skinner's life and might have led to the disbanding of his regiment. In the other, the conduct of James and the regiment altered the course of the war. If they had not succeeded, Ochterlony would have been defeated, Delhi captured, the Emperor taken, and the war indefinitely prolonged.

## 19 The Crisis by the River

OCHTERLONY in Delhi had seven miles of city wall to defend with only a handful of men. Lake's small army had won a brilliant series of victories in the winter of 1803–4 but it was in urgent need of rest. Yet here was Holkar, a new and formidable foe, coming into the field just when the heat of the sun was reaching the most intolerable extremes and when marching was becoming daily more exhausting. To Lake it was a principle of warfare, particularly in India, to keep up the momentum of attack. But even he did not feel that, in the hottest of the hot weather and after such a winter, he could call on his main force – particularly the English soldiers – for a further effort that would involve chasing an elusive enemy hither and thither across the rugged country of Central India. Lord Lake therefore decided on operations that would occupy and annoy Holkar though they could not bring him to book. That must be left till the next cold weather, the winter of 1804–5.

On 23 April 1804, Lord Lake moved a force into the Rajput country, which Holkar had invaded; the enemy quickly moved away south and Lake then took his main strength to rest in cantonments, at Cawnpore far away to the south-east. Colonel Monson, however, with six battalions of Indian infantry and some guns and cavalry, was ordered to advance into Holkar's own country. He was to advance southward until he met a similar force from Bombay under Colonel Murray.

Monson made good progress at first but by the beginning of July he had learnt that Murray could not keep the rendezvous. The rains were vigorous, torrential rain alternating with sweltering damp heat; many of his men were sick. He decided to retreat. It was a fatal decision. The neighbouring chiefs and petty princes, who had been eager to show their friendship when he was advancing, became hostile; the rivers had risen, the roads were bogs; the enemy cavalry harassed him by day and night; the sickness grew worse. He had to abandon his guns. On one occasion his troops had to leave their wives and families on the far side of a river and had no sooner crossed themselves than they saw them slaughtered by jungle tribes from the hills. Towards the end, the retreat became a disorderly flight. Remnants of the force began to reach Agra at the end of August 1804.

This retreat had an effect on opinion everywhere in India and particularly in the country south-east of Delhi, which had once been allotted to de Boigne and had now been taken over by the British. The star of the British had set, people began to say. The feeling spread everywhere and there were sulky looks where there had been smiling faces. It spread among the troops too. James's own men felt it. The corps was barely a year old; some of the men had known Sikandar when they were part of de Boigne's brigades, but they had not been under his direct command, they being cavalry and he infantry. And, then, they remembered how suddenly the star of George Thomas had set. He had once seemed invincible. Perron, too, had seemed all-powerful but he had come and gone. The famous brigades themselves had not lasted twenty years. How could even Sikandar's men feel certain of anything?

The English troops, who were certain that the English always won the last battle, had all gone away to Cawnpore. The Indian troops came from villages that had seldom known ten consecutive years of peaceful rule by one master. They had no cause to fight for. Only personal allegiance could give them any confidence in the future and at this juncture their commanders were wretched – sick old men who should have been pensioned long ago.

There was something approaching panic all around them. A shiver ran through the ranks even of Skinner's Horse. James felt the shiver; he knew it was there. He talked it over with Robert and Shadul Khan. Robert's allegiance to the Begam Somru had not lasted long. She asked too much of a man and gave too little. He had come back to James soon after the interlude at Saharanpur. Now, just as before, he and Shadul Khan were James's chief advisers. Shadul Khan told them that the men could not help hearing talk.

'But I can answer for every man in our own squadron. Not one of them will listen to such talk.'

He meant the squadron which he himself commanded. The men of this squadron were called *bargirs*; their arms and equipment were supplied by James Skinner himself at his own expense. In the other squadrons, each man owned his own horse and equipment.

James said: 'We must get rid of any traitor at once. For a whisper – dismissal. For an act – death. Keep with them, Shadul, as much as you can. Tell me at once if you hear anything.' He paused. 'Shadul – what about Altaf?'

'Ah,' said Shadul Khan. 'You have said that name. I have heard not a whisper. A month ago I would have given my throat to be cut for him. Now – I am not sure. There is something – in the glance of an eye – in the turn of head – something that makes me think. He is richer than any of us. He has much land.'

'Strike at once,' said Robert. 'Seize him!'

James shook his head. 'He has friends and followers – half his squadron are *bargirs* of his own. And we have not the least grounds for supposing – anything. . . .' He paused and considered. 'I must trust him. Not by a word or a glance must I show the least doubt. I must *show* I trust him. I must *really* trust him. So must we all three. We must watch but not be seen to watch. We must be open, confident – but always ready.'

They watched and waited. They were open and cheerful. They laughed at gloom. What were Monson's six battalions to the English? They would raise another six. But the rumours got worse.

Orders came for Skinner's Horse to join a force at Muttra under Colonel Brown, whose instructions were to support Colonel Monson. They were marching from the north, nearing Muttra, when the crisis occurred.

The Jumna lay across their path and had to be crossed. It was a well-known ford, much used, but deep and difficult, a bad place to be caught in by an enemy. James decided to keep six squadrons with himself and wait until he was quite sure the other six had crossed under Robert's command. That first part of the crossing was carried out successfully. The six squadrons still on the eastern side with James had unsaddled and were resting. He decided that it would be best to give them another half-hour's rest; then they would be fresh to go straight on to Muttra after the crossing. It was a cool shady grove of mango trees; there was a well and the men had filled canvas waterbags, which were everywhere hanging from the trees in the wind, so that they might cool. He went towards the lines where the men lay resting; it was routine to make sure that every man had unsaddled and that the horses were getting as much benefit from the halt as the men.

In the first squadron that he approached he could tell at once that there was something wrong; the men were not relaxed as men should be who are taking advantage of a halt. They were moving about and talking in low voices. He remembered that this was Altaf's squadron. There was a knot of men round some object of interest; they fell back and were silent when he approached. There was a stranger among them.

'Who is this?' he asked.

'He's a Gujar who has just crossed the river from Muttra with his cattle. There they are,' said one of the duffedars,* pointing to the Gujar's cattle.

'And what has he been telling you?'

'Oh, tittle-tattle, rumours, nothing at all,' said the duffedar, evasively.

'Come, tell me what he has been saying,' James said.

The duffedar looked at heaven and then at the earth.

'Rumours,' he said. 'He knows nothing. But bad news. That Colonel Monson's army has lost its guns and is in flight.'

'We knew that before,' said James. 'We have known three days.'

'And that Holkar is close behind him,' the duffedar added. 'But it is nothing, Sahib. He does not know.'

'I see,' said James. 'Bring that Gujar to me.'

He led the Gujar away from the men and questioned him further. All that he had to add was that he had heard that the British were preparing to retreat from Muttra. On top of Monson's disaster it was one more sign that things were going wrong; it was something to make the men uneasy.

But there was nothing to be done except to keep the men

* Duffedars are sergeants; first syllable rhymes with muff.

busy and to behave exactly as though nothing was amiss. He did just what he had been about to do anyhow. He ordered three squadrons to saddle up and make ready to move away. One of them was the squadron where he had found the Gujar. He called its commanding officer, Mohammad Altaf Khan, who happened to be the senior risaldar of the three.

'You are in command of all three squadrons, Altaf,' he said. 'March them down to the Jumna and send each squadron across in turn with orders to report to my brother as soon as the crossing is complete. God be your protector.'

'God be your protector, Sahib,' replied the risaldar: he saluted, and rode away to lead his three squadrons down to the river.

It was late afternoon, past the time of greatest heat. The grove of mango trees where they had halted, a cool grassy place, lay about a hundred yards distant from the sandy track from the north by which they had come. From the grove, the track led away towards the ford; it was in sight for about two hundred yards, as far as the point where it dipped over the low escarpment that marked the edge of the belt of river country. The river country here was nearly four miles across – a flat expanse of white sand strewn with the wrecks of trees left behind when the river was in spate. James watched the men and horses to the crest of the escarpment, saw the lances and the gay fans of the Muslim turbans outlined against the evening sky, saw them dip and descend towards the river, still two miles away. When they had all gone he moved away from the men, in the opposite direction, idly and casually, as though to relieve himself. It was the end of the rains and the low ridges that marked the field boundaries were outlined by plumed thatching grass, higher than a man. As soon as he was out of sight, he turned and walked, under the cover of such a line of grass, towards a knoll that he had noticed to the west of his halting ground. It was part of the escarpment the troopers had crossed; the loose sand of its crest was held together by a patch of *jhao* – tamarisk scrub. He could stand there unobserved by Altaf's three squadrons and see what they were doing.

As he moved into the *jhao*, his eye caught a movement, a flash of yellow. There was someone there already. He froze. He held his breath. But whoever it was seemed unaware of his presence. He moved cautiously, inch by inch, two feet forward and was able to see a trooper wholly absorbed in watching the squadrons who had moved off towards the river. There was enough wind to shake the *jhao*, and to drown the rustle of his movement. The trooper did not see him; he was intent on the scene by the river. James shifted his gaze in the same direction. The three squadrons had halted, a mile from the river. There was a group of men – they must be the risaldars and duffedars – apart from the motionless column, apparently in discussion. The group broke up; the men who had been conferring rode back to their squadrons and then the whole column moved off, still orderly, at the walk. But not towards the ford and to Muttra. They turned away towards the east, where a converging road from Hathrás* approached the ford at an angle with the track on which the regiment had been travelling. The three squadrons were deserting in a body.

James had half expected that blow. It was none the less a blow, a savage jolt to the pit of the stomach. Three of *his* squadrons! He turned his eye back to the man near him in the *jhao*. He too had clearly seen what he had come to se
He turned and started to run back to the grove where the remaining three squadrons were still supposed to be resting. James recognized him now – with a sick feeling. It was a man from his own squadron. That squadron of his own *bargirs* he had thought were as closely linked to him as men could be. They were almost his personal servants, his personal bodyguard. He had put up the stake for them; he knew everything about their personal lives, their villages and homes. If *they* were going to desert him, he did not want to live.

He went back to the grove by the way he had come and walked into it, still casual and unconcerned. But his heart

* Pronounce to rhyme with 'cut pass'.

thudded and the nausea returned when he saw that his own squadron were saddling without orders. They must have killed Shadul already. Now they were coming to kill him. He did not much mind but he would take one or two with him. He loosened his sword; a dying bite, he thought. The next minute they were mounted and moving towards him. He spoke sternly to the jemadar, Sayyad Karim Haidar. But he felt very sick.

'What is this, Jemadar Karim Haidar? There were no orders to mount. Where is Risaldar Shadul Khan?'

'Lead us, Sahib,' cried the jemadar. 'Those men without faith and honour have not gone to the ford. They have turned east. They are cowards and deserters. Lead us to punish them.'

And the men behind shouted in chorus:

'Lead us!'

Sikandar's heart leapt up. The sickness had gone. He was himself.

'Get my horse!' he said. 'Will you swear, every man of you, on the Holy Q'uran that you will follow me to the death?'

'We swear!' they cried. 'We will follow Sikandar to the death.'

By this time Shadul Khan had galloped up and was leading the cheering. James too was on his horse. He called to the other two risaldars – whose men were still peacefully resting:

'O Risaldar Mohammad Raza Khan! O Risaldar Diwan Singh! Stay here till I come back! One squadron of my Yellow Boys will be enough. Come on, Shadul Khan! Come on, Karim Haidar! Come on, my lads, my own lads.'

Every man felt some share of his relief and joy. They shouted: 'Sikandar! Sikandar!' They swept out of the grove behind him at the gallop and disappeared over the escarpment – yellow coats and scarlet turbans melting into a cloud of dust through which the afternoon sun cast sulphurous yellow beams.

Things had moved so quickly that they came up with the

deserters before they had gone two miles. They were marching in column of squadrons and did not seem to be expecting pursuit. The rear sections of the rear squadron first heard the thunder of pursuing hooves and turned in surprise. There were shouts and Risaldar Mohammad Altaf Khan came spurring back from the head of the column.

James shouted to Shadul and his own squadron to form line and halt. He walked his horse forward to meet Mohammad Altaf, who advanced to meet him. James said:

'What is this, Risaldar Sahib? Your orders were to cross the river. You are marching in the opposite direction.'

Altaf was a few paces from most of his men, as James was from his. But he had four troopers close behind him; James was alone.

'There is no point in going to Muttra,' said Altaf. 'The English are already starting to run away from Muttra. They have been running away from Holkar for weeks. The star of the English is setting, as the star of Perron set. It is all over with them now. We are going to join the Raja of Hathrás or, if he will not have us, to our villages, to protect our homes.'

'Do you mean to say,' James broke in, 'that you would desert your colours and leave your service for an idle rumour heard from a Gujar?'

'It is no rumour, as you will find,' Altaf went on. 'Everything is going against the English now.'

'Faithless cowards!' cried James. 'Without shame, without honour! Turn and come with me. Back to your colours! I give you a last chance.'

He raised his voice on the last words so that the men behind could hear and at that Altaf made a gesture to the trooper behind him on his right and cried:

'Fire!'

The shot hit James's horse in the head and the horse fell dead on the spot. James kicked his feet clear of the stirrups and managed to spring clear. But the men behind saw him fall and charged with a great roar of rage.

'Sikandar!' they shouted. 'Sikandar!'

They were in line and their swords were already in their

hands. Their opponents had been in column and had had no order to change formation. But knots of two or three had left the line of march to see what was going on. The knowledge that they were deserting had already led to behaviour that they knew was casual and unsoldierly. When they were attacked, their consciousness of wrong-doing fought against them. They were ashamed; they were, many of them, already so much ashamed that their first instinct was to run rather than to fight. Some had not wished to desert and now, too late, had half a mind to change sides again. The mutineers were divided against themselves and against each other. They had no chance against the charge of Sikandar's own squadron, flaming with loyalty, furious in their rage, whole in their allegiance and still under their accustomed discipline. It was a short and sharp affair. James found himself another horse, and in barely twenty minutes his trumpeter was sounding the recall. There were ninety dead or dying from the faithless squadrons; ten of his own devoted band.

They rode slowly back to the mango grove and told the others what had happened. There was no more talk of mutiny or desertion. There were nine squadrons now instead of twelve but Skinner's Horse were one regiment once more.

## 20 The Duck Are Flying

THERE followed a period on which James looked back with distaste till the end of his life. At Muttra he came under the command of Colonel Brown – that same Colonel Brown who had refused a guide to James and Carnegie when they were looking for Lord Lake. Brown was irresolute; he called councils of war and endlessly discussed what he should do. He gave orders and changed them next day. In the end, the Gujar was right and he abandoned Muttra without a blow. Though it had been so long debated, the retreat was undertaken suddenly and with so little preparation that Skinner's Horse, who were providing mounted picquets, were not even told that the army was moving.

They had formed a line of picquets to the south of Muttra, across the route by which Monson's stragglers had been coming in. Each picquet had mounted sentries in the saddle keeping a look-out; all horses were saddled and the men had the bridles on their arms. Squadrons took turn about for this duty. It was midnight when James handed over command of the picquets to Robert. He gave him orders to send out patrols at dawn an hour's ride into the country to find out whether there was any news at all of Holkar.

'But I don't believe there's a man of Holkar's within sixty miles of us,' he said. 'I wish to God I could convince Brown of it. Old men who've never been out of cantonments!'

He went off to get some sleep. By the middle of the forenoon, Robert had heard from the last of his patrols that there was no sign of an enemy in the villages to the south. It was at this point that James rode back, tense and angry.

'Robert,' he said, 'it's beyond belief. They've gone! The force we were supposed to be guarding. They've bolted. Lock, stock and barrel. Never told us.'

'God damn the bastards!' said Robert.

'You forget. It is we who are the bastards. It is those born in wedlock who run in panic from an enemy who isn't there. Those with regular commissions. Well, we must set them an example. We will show them that irregular troops, commanded by bastards, do not get in a panic even when regulars do. We shall move as though Lord Lake were coming to inspect us. We shall move in review order in column of squadrons; I shall inspect each squadron. We have plenty of time; there *is* no enemy.'

So they cleaned saddlery and horses, formed up as a regiment, were inspected, and trotted back exactly as though they were on parade. They overtook Colonel Brown's infantry, straggling haphazard and undisciplined in flight from an imaginary enemy. In one village, the population had turned out to jeer and the dregs of the people were actually throwing fragments of brick and old pots at the shambling troops when Skinner's Horse trotted up–spick and span, the horses shining from their grooming, the turbans of each squadron tied at the same angle, saddlery polished, drawn swords burnished and carried at the present. The jeering and stone-throwing stopped; the crowds fell back and began to slink away.

James found Colonel Brown, a tired old man, carried in a litter.

'There is no enemy within fifty miles of us to the south, sir. I had no information that this force was retiring but thought I should use my discretion to follow and protect you.'

'I'm sorry you weren't told of our decision. Bad staff work somewhere, I'm afraid. But I think you must be mistaken about the enemy. My advisers were all of the same opinion.' He settled back in his litter.

Ill-led, panic-stricken, Brown's force stumbled for a week in the direction of Agra, as utterly disorganized and unmanned as Monson's but without the excuse of having fought a battle. At Agra, there was a halt and the beginning of a change in feeling. In the course of Monson's retreat, some soldiers had deserted and some of those deserters had gone over to Holkar. Perhaps they now tried to desert again; perhaps they were merely suspected of such an intention. At any rate, some two hundred of them came into Agra with their ears, noses, and right hands cut off. It had a marked effect on the forces round Agra; desertions dropped sharply. Waverers judged it safer to stay than to fly. And then Lord Lake arrived with his army from Cawnpore. This was on 3 September 1804. Now the tide of opinion turned and ran strongly the other way; not only had he brought fighting strength but he had brought a fighting spirit. Once again all was brisk, all was directed to an object. The irresolute and incompetent were replaced. Everything began to be set in order again.

Lord Lake reviewed Skinner's Horse. He was very pleased with them. They were superb. They looked like regulars, every horse well-cared-for, every buckle in place. And he knew what they had done. They had stayed staunch and remained in being as a corps when irregular horse were deserting by the thousand. He raised their pay and allotted four galloper guns to the regiment, a great asset to cavalry. They were back to twelve squadrons again now.

The problem that confronted Lord Lake beyond all others was the supply of food and forage. Indian armies were usually supplied by long columns of nomadic grain dealers known as Brinjaras. They, with their pack animals and some bullock carts, moved more slowly than an army and for any organized campaign it was essential to make plans in advance. Vast numbers of Brinjaras must have warning that they should be at certain points by fixed dates. And they must be confident that when they arrived there would be silver rupees to pay them.

When Lord Lake left Cawnpore he had of course made plans of this kind and there was a train of more than sixty thousand bullocks loaded with grain winding its way across Northern India towards Agra. They had been given advance payments; it was Lake's grain. But it was a month behind him when he reached Agra. He moved on to Muttra, covering again the ground over which Brown had fled so recently. But for the whole month of September, the army was short of supplies. James and his men were out every day, scouring the country for grain and fodder for fifty miles around and seldom bringing in more than enough for one day.

Then suddenly things came to a sharp head. Lord Lake sent for James.

'I believe you're the one man who can help me,' he began in his usual brisk open way. 'Do you know what's happened? I see you don't. Holkar has made a pounce at Delhi, just as we thought he might. What he wants of course is possession of the Emperor. Ochterlony had foreseen it and had called Burn in from Saharanpur but he's terribly weak. He's got seven miles of ramparts to hold and they're in the most appalling condition. He can't relieve his posts. He has had to put every man he has on the ramparts and leave them there. They snatch a wink of sleep when they can – but they're never out of the line. He thinks he might hold out for ten days at most – and that would need luck – but not a day longer. Burn's in command of the defences. You know Burn, don't you? Holkar would move away if I marched for Delhi – but the devil of it is that I can't stir. You know how short we are of grain.'

'How close are those Brinjaras?' James asked, picturing those sixty thousand bullocks loaded with grain.

'That's the point. You've put your finger on it. They should have been here. But I've just had news that they've been stopped by the Raja of Hathrás. They'd reached a camping-ground within two miles of his fort. He's forbidden them to go another yard towards me and has said he will buy all their grain himself. My information is that they haven't moved it into the fort. Still bargaining, I suppose. I dare say they're not sure they'll be paid. Quite a lot of money. He can't be proposing to pay cash. Now! Can you bring them in? I'm sure no one else can.'

'Have I a free hand?' James asked.

'Entirely. Do as you like – but don't hang the Raja without letting me know. *With* that grain I can raise the siege of Delhi. Without it I can't – and Holkar will get possession of the Emperor.' He struck his hand on the table. 'I *must* save Delhi!'

'We shall have to move quickly or the grain will be inside the fort,' said James, thinking aloud. 'It would be very difficult to get it out once it was inside.'

'Exactly. And apart from that, I'm in a desperate hurry to have that grain. Even with the grain, it will take six days to get to Delhi – probably more – and Ochterlony can't promise me more than ten. Can you do it?'

'Leave it to me, my Lord. I will do it or, if I cannot, I shall die. You shall not see me again if I fail.'

That was the fourth time James had made such a vow. The moment he said the words he felt a change go through him. He was tense, sharp, keyed up – determined to do what he had to do. But he was quite free from worry. He would do it or die – but at death he had always looked with indifference. All minor anxieties had gone; he was possessed by a calm dedicated determination.

It was evening already. James went to his tent and sent messages for Robert and Shadul Khan and for Mangat Das, the leader of his *harkaras*, a man whose life he had once saved from brigands. They had had the rope round his neck when James rode up.

'We haven't a moment to lose,' he said to Robert. 'I'll explain to you afterwards. I must first give orders to Mangat Das, on whom everything depends. Mangat Das, you know the camping-ground at Hathrás?'

'I was born within two *kos* of Hathrás, Sahib.'

'There are many Brinjaras there with grain for Lord Lake. They are bargaining with the Raja and he is trying to get the grain into his fort. I *must know* when that grain is loaded on the bullocks and ready to move. I must know exactly.

'You must have a watcher there tonight – by midnight – and you must have a line of relays back to me to give me the news. They must have horses to bring the news. I shall be moving towards you with the regiment. I shall start on the road to Hathrás at midnight. It is how far? Twenty *kos*?' Twenty *kos* is thirty miles.

'Eighteen to the camping-ground. It is two *kos* on to the fort.'

'I shall start at midnight, canter easily for an hour, rest, and canter again. I shall aim to be close to the place two hours before dawn. Send word back along the road by the relays hour by hour. Keep sending news. Let me know at least once an hour whether they are loading and when they are likely to start. When they start loading, send word at once. Put your relays in position as you go. The password for tonight is Aflatun.* The answer is Sikandar. The messengers are to tell me whether the duck are flying and how much further it is to the *jhil* where we expect the duck.

'We *have* to catch them when they are ready loaded. Then

* Pronounce Uff-la-toon.

we can start them at once on their march to Muttra. If possible, we must catch them before they start for the fort. Without any doubt at all, we must catch them before they reach the fort. You understand?'

'Yes, Sahib, I understand.'

'Mangat Das! You are my man! Altogether my man. Do not forget. Absolute silence. Absolute speed.'

Mangat Das took off his turban and laid it at James's feet. James caught him by the hair, drew his sword and put it to his throat. 'I have sworn to do this and if I cannot do it I mean to die. You understand?'

'Sikandar Sahib, I am your servant. You know I am yours altogether. On my head be it. On my head and my son's head. May my son die if I betray you.'

'Good. Go. Remember – silence! Speed! Robert – Shadul – do you understand?'

'As much as I need understand for the moment. You want the whole regiment to start at midnight?'

'Yes. Now they must sleep. They don't know where they're going. Nor do you – neither of you. We shall start as though for Agra.'

'Good. All the regiment?'

'Yes. Twelve squadrons.'

'And the galloper guns?'

'Yes. Everything. We may have to fight the Raja.'

They started at midnight as though to Agra. But once out of the camp they turned east and went across country to the ford. They crossed the ford and cantered along the road to Hathrás. Now James explained more to Robert.

'If the Brinjaras have reached an agreement with the Raja and are moving the grain today, they will aim to deliver it before noon, then eat and sleep. It is two *kos* from the camping-ground to the fort, which will take them about an hour, but it will take them, say, three hours to load and the same to unload. I want to arrive just when they are loaded and ready to start. I think they will start to load three hours before dawn or perhaps earlier. They will want to march at dawn. I should like to be distant by not more than an hour's ride when they begin to load. But there is a lot of guess-work in my plan.'

'And if they're inside before we get there?'

'We shall have to plan again. But let us stick to one plan at a time. When we are distant from the camping-ground about one *kos* I shall go forward with four squadrons at the gallop. You will wait with eight squadrons for half an hour – no, less, a quarter of an hour – before you follow and then you will gallop round them and put yourselves between them and the fort. That should bring the milk to the boil.'

They moved steadily, not hurrying the horses, cantering easily and resting when they could. They had to save the horses, because there might be serious work at the other end. There was no moon yet. The stars were bright. It was windless and the dust hardly rose above the horses' bellies. It was about two hours after midnight when the first spy grew up suddenly like a shadow from the ground at James's stirrup.

'Aflatun,' he breathed. Aflatun is the Muslim name for Plato who, the villagers used to think, was a great king in the time of Sikandar – Alexander the Great.

'Sikandar,' James said.

'The duck are not yet flying but the head *shikari* says they will fly before dawn.'

'And how far to the water where we shall find the duck?'

'Six *kos*, *Khudawand*,' the man replied. There were still nine miles to go.

'Good. Good. He is a good man, that Mangat Das,' James said to Robert. They rode more slowly now.

An hour later, a second spy.

'Aflatun!'

'Sikandar!'

'The duck are not yet flying. Three *kos* to go.'

They rode quietly on, at the walk. There was a half moon now, still low in the east. The yellow coats by that light looked indeed the colours of the dead.

Half an hour later, a third spy:

'Aflatun!'

'Sikandar!'

'The duck are not yet flying. Two *kos* to go.'

About three hours till dawn. It was hard to wait. Both brothers felt the heart quicken. But they rode on at the same steady pace. Then – half an hour later – a fourth spy:

'Aflatun!'

'Sikandar!'

'The duck are flying. One *kos* to go.'

'Keep on,' said James. 'Same steady pace. A little longer. Not much longer. Must give them time to load.'

Then a fifth shadow, Mangat Das himself.

'Less than half a *kos* now. Beyond the next grove. Can you not see, behind the trees of the grove? There – it sparkles! The fires of their camp. They will be ready an hour before dawn. You have an hour to wait, Sahib.'

It was the worst hour of the night. In that windless air, the trees of the grove hardly stirred but the movement was enough to make the reddish fires of the encampment tremble and glitter like Mars on a frosty night. They dismounted but did not unsaddle. They stood, bridle on arm, waiting.

'Now!' said James at last. 'You follow in twenty minutes. Make them feel surrounded. Head them off from the fort. Goobye, Robert. Khuda hafiz – God be your protector.'

He did not know why he used the Persian phrase.

'Khuda hafiz, James. God bless you!'

James gave orders to four squadrons to mount and they went off at a canter, leaving eight with Robert.

They came into the camping-ground at the gallop. It was a huge open space, dotted with open fires; men moving about with torches; bullocks everywhere, but all standing, a few yoked to wooden carts, most of them patient under the loads fastened in panniers on their backs, their eyes shining green in the firelight. They snorted and shied away at the sudden irruption of horses.

'Your leader?' James shouted.

The men pointed, open-mouthed, not understanding.

There was a group a little apart from the rest, in the corner nearest the fort. Here were the leaders.

'I have come to save you from the Raja,' cried James at

the top of his voice. 'I come by orders of Lord Lake, with whom you made an agreement. From whom you took advances. I have come so that you can fulfil that agreement and march to Muttra. I am your escort and will see that the Raja does not molest you.'

'We have made an agreement with the Raja now,' said the leader, a big bearded man with a dirty green turban and a silver bangle round his neck. 'We are just starting for the fort.'

'Oh, no, you are not. You are going to Muttra – as you agreed.'

One of the men near the leader gave James a defiant look and began to walk towards a pack bullock as though to unload it.

'Swords!' shouted James. Everyone had fallen silent and the clean *wheeep* of four hundred drawn sabres was distinct above the tinkle of bells and the occasional rattle of bullocks shaking their gear.

'Stand still, you!' he said to the man who had moved. 'The first man to throw down his load I shall put to death.'

The man who had begun to move had stopped when the swords were drawn. Now he tossed his head in another gesture of defiance and went on towards the bullock.

'Touch it and you're dead!' said James.

He signed to a trooper to move closer and stand over him with drawn sword. He flinched and drew back his hand. But another man ran to a bullock and with a quick hand on the fastenings threw down the load.

'Cut him down!' said James.

The trooper's sabre flashed and the man fell with a terrible cry.

'I mean what I say,' said James. 'You are going to Muttra as you agreed. I shall escort you. If the Raja has bribed you to break your contract, that will be his loss. I shall settle with him. Tell your people to start now and tell them that any man who throws down a load will be put to death. Look! Here are more of my men.'

Robert had galloped up with eight squadrons. He had

divided into two wings and each had gone round one side of the camping-ground. On the far side, towards the fort, they formed a single line barring the way.

'You see, we can surround you. Give the order to start for Muttra at once.'

James drew his own sword and moved nearer the green turbaned leader. This man now made a gesture of acceptance.

'It is the will of Lord Lake,' he said. 'We must accept it. To Muttra, then. Start!'

The cry ran up and down the lines of bullocks.

'It is the will of Lord Lake! To Muttra.'

The first of the line of bullocks started slowly to move westward to Muttra on the track by which James and his men had ridden. The sky before them in the west began to turn a pearly grey. Men moved like ghosts instead of shadows. The sun would soon be up.

'See that they keep moving, Risaldar,' said James. 'And remember – if any man attempts to throw down his load or refuses to move, put him to death. At once. One quick blow will save many deaths later.'

He rode over to Robert.

'I had only to strike once!' he said. 'Robert, you take over the escort. Send Karim Haidar's squadron back to me. And Diwan Singh's. Keep them moving. Instant death at any sign of treachery. I shall cover your rear with six squadrons. You take the six that make the right of your line. If the Raja comes out, I shall have to stand and face him and hold him. Send a message back from time to time to tell me your progress. Eighteen *kos*; a long march for bullocks – very long – and they will have to stop for water and rest – fourteen hours – but if you keep them going, they should do it not long after sunset. Everything depends now on whether I can stop the Raja. I shall.'

It was a sore trial to tired bodies and strained nerves to see how slowly the column moved away. The leaders had gone more than three miles before the tail of the column was clear of the camping-ground. James did not unsaddle; he let three squadrons water their horses and rest with bridle in hand while two shepherded the bullocks on their way and one watched the road from the camp to the fort. Then they took turn about. The sun showed a burning rim and suddenly became a blinding disc.

The tail of the column of bullocks was half a mile clear of the camping-ground when the gate of the fort opened and a rider came out. He was not in a hurry. He walked at a leisurely pace towards the camping-ground, then suddenly pulled up. He must have rubbed sleepy eyes. Last night there had been a square mile of ground packed tight with men and bullocks; now there was nothing but the ashes of fires, dogs nosing for leavings, crows fluttering and squawking over horse droppings, rags, straw – nothing but that! He sprang into sudden life and galloped back. Inside the fort, a conch sounded a hoarse and prolonged shriek, like the trumpeting of an elephant.

'Not long now,' thought James. His six squadrons must find a place where they could stand if need be. But the further from the fort, the better. He left a line of scouts and moved back with the rest, scanning the country for a good place to stand, watching the road by which he had come, sending messages back to his scouts, getting their reports.

He had covered in this cautious way some three *kos* – between four and five miles – and he knew by the constant reports from Robert that the tail of the column of bullocks was ahead of him by as much again – when the news came that the Raja was out of the fort with a considerable body of horse who were coming on briskly. He called in his scouts. There was a slight rise in the ground – no more than a fold in the level plain – not far ahead; that would make a place to stand. There was a patch of broken ground on one flank of this position. Here he formed up his men in line across the track with his galloper guns in the intervals between the squadrons. He spoke to the men. He told them what he had told his brother; that he had resolved that he would not go back to Lord Lake without that grain. If he could not save it, he meant to die on this spot. They kindled at his speech and shouted that they would die with him.

They waited for death in the bright sunlight, drawing shallow breaths. A single peacock uttered its long mournful cry in the broken ground to the right, an evening cry that was strange when the sun was near the zenith.

The Raja and his men were close. They outnumbered the Yellow Boys many times. But they did not at once attack. They drew up and a man with a flag rode out, followed by a person who seemed to be of some consequence. He came on as though to parley. James was determined not to yield an inch but he was quite ready to parley. One half-hour would be a gain; the bullocks would be almost a *kos* nearer Muttra. He went a short way ahead of his men to meet the stranger – but not too far.

The flag-bearer stood aside and the nobleman addressed James:

'Who are you?' he asked in ringing tones. 'And by what authority have you stolen the Raja's grain and compelled the Brinjaras to go with you?'

'I am Captain Skinner commanding Skinner's Horse and I have the authority of Lord Lake for what I am doing. It is the best authority in Hindostan. As to the grain, those Brinjaras made a contract, in Cawnpore, to deliver it to Lord Lake. It is his grain. It is your Raja who tried to steal it and who tried to force the Brinjaras to break their contract.'

'Unless you hand over the grain, the Raja instructs me to say that he will punish you severely.'

'You may tell your Raja that before he takes the grain he must take my head.'

'Do you not see that you are outnumbered many times?'

'Do you not see that the men facing you are Sikandar's Yellow Boys? It is not often that the odds against us are so trifling as today's.'

'I shall inform the Raja of your insolence.'

He rode back and there was a pause, during which a message came from Robert. He had crept on another mile. Then skirmishers came out on the Raja's flanks, little parties of horse, who galloped towards that steady line of troops as though to charge home but turned away and fired and galloped back. They went back with some empty saddles; every trooper in Skinner's Horse had practised firing at the bottle while at the gallop. But the Raja seemed to have no guns with him and after about an hour of demonstrations which did him no good at all he sent out his messenger again.

'If the Raja allows you to go on your way without punishment, will you take me with you and bring me to Lord Lake so that I may ask him for a suitable reward for the Raja?'

'Certainly not. The people would think I had made you some promise. I have made no promise and in no circumstances will I make any promise but this. If – when the grain is delivered – you will come to the camp and ask for Sikandar, I will take you to Lord Lake and you may ask him what you like. I will be surety for your life – and safe return – nothing more.'

They agreed on that. The Raja's force rode back to his fort. When he was sure this was not a trick, James drew a long breath. Once again, he was alive. He had been spared. All that remained was fatigue, care, constant vigilance. He ordered one squadron to act as a rearguard and with the other five closed gradually up to Robert. Mile after mile at the pace of a bullock – two miles an hour; the road seemed interminable. Bright sun all day and dust hanging in the air until at last the light began to turn to gold and then to green and the dust did not rise above the bellies of the bullocks. Now the long melancholy cry of the peacocks came from every grove as they went to roost. It was long after dark when they reached Lord Lake's camp and he was already at dinner. But he came out to see them.

'Have you succeeded?'

'Yes, my lord, I have brought sixty thousand bullocks.'

'Hurrah! No one but you would have done it! I shall never forget either Skinner or Skinner's Horse! Never! Here, take my sword. It is yours. And tomorrow, we will arrange a more practical reward. Come in and have dinner.'

'My lord, I have been on horseback since midnight; I beg to be excused. I must see to my men and horses. But tomorrow I will make you a full report.'

'Yes, yes – but tomorrow evening I shall march for Delhi. Skinner, I shall never forget you.'

Skinner went to see that every one of his troopers got two pounds of sweetmeats that night and every horse an extra ration of gram and some boiled linseed. Then he ate something himself and fell into bed.

## 21 If I Am Found Dead

NOT long after this, James spoke to Robert about the arrangements he wished to be made for his dependants if he were found dead on the field of battle. He had been afraid that his body might not be identified; someone might take off his head or it might be crushed by a cannon-ball. But he had had his chest tattooed with the griffin's head and bloody hand of the Skinners – the same device that was used as a regimental colour. This Robert knew. Now James gave him a list of his possessions and another of his dependants.

Robert said: 'But, James, I might be dead too. In fact, it is likely.'

'I know. But I shall tell Colonel Burn as well and I shall send a letter to our brother Templeton – though he is a cold fish. But you would be responsible if I am found dead and you are alive. You would need a list of what I have. Here it is. There is Rs. 20,000 to be added to that, which Lord Lake has given me for bringing in the Brinjaras. There! I have added it.'

He had never saved anything from his pay. But he was a soldier of fortune and it was regarded as proper that he should acquire such loot as the idols with diamond eyes he had taken at the same time as the Fish of Honour or such presents as Harji had given him. And now he was commanding a regiment. Even in the regular army, the commanding officer drew an allowance for every man on his strength, from which he was expected to meet not only the man's pay but all other expenses. In the case of a cavalry regiment, this came to a considerable sum – and Skinner's Horse was the size of at least two cavalry regiments. By good management, a man ought to be able to keep his men smart, well-equipped and well-mounted and be left with a profit. It was a bigger profit if he supplied the horses for his own *bargirs*. So there were some investments in East India Company Stock and some deposits with Indian bankers. It was not a great fortune.

James paused when he had given Robert the list of property. He went on:

'I know Lord Lake means to reward me after the war and perhaps he would do something for my dependants. But in any case, there will be *something* for them. Here is the list of my dependants. Robert, you will understand – not Templeton. He has ink in his veins. These are the women who are truly my dependants. I have written the shares against each and the names of their children. But, Robert, if any other woman comes to you, she has no claim. You know the life we have led, far from home for weeks on end; I have enjoyed female society, of course, but there is no woman I have wronged. I can swear to that. If any woman comes to you who is not on that paper, you can be sure that she knew what she was doing and has been generously rewarded. But these women, here on this list – I look on them as my wives by law – they were given by their fathers with their own consent. They are Muslim women of good family and entitled to a share in anything I leave. All but Mannu were given me by their fathers; her I rescued from her husband's funeral pyre. She was too young to die. Too young and too pretty. But she should be treated like the rest.'

He thought of his dependants. He remembered the negotiations for the first of them. It had been in Agra. He remembered her father, a most respectable Muslim with what is called in India a wheat complexion, lightly pock-marked, his beard clipped short and tinted with henna, his eyes light-coloured. He was wearing a *sherwani* of maroon velvet with a little round cap of the same velvet, embroidered with gold lace.

James had said to him: 'I am not of your faith. You understand that. But I take your daughter Mumtaz-ul-Nisa as my wife according to the customs of Islam and the Holy Q'uran. We have exchanged gifts and she comes with your full consent. That is so?'

The old man had agreed to that.

'And on my side,' James continued, 'I swear that I will honour and protect her as a wife and leave her a share of my possessions when I die.'

'It is just,' said the old man. 'She is yours with my full consent.'

She had been a good wife, he thought, kind and generous and a good mother.

But Mannu had joined his family in quite another way. They were beating through the *jhao* along the bank of a river, looking for a gang of armed robbers, who had looted and burned a village and broken the 'strong peace' James was trying to impose. A trooper brought him the news and he went at once to the spot.

There was a sandy beach by the side of the river and a track winding down to it through the *jhao*. The escarpment rose sharply from the beach; it was not a large river and the stage for the drama was a small one – the strip of sand white in the moonlight, the dunes and the *jhao* dark all round, the river gleaming silent in the foreground. It was dusk and a moon near the full had just risen. Near the water's edge was a pyre, a pile of wood carefully built up; on it lay a corpse swathed in white. Men with torches, all in white clothes, stood around; between the pyre and the *jhao*, away from the river, stood a knot of figures all in white – a priest, a woman with her arms held by two men, a small crowd of spectators. Between the priest and the pyre was a line of eight troopers.

The duffedar in charge of the section made his report. He had heard a cry – a woman's voice, a cry of fear. He had ridden to the sound – and there was the pyre with the dead body just laid upon it – and the girl, standing there, trembling and afraid. It was she who had cried out. She did not seem to be a willing victim so he had stopped the proceedings and sent word to James.

'What people are you?' asked James.

'We are Gaur Brahmans,' said the priest sulkily. 'This is no place for barbarous infidels.' He used a word – *mleccha* – that high-caste Hindus apply to both Christians and Muslims. 'This is no sight for you. Go away from here. It is the custom of our people.'

'It is the custom of your people – if she is willing,' said James. He remembered his mother's tales of proud Rajput ladies who flung themselves into the fire beside their warrior husbands – but this! This was very different. The dead man was not a warrior but a Brahman and in the light of the moon and the torches the girl's smooth rounded face seemed that of a child.

'Of course she is willing,' said the priest. 'She would not be here if she were not. She gave her consent this morning. There is often a little reluctance at the last but this is her settled will. She has only to walk three times round the pyre and lie down by her husband. It is no business of yours.'

If she did that, the priest would pour clarified butter over the living body and the dead, the torches would be put to the four corners and the whole would go up in a blaze.

James said: 'I shall not allow her to be sacrificed unless she is willing.'

He spoke to the girl, more gently: 'What is your name, lady?'

She gave a frightened look to the priest.

'Come, sister, do not fear. I shall do you no harm. Tell me your name.'

Terrified, hardly to be heard, she breathed, as though to herself: 'I am dead already. They say I am dead already. I must not speak.'

'You are not dead unless you wish it. Ah, sister, you are too young to die. If you do not wish to die, I will protect you. Speak without fear. Do you wish to die?'

She looked at the priest again, the whites of her eyes gleaming in the moonlight, then back at James. Suddenly she made up her mind.

'No!' she said in a low strained voice. 'No!' she said, louder and more determined now. 'No! No! No! No!' in a more and more desperate crescendo. 'He was old. He was my husband but he was horrible. No! I am young. I want to live!'

'You have spoken,' said James. 'You shall live and I will protect you. Duffedar! Swords! Push these men aside from her. Do them no harm unless they resist. If any man resists, cut him down. You, priest – burn your corpse but you shall burn no live woman against her will. But I will pay for her. Here is silver.' He threw silver on the ground. 'Buy a cock and put it to death in her place if you must have blood.'

He caught up the girl.

'Put your foot on mine. There! Behind me. I will protect you.'

They rode away in the moonlight.

That was how Mannu became part of his family. She too had been a good wife, he reflected. The only Hindu. But not at all like his mother, gentle and pliable where his mother had been proud and often fierce.

He turned again to Robert.

'So – that is clear and off my mind. Women – no man that is a man can live without them. I love all these women. I love them as I loved my mother. It is a duty to respect them and protect them. But no man that is a man makes women the main business of his life.'

## 22 Lord Lake is Coming

When Skinner's Horse brought in the sixty thousand bullocks, Lord Lake was able to move towards Delhi; he started the next day. As he had foreseen, Holkar broke off the siege and moved away. He did not want a pitched battle; he wanted to keep to the old Maratha methods of warfare, sweeping over the enemy's territory with great hordes of cavalry, living on what they found, looting, burning, killing. It was his aim to keep Lord Lake moving ponderously after him, always fifty miles behind. There was intense speculation in the British camp; where would he go? What would be his next move?

Things were at this stage when a Pathan trooper came to Sikandar secretly by night.

'Sahib,' he said, 'I have a plan.'

'Tell it,' said James, who had a feeling of dislike for this man, though he could not say why.

'You will not be angry?'

'I cannot promise what I shall think till I have heard your plan. You may either tell it me or keep silent and go away.'

He stuck to that and at last the Pathan overcame his fears.

'I have relations in Holkar's service,' he said, 'and I can easily get employment with Holkar. If the English will promise me a grant of land and a hundred thousand rupees, I will stab Holkar secretly and escape.'

James looked at him in silence but with mounting anger.

'Get out of my sight!' he said at last. 'You were right to think I should be angry. It is treachery. I hate treachery. Go!'

The man fawned and begged forgiveness but James would have nothing to say to him but:

'Go!'

Thinking it over, however, he decided that he should tell Lord Lake. Such a man would have accomplices; there might be talk. He would hate it to reach Lord Lake's ears that he had refused something that might be regarded as an advantage. He must be entirely open with Lord Lake if he was to be trusted; trust between them was essential. He asked for an interview and recounted what the man had said.

'Well,' said Lord Lake, 'and what do you think? Would he do as he says?'

'I think very likely he might. But such a man is not to be trusted. He is a traitor self-confessed!'

'What do you think I should do then?'

'Does your lordship wish me to speak quite freely – saying just what I think?'

'Of course.'

'Then I think he might very likely do what he says if he were promised the reward. But what would be said throughout Hindostan of Lord Lake and the English? People would say they were not strong enough to beat Holkar in the field. So they turned to treachery and assassination. If you will be advised by me, let the man be told publicly that we do not encourage treachery. He will be disgraced – but we must see that he does not starve.'

Lord Lake agreed and James announced in public – before a parade of his own Yellow Boys – that this man was a traitor who deserved death, but that since he had at least shown good will, he would not be punished and would still be employed, though in a position where he could not do much harm.

'But if any man,' James added, 'brings me the head of Holkar, slain fairly in battle, that man shall have a splendid reward.'

The end of that story came not long after. The man could not stay as a trooper in Skinner's Horse; they would not have him. But he was given a post as messenger and a strange thing happened. There was no general engagement but there were enemy forces not far distant. James Skinner was with Lord Lake at the time, well to the rear of the front line, when he saw that very man pass them, engaged on some errand. Hardly had he passed when a stray shot struck him and killed him instantly. It seemed to come from nowhere.

'Look, Lord Sahib,' cried James. 'The man who wanted to be a traitor! Killed before our eyes, when not another man has been hurt. That shot surely had its orders. Treachery has had its wages.'

Perhaps Lord Lake smiled but to James it was a confirmation of his deep belief that nothing happened without a purpose. It was a feeling that his own men would all have understood, whether they were Hindus or Muslims.

Now Holkar's intentions became more clear. He divided his army into two. Leaving the guns and infantry to move slowly south, he himself, with an army of cavalry some sixty thousand strong, went back to traditional Maratha methods of warfare and swept first north, to Saharanpur, and then eastward and southward through the rich country between the Ganges and the Jumna, plundering and burning in a swathe thirty miles wide.

Lord Lake was quickly on his heels. He too left his guns and infantry and pursued Holkar with his cavalry, following him through blackened and ruined villages, hoping to bring him to battle. Two hundred miles from Delhi, near Farrukhabad on the south bank of the Ganges, Holkar halted, convinced that Lake was so far behind that he could rest in safety. But Lake, though nearly forty miles behind at sunset, determined to press on all that night and after an exhausting march surprised him as dawn was breaking on 17 November 1804. Holkar had been utterly confident that he was safe and had taken no precautions. Farrukhabad was more a slaughter than a battle but it was the turning point of the war. From that moment, Holkar was beaten and everyone knew it. He turned back and fled towards the west. He lost men by desertion as he went. But though his army was half the size it had been, it was still ruthlessly destructive, plundering to support itself but also burning and killing in the anger of frustration and defeat.

On 19 November, Lake sent for James Skinner.

'I have a task for you. Exactly the task for which I told you I needed light cavalry and you of all men to lead them,' he began. 'Holkar has doubled back westward, as you know. He moves fast and if I am to catch him again, I must know just where he has gone. I can't afford to zig-zag across country here and there, looking for him; I must take the shortest path. That means light cavalry hanging on his tail and sending back accurate news to me all the time. Now, would your corps undertake this task?'

'My lord, you know me too well to ask such a question. Of course, we will obey any orders your lordship gives us. And this – I welcome it.'

Lake sprang to his feet and seized his hand.

James and his regiment had been in the pursuit from the beginning. Again and again they had ridden into villages where not a living soul was to be seen. The walls of the houses were of dried mud; they had resisted the fires and stood there, like the discoloured remnants of old teeth, crumbling and misshapen. The rafters and thatch had gone up in the blaze and lay in blackened ruin. Here and there dead bodies; dogs and vultures squabbling over the sordid remains; here and there a broken chest or the shattered remnants of the great earthenware jars used for storing grain. But no food, no cattle, no people. The Marathas had made a clean sweep.

In the early stages of the chase Skinner's Horse had been in close contact with Holkar's rearguard and had been in a number of skirmishes; they had covered far more ground than the dragoons who made the main striking force. But for that last prodigious night march they had been a rearguard and they had had no part in the attack on Holkar's army at Farrukhabad. All the same, they had had a gruelling time.

James went straight from Lord Lake to his regiment and picked the six hundred men and horses that seemed fittest for what would clearly be still harder work. He left as many more behind. He was on the road by two in the morning of 20 November and that evening rode warily into the outskirts of Mainpuri, fifty miles away.

This was the headquarters of a district which had once been part of the kingdom of Oudh* but had recently been ceded to the British. There were a dozen or so civilian officials at Mainpuri and two or three subalterns; the senior military officer was Captain Martin White, but he had under his orders no regular soldiers, only *sibandis*, men armed with

* This is more correctly Awadh, rhyming roughly with coward, but our ancestors spelt it Oudh and rhymed it with proud.

sword, shield and matchlock, collectors of revenue and policemen as much as soldiers. The Europeans had had some warning of Holkar's approach and had collected at Captain White's bungalow, which he was preparing to defend. He had some of his *sibandis* guarding the Treasury and some the gaol; the rest he had concentrated at his bungalow, where they were sulkily digging a shallow trench to surround the building. But he had grave doubts as to whether they were reliable.

Holkar had arrived in the late afternoon. He had camped near by and sent out plundering parties into the neighbouring villages and into the city, also parties to the civil lines where the Europeans had their dwellings. The main purpose of these parties was to collect information. They might find the servant of some official who could tell something if he chose – and he *would* choose, once they laid their hands on him. There would be a chance of loot as well – but when all the information and the loot had been squeezed out, then a blazing house would make a satisfactory end to the day. The squeezing was pretty complete when darkness fell and all round White's compound the thatched bungalows of the officials were going up with a roar and a torrent of sparks. The European women were clustered in the *gol-kamra*, the room at the centre of the house, like the nest of a queen termite, protected against the heat by surrounding rooms and deep verandas. One or two were firm and pale, one or two helplessly sobbing, six or seven anxiously waiting for a lead. Mrs White heard her husband's step and went to meet him.

'Could we not help by loading?' she asked.

'I was coming to suggest it. Get any lady who is quick and collected to stand by a man with a second weapon and load for him. The men are on the verandas, two on each side of the house, keeping behind pillars as far as they can. Any mattresses or stuff like that you can take to them would help. Even a quilt over a chair will hide a man. They have time to show you how to load. There's no enemy inside the compound yet. In fact, there are only a few parties of Marathas about and they have no cannon. A lucky shot or two and they'll sheer off. I shall be with the men in the trench round the compound. I'm going back there now. All is well as long as they hold that ditch. And at present, they can and will. But – for your ears only; not a word to anyone else – I've no hope of the *sibandis* staying loyal if there's a general attack. But there's no danger of that before morning. For the moment, we can defend the bungalow.' His voice softened. 'My dearest. You're wonderful – so brave, so calm. Keep their hearts up. I'll be back when I've been round the trench again.' He went into the middle of the *gol-kamra* and spoke in a public voice. 'Ladies, please do as my wife asks you. It's not for long. Lord Lake is coming. He will soon be here.'

Mrs White began to tell the women what to do, sending some to collect mattresses on the verandas, others to learn how to load. Her husband went out again to the trench round the compound. There he met the subedar of one of his three companies of *sibandis*. This was Amrit Singh, a fiery old Rajput, very lame in one leg. Amrit Singh was the one man he trusted.

'Is all as it was, subedar?'

'Yes, Sahib. All as it was. So far, we have seen only small parties of enemy. No serious attack. As long as there are only small parties, the men will be faithful. But, Sahib, I am not sure that they would stand a serious attack. Perhaps that will come in the morning.'

'Perhaps by then Lord Lake will be here. Do the men not know what Holkar did to Colonel Monson's sepoys who deserted to him?'

He broke off suddenly and gazed into the darkness. 'What's that? Who are those men? Can you see? To the right of that burning bungalow?'

'Yes, Sahib. I see. Maratha horse. Another party, like the last, who will come towards our line but sheer off when we fire. We will hold our fire till they come closer.'

He crept forward and spoke to a man lying in the trench. 'Understood.'

Amrit Singh came back to White and stood, peering into the darkness.

The Maratha horsemen had stood in a knot, as though conferring. Now suddenly they uttered wild ululating howls, as jackals howl, rising and falling, and galloped towards the line of *sibandis*, then swerved to the right, dropping the reins and firing over the bridle arm as they turned.

'Fire!' cried Amrit Singh and a dozen shots rang out. Two or three horses came down and there was one empty saddle. The rest swerved away to the right again, turning like a wedge of teal.

'Just as I expected,' said Amrit Singh. Then suddenly he stiffened.

'There's another party. There, behind them, coming through the smoke. Who can they be? Men in pale clothes. Long coats. They don't look like Marathas.

'And they're charging the Marathas! With the sword! It's the Yellow Men! It's Sikandar's men! Lord Lake is coming! He must be close!'

The two parties met and clashed in the gloom, visible for a few seconds against the blaze of the burning bungalow, swords flashing high above men's heads, horses rearing and screaming, a wild confusion of struggling forms. Then they disappeared in darkness and smoke. Five tense minutes later, a trumpet sounded and a score of yellow coats came trotting towards White and Amrit Singh.

'Captain Skinner of Skinner's Horse. Let us in, will you?' came a voice from the leader of the troop. 'What, is that you, Amrit Singh? Ah, that day when we lay side by side on the battlefield at Uniyara! We thought we should die – and both of us are still alive!'

'Sikandar Sahib! My heart is happy! My heart is full!' Amrit half drew his sword and thrust the hilt towards Sikandar, who touched it as *nazrana* is touched. 'Lord Lake is coming?' Amrit went on eagerly. 'He is close?'

'Yes, he's coming. Hot on the trail,' said Sikandar carelessly. 'Have you someone to hold my horse for a moment?'

'Yes, Lord Lake's coming,' he went on, rather loudly and still speaking Hindi. He was dismounted now and turned to Captain White, to whom he bowed.

'White. Captain Martin White. 2nd/7th Bengal Native Infantry. I can't say how pleased we are to see you. Is Lord Lake close?'

'Shall we take a turn, Captain White?' said James. As soon as they were a few paces distant, he said:

'For your ear only, Captain. I left Lord Lake's camp this morning, soon after midnight, near Farrukhabad. That must be fifty miles away and he cannot yet have come half that distance. I am sending back messages to tell him where Holkar is, and he will follow as fast as he can but his men and horses are very tired. They marched all day on the sixteenth and rode forty miles that night and fought a battle after twenty-four hours in the saddle. I doubt whether they'll be here before tomorrow evening at the earliest. What strength have you here?'

'Only three companies of *sibandis* – and a poor lot except for Amrit Singh. And one gun. We couldn't stand a direct attack by a force of any size. I could not rely on them.'

'We must make Holkar think that Lake is closer than he is. You must tell all your people that Lake is close. Don't breathe a word to anyone of how far he really is. I must try to take some prisoners; they would be useful. Stuff them with information and let them go. There will be no rest for us tonight, but I shall hope to see you in the morning. Good night, Captain White.'

'But you can't go like that. You must come in for a moment. The ladies will want to thank you. You have saved all our lives. Do come!'

'Very well, for a minute, but only for a minute. Don't relax, White. Mind you keep up your defences against the danger of parties of looters – but I don't think you have to fear a general attack now.'

He went into the *gol-kamra*. The women saw a sturdy compact figure in a blue uniform with silver lace, a face altogether Indian in complexion, but clean shaven, the lips and chin firm and resolute, the eyes kindly. They came to thank him. They all wanted to touch his hand.

'Thank you, thank you, Captain Skinner!' said Mrs White. 'I am sure you have saved us. We shall always remember our preserver.'

She had a broad brow, eyes set wide, nose, lips and chin firmly chiselled in clean lines, but in repose her expression might have been thought severe and at such moments some men might have judged her plain. But her face lighted up when she spoke, when she smiled, when she turned her head to listen, showing the very clear whites of her eyes. Then she was beautiful. Her face was alight now, as she thanked James.

'Goodbye, ladies,' he said. 'I am sorry I cannot stay. I am glad I have been of service. I too shall remember you.' He kissed Mrs White's hand and looked at her with admiration.

'There is a woman – a woman who might have been a companion,' he thought, but he dismissed the thought.

'Keep up your spirits,' he continued, 'Lord Lake is coming.'

He was off again. He sent messages to his risaldars to take prisoners if they could; if they could not take prisoners, they were to chase any parties of looters back to Holkar's camp. They were to sound trumpet-calls wherever they could, on all the approaches to the camp.

Within an hour or two, he had a score of prisoners. He made them a short speech. He did not want to make war, he said, on men such as they were, humble troopers who earned their bread as he did – soldiers of fortune who fought to earn their pay. He was going to let them go without harm, when they had answered a few questions. He then asked them for information about Holkar's strength, the names of his generals and the state of mind of his troops – matters of which he already knew a good deal, matters of general knowledge. Then he wished them good luck and gave each of them a rupee, adding that they should be careful not to fall into the hands of Lord Lake's terrible dragoons, who were close behind and would certainly not treat them as he had done. They made him deep salaams and went off towards Holkar's camp, jubilant at getting off so lightly.

And there, in Holkar's camp – he would say with relish, years later, when he told the story to his friends over the dinner-table at his home in Hansi – there, in Holkar's camp, they said they had *seen* Lord Lake's dragoons and narrowly escaped them!

The ruse worked and early next morning Holkar's camp was breaking up and making for Etah. Captain White and his party were saved. James went to see them briefly but could not stay; he must keep close on Holkar's tail, sending back news all the time. He had been two nights now without more than an hour or two's sleep, snatched in a grove by the side of the road.

Etah repeated the story of Mainpuri. Skinner's Horse seemed to be everywhere and Holkar could not doubt that Lake was close behind them. He pressed on, leaving the city of Etah untouched and its small European population unhurt. For seven days, Sikandar was snapping at his heels. The horses were never unsaddled and the men rested, when they could, with one end of the rein buckled to the bridle and one round the wrist. They changed their ground two or three times in a night for fear of being surprised. When they stopped to eat they would make a kind of broth, taking ears of the millet that was still standing in the fields, husking them as best they could and boiling the grain with anything they were lucky enough to get, the meat of a goat perhaps or a pot of clarified butter. All shared alike. James would remember this with special pleasure.

'This broth,' he told his friends, 'was served out in earthen pots, my share being always brought to me by the men, who showed me great love and attention, and were willing to act as my private servants, and tried in every way to please and add to my comfort.'

And then he would add with a smile, raising his glass to his lips:

'But I felt the want of my dram.'

There were compensations. They captured a great many horses and camels and, when Holkar had been chased back across the Jumna, and when the regiment went back to their headquarters at Sikandra, Lord Lake visited them. He reviewed the regiment and praised them highly, promising that they should have 'bread for the rest of their lives'. To James, he was specially warm in praise, giving him a present of a splendid horse with silver trappings, a present to himself from some Raja, and raising the strength of his corps from twelve hundred to seventeen hundred men. This was not only gratifying but remunerative, since he received a monthly sum for each man on his strength. Since he had plenty of captured horses, he was able to increase the number of his *bargirs*; this was an additional gain, since he paid out much less for a *bargir* than for a man who found his own horse and equipment. He had no difficulty about finding men; the countryside was full of men from de Boigne's brigades who were looking for employment and were only too glad of service with Sikandar. But there was not much time for rest and recruitment. Within less than a month, a summons came for service almost as arduous as the pursuit of Holkar.

## 23 Hired to Die

In the three months that followed, James and his Yellow Boys were constantly employed in operations that were exhausting and sometimes dangerous, though less spectacular than the seven days spent in pursuing Holkar. For most of this time, Lord Lake was besieging Bharatpur and the regiment provided escorts to columns of Brinjaras and their bullocks; they also helped to subdue petty chiefs who were reluctant to give up their habit of plundering their neighbours. They distinguished themselves in this work and Lord Lake presented James with another sword and on another occasion with a pair of valuable pistols. Both brothers won golden opinions from the whole army and their fame grew in wider circles too.

In February 1805, however, it seemed as though the old days of the pursuit of Holkar had come again. Holkar had an ally, a freebooting chief with men at his command, one Amir Khan. His forces were not disciplined; they were no more than robber bands, of a particularly cruel and atrocious kind, expert at extorting from a village every scrap of loot that was to be had. It was said to take thirty years for a district to return to normal after Amir Khan had swept through it. He would avoid battle if he could; his horsemen, loosely organized under various lesser chiefs, lived off the country and moved with extreme speed.

Amir Khan now started on one of those destructive expeditions for which he was famous. The raid may well have been meant to draw Lord Lake away from Bharatpur, but its main purpose, as always, was plunder. He crossed the Jumna near Muttra with thirty thousand men, swept across the Doab, which Holkar had so recently ravaged, crossed the Ganges further north, and moved on Moradabad, the headquarters of the most westerly district of Rohilkand. But Lord Lake did not raise the siege of Bharatpur. He stayed where he was, with the guns and infantry, sending his cavalry with its galloper guns under General Smith to chase Amir Khan and try to bring him to battle.

Skinner's Horse were the advanced guard as well as the antennae of this pursuing force. It was like the chase after Holkar all over again, except that Amir Khan was even more elusive than Holkar and every bit as destructive. Once again they rode into villages where only the stumps of mud walls stood in the ashes of their thatch, where no life was left and the vultures tore at the distorted bodies of the dead. Sometimes the ashes were still smoking and they knew they were close; sometimes they lost the trail. At Moradabad, it was the same tale as at Mainpuri; Skinner's Horse arrived just in time to save the score or so of Europeans who were besieged in the gaol. Amir Khan fled at the sight of the yellow tunics because he thought the dragoons and the galloper guns must be close behind.

The hunters lost his track. They captured two of his

foragers and found out where he was. But where would he be tomorrow? James decided to enter his camp in disguise with a few of his troopers and see what clues he could pick up. Some of his men had relations in Amir Khan's gangs but he knew he could rely on their personal devotion to himself.

That night, in Amir Khan's camp, sitting quiet by the camp fire, listening a great deal, saying very little, James was soon aware that the men around him did not think they were closely pursued. But there was much ill-feeling between the groups who were mostly Pathan – like this among which he sat – and those who were Maratha. The feeling suddenly flared up, some time after dark, when it became known round the camp fires that the Maratha leaders had complained to Amir Khan of offensive language used by the Pathans. They had questioned their courage, said the Marathas, and they insisted that the Pathan leaders should make reparation or be punished.

The scene was outwardly familiar – camp fires in every direction, men sitting near them huddled in their *rezai* quilts, tripods of lances with shields and water bags slung from them, horses hobbled and haltered. The fires were beginning to die down and one by one men were turning from the warmth of the fire to wrap the quilt more closely about them and sleep. All that was familiar, but added was a hum of gossip, a coming and going of men from one fire to another, a sense as of bees not yet swarming but uneasy, disturbed, ready to spring suddenly into furious activity.

What was happening was hard to know. James decided he must be patient; whatever he did, he must not act in a way that would rouse suspicion; he rolled himself in a *rezai* and went to sleep. But in the morning the buzz of rumour rose to a shriller note and soon the news came that the Marathas were so incensed that they had refused to move. The whole camp was to have broken up, but now the Marathas had said they would stay where they were till they got satisfaction.

It was too good a chance to miss. He and his troopers

slipped away, ostensibly to find villages near by that had not yet been plundered; he got word to General Smith. Smith had just decided that he must halt to rest his men and horses, but at this news he broke up his camp and marched again, just as Lake had done before Farrukhabad. He did not repeat Lake's success; by the time he came up with Amir Khan, it was too late in the day and Smith's army was too small and tired to inflict the crippling blow he had hoped for. Once again Amir Khan escaped and they had to hunt for the trail.

They found the little town of Chandausi burnt to the ground and this suggested to Smith that Amir Khan meant to cross the river Ramganga at the near-by ford and pillage new territory in the Bareilly district. He was so sure of this that he made for the ford and waited there for the Pindari host to come to him. Meanwhile, he sent Robert Skinner, with five hundred of Skinner's Horse, away to the west to Anupshahr, where he was to meet a column of Brinjaras and their bullocks and bring them in. Robert had greatly distinguished himself, both in the pursuit and in the inconclusive battle.

James, with the rest of his regiment, was with Smith's main force at the ford. Tents were pitched and picquets posted; it was the middle of the afternoon. James had lain down for an hour's sleep. Suddenly he was aware that someone was in his tent; he was instantly awake and his hands on his loaded pistols. But it was Mangat Das, the cleverest and most faithful of his private corps of *harkaras*, he who had told him when the duck were flying at Hathrás. He crouched by the bedstead and breathed in James's ear. He was secret by habit as well as by nature.

'I have had bad news, Sahib,' he said.

He had brought a letter from Robert.

Robert wrote: 'We suddenly found ourselves faced with the whole of Amir Khan's horde. There was nothing for it but to get into an old *serai*,* near Sambhal. Mangat Das will tell you

* A halting place for travellers.

all. We have beaten off one attack. They made three assaults. Supplies are very low. I am taking the shoes off the horses to make bullets. Only ten rounds left. Come if you can.'

Mangat Das told him the rest. He spoke so low that no one but James could hear. As he spoke, James saw the scene in his mind's eye. No sooner were Robert's men in the *serai* than they were surrounded. It was a place that had once been fortified but was now partly ruinous. They hung out the regimental colours – the griffin's head and bloody hand on a yellow ground – on one of the angles of the fort. There were parties of horse in every direction, watching the ruined fort like a cat at a mouse's hole. Then Amir Khan himself advanced; he sent a *chobdar* with a spokesman and letters. This person, whose dress showed he was of some importance, rudely announced that his message was not for Robert but for his risaldars. Robert haughtily replied that he had absolute faith in his risaldars and would leave them to receive the message. He withdrew, coldly and distantly, to a point on the ramparts. The herald then read Amir Khan's message to the five risaldars. He wrote that if they would give up Robert, everyone else would not only go free but be given three months' pay. The risaldars with hardly a moment's consultation sent him a contemptuous reply:

'Your mother was a harlot and a bitch and had no nose,' they said, 'but we are men of faith and honour and will never do what you want.'

That message, they thought, would slam the door on all negotiations. Having sent it, they went in a body to Robert and told him what they had been offered and what they had said. He said:

'Your message is what I should have expected. I knew it would be the answer to my trust. But if he does send word again, you must give me a chance to be heard.'

They went back to the broken battlements. They saw that Amir Khan had gathered round him a great gathering of dismounted men. Mangat Das had been with them when they occupied the little fort; telling the story to James, he thought that there must have been ten thousand of the enemy.

Robert and his risaldars saw to their surprise that Amir Khan was sending the *chobdar* and the herald a second time. Robert was delayed a moment on the battlements giving orders to a duffedar. When he got to the gate, he learnt that Amir Khan had sent the same message again, saying that he would excuse their rudeness. Before Robert could intervene, the risaldars had sent him back again with the same message, adding that, herald or no, they would shoot him if he did not go back at once.

Robert said he was displeased with them. He knew they did it for love, but they had disobeyed his orders. He summoned from the ramparts all his five hundred except the sentries. He told the men what had happened and said that in spite of this he was willing to go to Amir Khan as a prisoner.

'It will save five hundred lives,' he cried, 'and I will go at once if you wish to lay down your arms and are willing to be saved by such means.'

But they broke out in an angry though affectionate babble.

'Never!' they cried. 'When we are all dead you may go, but till then we shall not let you go. Are there not thousands being killed every day at Bharatpur? What are five hundred such as us to that? Are we not soldiers? Were we not hired to die? Have we not eaten your salt – yours and your brother's? We will die like soldiers.'

'Very well,' he cried, 'we will all die together.'

And as he said those words, a shout came from the sentries on the ruinous battlements that the enemy were moving.

'There is time for one thing,' Robert said. 'Let us say a prayer together, Hindu, Christian and Muslim, each in his own way, asking Almighty God to grant us courage to die as brave men.'

When they had done that they ran to the ramparts. The Pindaris were approaching on all sides and now made a determined attack. Each of the defenders took careful aim as he had been trained to do; each time he brought down his man. Three times the enemy came and three times they were beaten back; several parties gained a footing on the walls and were cut down with swords. As the darkness fell, the storming parties fell back for the third time and it seemed likely that the enemy would wait till morning when they could make the best use of their overwhelming numbers.

The defence were now desperately short of ammunition. Even with the bullets they were making from horse-shoes, they would have only ten rounds apiece. As soon as it was quite dark and before the moon rose, Mangat Das slipped out of the *serai* and, moving very slowly and cautiously, crawled past the surrounding groups of Pindari camp fires. There was nothing like the organized picquets and sentry lines of disciplined troops and it was not difficult for Mangat Das to avoid being caught. But he had to be careful and caution slowed him up. After that he had to cover thirty miles on foot over country he did not know well and in which he must take care not to fall into the hands of Amir Khan's foraging parties. That was why he did not reach James till three in the afternoon.

James was in great distress. He went at once to General Smith, a man whom he respected though for him he did not feel the affection and admiration he felt for Lord Lake. Smith listened to him carefully and then said:

'What exactly is it that you want me to do?'

'I want you to march at once for Sambhal and attack Amir Khan.'

'It is thirty miles,' said Smith reflectively. 'Men and horses are tired; they have just finished a day's march and must have some rest. It would be madness to start at once and arrive exhausted for a battle against superior forces.'

'It's what Lord Lake did before Farrukhabad,' Skinner broke in. He was too much moved to be respectful.

Smith looked at him not unkindly.

'True,' he said, 'but I am not Lord Lake. He has an extraordinary capacity for getting men to perform the impossible. It is what I did before that inconclusive battle. It is a mistake I do not mean to repeat. But let us consider what is likely to happen. You want to save your brother. Of course you do. But he was expecting to be attacked again this morning. I am afraid the probability is that he has been and that he has already been overwhelmed. I am sorry, Skinner, but in war we must act on probabilities. You must see that that is the most likely thing to have happened. It is possible, however, that Amir Khan did not attack him – or that ten rounds were enough and he was beaten off. In that case, it seems probable that Amir Khan would move away. I still think he will want to cross the river and get into the Bareilly district; we all thought so when we discussed it yesterday – you agreed yourself – and this news does not alter my opinion. He never takes the direct route. At Sambhal he is further away than I had expected but I still think he will have made for the ford. I think we should rest the men and horses now but start at midnight towards Sambhal. I think we shall meet Amir Khan on the way.'

'But if you started at nightfall, sir – six hours earlier – you could be there before dawn. And if Robert and my men had survived today, that would save them from being destroyed tomorrow morning.'

'But – I am sorry, Skinner, but I have to say it again – I think that most probably they have already been overrun. And in that case Amir Khan will already be moving and I hope in this direction. He will pitch camp somewhere tonight. I don't want to go past him in the dark. Nor do I want to meet him when my men and horses are half dead with fatigue.'

'Then, sir, will you allow me to start with my men for Sambhal at once? I could cut my way through the Pindaris and into his fort and at least bring him powder and shot.'

'Skinner, I'm sorry, but it wouldn't be right. It would be throwing good men away. And if we are to start at midnight, I must have you with me. I shall want a screen of light cavalry moving ahead towards Sambhal. No, you must stay with us and march at midnight.'

'Then I must make Amir Khan *think* you are marching at once. By a ruse. Do you mind if I do that?'

Smith reflected.

'He must by now know where I am. And if he thinks I am near him, and if he means to cross by the ford, as I believe he does, he will try to slip past me. He will think I am moving by the main road, well away from the river. He will get down to the river and move with the river on his left. Then I should be able to wheel to my right and catch him with his back to the river. That would suit me very well. Yes, you may do that – but you must yourself get into touch with him as early as you can and let me know where he is.'

James almost ran back to his tent.

'Where's Mangat Das?' he asked his orderly.

'Asleep, behind the tent, Sahib.'

'Let him sleep all he can; he's going to need every minute,' said James. 'Get me the ten troopers who went with me into Amir Khan's camp. Quickly, quickly.'

He himself sat down to write a letter to Robert.

'I have your letter,' he wrote, 'and informed the General who will march before nightfall. He should reach Sambhal with his main force not long after the bearer of this reaches you. Try to keep Amir Khan in play by discussing terms for surrender.'

By the time he had written and sealed this letter, the troopers had arrived. Mangat Das was aroused and told that he must go back with these men.

'Here,' he said, 'is a letter for my brother. You must contrive that it falls into the hands of Amir Khan. He must think it was for my brother's eyes only. Understood, Mangat Das? Now – you ten – the ten of you must do everything you can to give Amir Khan the impression that the English are very close. I want him to think our army started before nightfall. It is really going to start at midnight. Understood? Does every man understand? Then be off. You will be well rewarded – a thousand rupees to each of you.'

They were gone. James must wait. He pictured the fort, full of dead men, his colours captured, five hundred of his men lost, his brother torn by crows and jackals. But he must wait.

At the very moment when James was trying to persuade General Smith to march at once, Amir Khan and his Pindaris had launched another attack on Robert and the five hundred

Yellow Boys at Sambhal. All morning the sentries in the fort had been watching every movement in the Pindari camp; all they could discern was bustle without obvious purpose. In fact it was the old tale of divided counsels. Some chiefs wanted to march away at once; others to attack Robert in the morning and march in the evening, whether successful or not; a third party thought that if they were ever to hold up their heads again, they must take the *serai* from which so pitiful a party had so long defied them. After arguing all morning, the chiefs at last agreed to an attack that evening.

The assault met determined resistance; the defenders aimed every shot with the knowledge that they had only ten rounds and they made every shot tell; none the less, some attackers got on to the rampart and were cut down by the sword. When at last the assault force fell back, many of Robert's troopers had not a round left and none had more than one or two. They were very tired; they were on half rations, hungry and faint. If they were attacked again, there would be nothing for it but to open the gate and die sword in hand.

Mangat Das and the ten troopers rode through the night and were near the *serai* at Sambhal an hour before dawn. They did not know what they would find. They must first discover whether there was still anyone left in the fort. But as they moved warily round it, the besiegers seemed everywhere to have posted rudimentary picquets, as though it were still occupied. The moon had risen late and was past the full but when they drew closer it gave enough light for them to see something very like the regimental colours still flying at the angle of the fort.

'They are still there!'

They separated; the troopers moved back to where they had left the horses. They waited a little, then circled round the camp and found a party of grass cutters whom they chased noisily towards the sleeping Pindaris. They repeated this from another angle and then set fire to some stacks of corn-stalks. Smoke and flame and wild shouts and trumpet-calls – they were experienced in this kind of thing and enjoyed it. Meanwhile, Mangat Das had clumsily blundered into a party of sleeping Pindaris. He began to blubber and snivel as soon as they laid hands on him.

'Let me go, let me go!' he cried. 'I am a poor man, nobody at all. Let me go!'

They questioned him angrily. What was he doing, wandering about at night near their camp? He must be a spy and should be put to death at once.

Torrents of tears and protestations. No, no, he wasn't a spy, he was nobody at all. They searched him.

They soon found the letter and dragged him before Amir Khan, an unimpressive man, small and sneering, though clever and quick of decision. Here Mangat Das continued to weep and ask for mercy and to protest that he was nobody. But when Amir Khan had read the letter and threatened him with torture he gave in at once and said he would tell everything.

'Yes, it is true, I came from the big Sikandar, who had a great love for his brother. It was a message to the little Sikandar. I don't know what is in the message. I am a poor man, nobody at all. I will tell you all I know but I know nothing. Yes, I heard it said before I left that the army would start at once, before nightfall. I know nothing but I heard it said. It is a big army, thousands of men and horses. Yes, they have the little guns that can be pulled by a galloping horse. I know nothing. I am no one. Let me go.'

It was at this moment that men came hurrying in with the news that the grass-cutters had been chased in by mounted men in long yellow coats. And then came others to report burning villages all round them.

'Beat him and let him go,' said Amir Khan. 'We must go. Saddle! Mount! Away! Away!'

They were in too great a hurry to beat him long.

It had been a tense night for Robert's sentries on the wall of the *serai*, not much less tense even for those supposed to be resting. A little before dawn, a blaze of fire beyond the

Pindari camp made the sentries call their officers. What was burning? Villages? Stacks of straw? One sentry thought he had seen a yellow coat by the light of a blaze. Then there were trumpet-calls – calls they knew. Then a confused hum rising to a roar was heard from the Pindari camp – orders, shouts, quarrels, the jangling of metal, horses whinnying, bustle, hammering, all merging in one mounting hubbub. Another attack? That meant death; they had not one round apiece. Or flight? Or a battle against the advancing English? Then the first horsemen were leaving the camp – there could be no doubt any longer. It was flight.

Everyone was on the battlements – the men of all five squadrons. A great shout of triumph went up. Robert made his voice heard.

'Sentries, stand fast! You are still on duty till you are relieved. Kot-duffedars in each squadron, have your new guards ready to relieve those coming off duty.'

As soon as the relief had taken place, he sent his five trumpeters to the angle of the wall where the colours hung. There in the bright sunlight of early morning, the five trumpeters together sounded the rousing call that starts the day. It was a new day, sharp and clean and cold, and there was new life for men who had counted themselves dead.

But it was still some time before the enemy's camp was altogether deserted and one of James's ten troopers could trot to the gates of the fort. Then at last Robert could relax some of his precautions. Meanwhile, another of the ten was riding back along the road they had travelled in the night to bring the news to James. They reached him when Smith's army still had fifteen miles to go. Mangat Das and the ten troopers had saved five squadrons of Skinner's Horse.

But Amir Khan did not, as Smith had hoped, try to double back and make for the ford into the Bareilly district. He had had enough. He went the other way to the ford of the Ganges by which he had entered Moradabad district and did not stop until he had gone back across the Jumna with only ten thousand men of the thirty thousand with whom he had begun his raid.

PART FIVE

# TREACHERY

## 24 These Are Sad Times

YEARS afterwards, James Skinner's eye would light and the fire of youth would come back into his voice as he talked over the dinner-table to his friends of those days in the winter of 1804–5.

'Those two chases made as severe a course of service as any corps ever went through. In the chase after Holkar, the army went five hundred miles and after Amir Khan seven hundred miles. I am sure my men went twice the distance the army went and endured twice the labour and twice the hardship of the regulars. We were never less than eighteen hours of the twenty-four on horseback. They never murmured; not once were my men accused of shrinking from any duty; not once did they turn their backs on the enemy.'

Those were the words he would use, remembering with intense pleasure those times when action had been everything, when there had been no doubts about where duty lay, when the pleasure of swift achievement had satisfied him so completely that he could fall asleep the moment he lay down and closed his eyes.

It was not quite the end when Amir Khan was chased back across the Jumna. Holkar was beaten, but he remembered the old Maratha saying, that for a Maratha soldier his home was the back of his horse. He left his territories and with his whole army marched away to the north, into the territory of the Sikhs, where he asked for protection against the English. But the Sikhs were not prepared to join him in war against the English. There was nothing left for him to do but sue for peace and hope to get it on good terms. He was very lucky; just at that moment, a sharp change of policy among the English got him much better terms than he had dreamed of.

James went with Lord Lake into the Punjab in pursuit of Holkar. They marched through the country of the friendly Sikh chiefs on the eastern side of the river Sutlej, which formed the boundary of the independent empire of Ranjit Singh. Indeed, James, at Lord Lake's request, was the first to cross the Sutlej and to show that there was a way across where a galloper gun could be taken. He liked to remember that he had gone into Sikh territory as far as the point where the first Sikandar – Alexander the Great – had turned back from the conquest of India. It was on the banks of what modern Indians call the Beas, and the Greeks called the Hyphasis, that Alexander had given in to his almost mutinous troops and turned for home. And this new Sikandar, James Skinner, was the first man in the service of the British to water his horse in the Hyphasis.

The crossing of the Sutlej was done at Lord Lake's request. It was not an order, because the British were not at war with the Sikhs and strictly speaking to cross the river was a breach of neutrality. But to know that a gun could get across would be a help in bargaining and Lord Lake let it be known that he would be pleased if it were done.

Not that Lake could do much bargaining. Lord Wellesley, who had been the Governor-General when the war began, had believed that peace and order under British rule were the best gifts he could bestow on Central India and Hindostan. Not only British interests but those of the Indian peasants demanded, he believed, that large areas should be annexed and firmly administered. But he had been recalled in the summer of 1805, and Lord Cornwallis had been sent out in his place – Governor-General for the second time – with instructions to make peace as soon as possible and at almost any price. Cornwallis had died within three months of taking office. His successor, Sir George Barlow, was glad of the opportunity to carry out the same policy. He believed the British had no business in India but trade. He thought they had no concern with the well-being of any Indians but those already their own subjects. He deplored expenditure on military operations and extension of territory. Profit was the only object.

Barlow was a man for whom none of his contemporaries had a good word. His manners, they said, were 'cold and repellent' and since the chief article of his policy was to avoid expense, no consideration of merit or long service would induce him to depart from rigid observance of rules which, to most of those who have written about him, seemed mean and pettifogging.

Lord Lake sent for Skinner. He rose when James entered his tent and came round the table to shake his hand and make him sit down.

'Skinner, these are sad times,' he said. 'We had times of glory, you and I, when we were chasing Holkar – we were always in the saddle and we knew what we wanted! To beat Holkar! That was all – nothing else. Now I have to make peace with him! And by no means the peace he deserves. Everything has changed since Lord Wellesley went. This man Barlow – I speak freely to you, Skinner; I know you won't repeat what I say – this man Barlow, who is now the Governor-General, has the outlook of a draper's assistant. He tells me to make peace as quickly as I can and on any terms. He has no thought for the lives spent in winning victory; no thought for the future peace and government of this countryside. He hasn't seen the villages you and I have seen – the thatch burnt, the walls bare, the roads strewn with mutilated bodies. I'm told to make peace on terms which mean that all we have done will have to be done over again in ten years' time. I wager you – in ten years' time we shall be forced to do it all again.

'However, we soldiers must do as we're told. Why I asked you to see me was about the future of your corps. At the moment, it stands at 1,700 strong. I have orders that all irregular cavalry are to be reduced and nearly all disbanded.

I've put in the strongest recommendation to make an exception of yours. It'll have to be reduced, but I've put it at 1,200. I've made only this one exception and I've pitched it in as strong as I can about all you've done. Not a word more than is true, mind you. I couldn't have managed without you. Even Barlow can't overlook such service as yours.'

After that interview, James went back to his headquarters with a good deal of satisfaction. It was 1806 and he was still only twenty-eight. To have command of 1,200 men at that age was something he could hardly have hoped for, ten years ago. He talked about it to Robert.

'No, Robert,' he said, 'I'm not dissatisfied. It is true that I'm still only a local captain and can be given orders by a boy straight from England with his mother's milk still on his lips. But I have 1,200 men and now we shall have time to look after them properly and make their training perfect. It'll be a pleasure to get to know the men really well and to know something of their homes and families. There's nothing like that. Too often we've had to go into action with men we didn't really know, men who hadn't been long enough with us to have the true spirit of our regiment. And then, there will be a grant of land. There must be. Lord Lake has always said he would reward me. Look at Amir Khan, whom we chased out of Moradabad, whom you defied at Sambhal with five hundred men against nearly thirty thousand. He's been recognized as an independent chief with a salute of thirteen guns. But, truly, Robert, I can be happy with command of 1,200 men and the knowledge that I did my best and that Lord Lake was satisfied.'

He paused and went on slowly. 'You and I are fighting men. It is our calling. It is part of our nature. Danger has brought us moments of intense life that we don't know in quiet times. These have been the moments of real living – when every tiny thing seemed beautiful and when it seemed certain we should die. A man who has not known this – he hasn't lived. If we are rewarded with land and money – that is good and right but it is something extra. A gift from Heaven. So, Robert, I'm not dissatisfied.'

Robert was a fiery character, more impetuous than James and less thoughtful. His affection for James restrained him but he was sometimes on the verge of mutiny. He said:

'Well, I *am* dissatisfied. I should like a grant of land and a proper commission and a decent rank. Local lieutenant! And Amir Khan has a thirteen-gun salute! Plunder the British and they make you a prince. Serve them faithfully and they make you a local lieutenant.'

A month later, James was again summoned to Lord Lake's camp. Sir John Malcolm was there too. Malcolm was a soldier who had turned political officer. A man of enormous energy, he was to turn soldier again, command a force and win a decisive battle; he was to become Governor of Bombay. He wrote a history of Persia and a life of Clive. He was not only versatile and vigorous but generous and open – indeed, sometimes he was criticized as too generous for a diplomat. In Sir Arthur Wellesley's mess, he would sometimes after dinner start some boyish game of exuberant physical exertion that was known as 'a Malcolm riot'. They called him Boy Malcolm because of his infectious high spirits. He had been Sir Arthur Wellesley's companion at the decisive battle of Assaye and was all his life a friend of the great Duke's. He had been trusted by the Marquess of Wellesley when he was Governor-General and he had great admiration for Lord Wellesley, and inevitably a corresponding dislike for Sir George Barlow and his policies.

James arrived in time for breakfast, then usually a large meal eaten late by men who had been on horseback since the dawn. Lord Lake and Malcolm came out to greet him when he dismounted; they were, as always, friendly and cordial.

'Skinner, my dear fellow, it's good of you to come over. Come into the tent and have some breakfast,' said Lord Lake. 'You must be hungry. We'll talk business afterwards.' But beneath his kindness and goodwill, James felt a constraint. There was something disagreeable in the offing, he felt sure.

After breakfast, the three of them moved into the office

tent. Here Lord Lake changed his manner. It was suddenly as though he had to announce the death of a son or a wife.

'I can't tell you myself,' he said gruffly. 'I'm too ashamed. You'd better read this.'

He handed him an official letter. James took it; he looked at it as though it were a snake. He turned to Malcolm.

'Have you read it?'

Malcolm nodded.

'Then tell me what it says.'

'It says that no exceptions can be made and that all irregular cavalry are to be disbanded. The only concession is that in view of the exceptional services reported by the Commander-in-Chief all ranks of Skinner's Horse are to receive a gratuity of one month's pay.'

James laughed at that.

'Three months' was what Amir Khan offered them. But that was for treachery, not fidelity.'

Lord Lake had tears in his eyes.

'James Skinner,' he said, 'I know what your regiment meant to you. And I know what fidelity and honour have meant to you. I can't say how much I regret this. That man Barlow! I can't serve with him. I shall go home. But before I go – there are some things I can still do on my own authority. Pensions for your men. I can pension all the duffedars and above. That's right, isn't it, Malcolm?'

'Yes, you have the right to do that.'

'And I can give the rest three months' pay, whatever Barlow says. That's one thing. Now the other is this. Ochterlony is to stay on for the present as Resident and he's to have an escort of three hundred men. We'll transfer your three squadrons of *bargirs* to be the Resident's Escort. You'll still be their commandant – you can appoint an officer to do the duty for you – and there'll be a remnant of Skinner's Horse. It'll be a foundation to build on when this decision of Barlow's is revoked. Mark my words, this won't last. As soon as I'm home, I shall go to the Horse Guards – I shall go to the East India Company – I shall go to the King. I won't see injustice done and take it lying down.

'Another thing. I am empowered to give *jagirs* – grants of land – for exceptional services. I want you to decide on four of your risaldars – whichever you think – it's entirely for you. Give their names to Malcolm. They shall have grants of land worth five thousand rupees each. And what can I do for you? Nothing, I know, to compensate you for losing the regiment. But there should be a *jagir* for you and your brother. I've talked about it to Malcolm. I haven't unlimited land at my disposal but from the allotment I have I want to put land worth twenty thousand rupees a year at the disposal of you and your brother. I know it's not enough – but will you take it?'

'My lord,' said James, 'you are very kind. You understand me. You know how I feel. To lose the regiment – I won't deny it is a heavy blow. I had hoped it would live after me. But such hopes are childish. Man dies and there's an end, on earth at least. To have satisfied you and won your good opinion means very much to me. I can always find satisfaction in remembering that. And then, my lord, this *jagir*. Of course we will most gratefully accept it. I am deeply grateful. It is to make us princes – small princes it is true – but we shall have a home, something to work for. It will be something we can come back to from whatever else may befall us. And we shall value it the more because it comes from you.

'You know, my lord – for we have talked of these things – that I believe a man is under orders – though I do not know from where or from whom – to do his best in whatever may be his proper calling. I thought my calling was to be a soldier. I tried to be a good soldier. Perhaps now it is to be something else. It will be a sad thing to say goodbye to so many of my men. But we have to face what is sent us. And I console myself by hoping that once again there may be a just man at the head of affairs who will listen to your lordship's recommendation and will take me by the hand again.'

Lake rose and again shook him by the hand.

'I told you long ago I'd never forget you and I won't.

As soon as I'm home I'll set about putting Skinner's Horse on its feet again. I'm your friend as long as I live. Never doubt that. And Malcolm here will be your friend in India. He knows what you've done.'

'The trouble is,' said Malcolm, 'I'm out of favour myself. I was Lord Wellesley's man – and Sir Arthur Wellesley's friend. I'm tarred with the same brush. But I do know what you've done and no man has a higher sense of what you deserve. I'll do what I can. Don't hesitate to tell me anything or ask for anything. Ochterlony's your friend too.'

James went away with a sad heart. But he had a letter in his pocket to the chief civil officer in the Aligarh district. This letter instructed him to place James and Robert in possession as landlords of part of de Boigne's old property – a tiny fraction only of what de Boigne had had, but still an estate that would give them a home, a base, something to which they could add, a property they could improve.

It was a sad day when he told his regiment what had happened and said goodbye to hundreds of them. His heart ached that night, for friendships interrupted, perhaps broken. It was the break in friendship that hurt. His men would not starve. They all came of families that had land. They would go to their villages and live on the land till another chance came. If the regiment was ever restored – though he had little hope of that – he would be able to find them again.

As for himself, he was young and in a few days a new interest began to claim him. He went to see the villages assigned to him, villages where he would be the lord of the manor, collector of revenue, dispenser of justice and principal farmer as well. He saw the District Officer in Aligarh, a friendly and helpful man who had chosen him a group of villages close together, with groves of mangoes, good soil and good wells, where the tenants were industrious cultivators, Jats and Kurmis for the most part, solid peasant stock, and where there was a good site for a house on a piece of rising ground. They went to look at it together and he was pleased.

It was a tract that had somehow been missed by Holkar's

marauders and under de Boigne they had had peace. There was a peaceful look about these villages. They were rich in trees, not only in orchards and groves of fruit-trees near the inhabited sites, but growing among the houses, in the centre of the village. In the largest village, near which his own house would stand, there was an open space with a fine *pipal* tree, a kind of fig, where the leaders of the village met to talk things over. There were *neem* trees too, tall trees with feathery leaves like an ash, trees whose shade is good to sleep under, whose leaves are fragrant for soap and make poultices for wounds. The walls were of dried mud, well-kept by yearly application, smooth as old ivory. As you walked between the houses, you would look through a gateway into a little yard where a light cart for a trotting bullock stood up-ended, where a couple of wooden ploughs rested against the wall. Men sat talking on wooden bedsteads. It was a peaceful place and, in terms of the life its own people knew, prosperous.

James saw some of the leading villagers and talked to them; peace and quiet was what they wanted more than anything, to be left alone to get on with sowing and harvest and not to have armies trampling over their fields every other year. And a landlord who lived on the spot and whom they could see.

He had signed the papers, he had been entered as the owner in the register. He had thought of all kinds of improvements he would like to make. He thought that gradually, year by year, he would pave those streets with baked brick so that they did not become a quagmire in the rains. He thought of tanks he would build to store water for irrigation. Here he would have a place of his own and a place among the village people, a known place. He would be happy here. He was thinking of these things, his mind full of seed and bullocks and the better use of dung, as he rode back to the bungalow at Ko'el where he was staying. It had been built for one of de Boigne's officers.

There was someone sitting on the veranda, someone who stood up when he appeared and came out in the evening light to meet him. It was Malcolm and though Malcolm was a friend his heart sank. A syce who had been patiently squatting by the corner of the veranda came running to take his horse. James dismounted with a sick feeling as though his stomach was full of bile. He remembered just that feeling at the ford near Muttra when he had thought his own squadron of *bargirs* was plotting to desert him. It was treachery not danger that made him sick and he smelt treachery now. Malcolm would not have come to see him unless he had something to tell him which he disliked putting in a letter. Treachery in a soldier, ingratitude in a prince – they were the same thing, the breaking of a bond, infamous, ignoble, dishonourable.

'What is it?' he asked. 'Tell me quickly.'

'I had to come,' said Malcolm, 'I couldn't write. Lake's on his way to Calcutta or he'd have come. All right, I'll be quick. That man Barlow says that *jagirs* are only for natives of India. He has confirmed the *jagirs* to the four risaldars. But he says you are not a native of India but a British subject and no British subject may be given land as a reward. He has disallowed your *jagir*.'

James walked past him without a word. He sat down on a chair on the veranda and waved Malcolm to a chair. A servant appeared and he said:

'Yes, bring tea.'

He still did not speak to Malcolm. At last Malcolm, deeply embarrassed, said:

'I know it's no use, Skinner – '

But James interrupted him.

'No,' he said. 'It *is* no use. I know what you would like and what Lord Lake would like. But that makes no difference to what I feel. There was no question of being a native of India when Lord Lake sent for me to bring in those Brinjaras with their bullocks so that the army could march to save Delhi. I told him he should never see me again if I failed. I made up my mind that I would do it and that if I did not it would be only because I was dead. He trusted me, I trusted him. He did not ask where my mother was born. He knew he could trust me. When my brother with five hundred men faced Amir Khan with thirty thousand at Sambhal, they made up their minds to die rather than give in because their honour as soldiers would not let them change sides. Do you know, Colonel Malcolm, a very common word that we natives of India use? It is *wafedar*, and it means a man who is faithful and keeps his trust. There is another word that means the opposite, without faith, ungrateful.'

He stopped. Then he rose and went to Malcolm.

'Colonel, I am sorry. I have made you even more uncomfortable than you were before. And you are my guest. I need not tell you that for natives of India it is a matter of shame to make a guest uncomfortable. But I forget, I am not a native of India. At least – not when it is a question of a grant of land. But I *am* a native of India when it is a question of the King's commission.'

He paused and went on:

'Things are very difficult for a man in my position. I am so ignorant. Is it good manners for an Englishman to make a guest uncomfortable? But I keep forgetting. I am not English either. I am sorry. I have done it again. I really will not embarrass you any more after this. You will stay the night, of course. Shall I order your bath before dinner?'

'You couldn't make me more uncomfortable, you positively couldn't. Yes, please, I should like to stay the night. But there is something else – two words more of business. The first is official. You are to have the retiring pension which has been authorized for a lieutenant-colonel in the Maratha brigades who came over to us. It is three hundred rupees a month for life.'

'I see. Less than my risaldars. Thank you. And the other point?'

'That is not official. It is highly personal. From Lord Lake. He has asked me to assure you once again that as soon as he is in England, he will make it his business to get your *jagir* restored and to bring your regiment back to life.'

'He is always very kind,' said James. 'I shall always be glad to have served him. *He* has been like a father to me.

But the English in Calcutta – Malcolm, Bourquien was right. The English are hard fathers to their children. Let us bath and have dinner. I know you are my friend.'

He called for Nagendra Singh and gave orders.

## 25 Lord Lake is Dead

'I LIKE to see them go by,' said Ochterlony.

He and James stood on the balcony above the porch of the Residency at Delhi. They were watching a procession of thirteen elephants, each with a howdah on its back. These were howdahs for ladies, each with a gay silk canopy and a screen of pierced work in gilt and tinsel through which the riders could see the world but not be seen. The elephants rolled in their walk, swaying indolently and voluptuously, like plump ladies of pleasure, an effect intensified by the long silk hangings and the tasselled gilt ropes that hung from the howdah almost to the ground.

'They like to sit indoors in the *zanana* all day,' Ochterlony continued. 'But I think it's good for them to take the air and see something of the world. So I insist that they go out every evening. Thirteen wives. Thirteen elephants. Wouldn't do to have two wives on the same elephant, you know. Sure to quarrel. So each wife on one elephant with a female servant to talk to. They must chatter of course. Their chief pleasure. Wouldn't deny them that. Good custom I think. Impresses the natives. But, my dear Skinner, we didn't meet to talk about my wives. Come inside and sit down.'

'You do indeed live like a Moghul prince,' said James.

'Well, I like to,' said Ochterlony. 'Besides, as you know better than anyone, everything depends on appearances. One must keep up appearances. Here I am, at the capital of India, the seat of the Emperor, with the Emperor to guard and this great city to defend, and I haven't one European soldier. Three hundred of your splendid Yellow Boys, two battalions of Indian infantry – that's all I've got in a country where Scindia or Holkar would have an army of a hundred thousand. My thirteen wives do their bit. Give an air of confidence. Some people say it's an unlucky number. I haven't found it so. Very fond of them all. Don't need any more.'

They moved back into the great vaulted room, at the centre of which stood Ochterlony's desk. Here they sat down and he continued:

'Now, Skinner, what about you? I've had a letter from Lord Lake, full of your praises – not that I needed that. I know what you've done – and how disgracefully you've been treated. I'm ashamed of that man Barlow. But what's to be done? You're not yet thirty. You can't sit still on a pension of three hundred a month and what you make from your *bargirs* – which can't, by the way, be much, for my escort is splendidly horsed and equipped. What are you going to do?'

Ochterlony was well aware that Lord Lake had promised to try to get Barlow's decisions reversed. James spoke of this and of his sense of Lake's kindness. If anyone could help him, Lake would. He went on:

'All the same, I have a feeling that fate is against me. You cannot fight fate. But you know the motto we took for my regiment? *Himmat-i-mardan wa madad-i-khuda*. By the courage of man and the help of God. The help does not come without the courage – and some effort. I fear that Lord Lake will not be successful – so it's no use my sitting still and building castles in the air. And since there is nothing else, I have determined to lay out in trade what little money I have saved. It is not what I care for – but what else is there? I am not a servant of the Company so I don't think even Sir George Barlow can find a rule that forbids me to engage in trade. You know that Hindostani saying – the washerman's donkey, who belongs neither to the house nor to the river, where the clothes are washed? Well, that is what I am, a washerman's donkey, but at least I can carry a load.'

'Trouble is, Skinner, you're a Rajput, not a *bania* – or at least, half of you is. Rajput in spirit. So am I. I sympathize with you. What sort of trade?'

'Oh, silks and muslins and cotton things I suppose. May I beg for the patronage of your distinguished and numerous family, Lofty Presence?'

'What you really want is a partner who knows something about such things. I will talk to the Hindu Rao. He's the richest man in Delhi. He knows everybody, and, what is more important, he knows everything about everybody. He's much wiser than you might think at first meeting. Bit too fond of cherry brandy.'

'That was Holkar's tipple too,' said James.

'I'll get you to meet him and, if he likes you, as I'm sure he will, he'll think of a way to help. You want a real *bania*, born to the trade, to buy and sell for you. You know nothing about silk. Nothing about trade. You'll never make anything of it by yourself. You're a soldier. I hate to think of you brought to this.'

'Thank you for your help. One thing I should mention, Colonel. My brother. He takes it much harder than I. He still has the rank of local lieutenant – only that, after so many years' service – and such service, Colonel! He wanted to resign and go to the Sikhs – who would make him a Major-General straight away. I managed to persuade him not to go. There will be war with the Sikhs sooner or later and there we should be – just where we were before! Twice we've started at the bottom and faithfully worked our way up – won confidence and trust – only to meet at the end with treachery.'

'Treachery?'

'I suppose I should say ingratitude. To me it's the same thing.'

'Yes. Must seem like that. But I don't think there'll be a war with the Sikhs all that soon. Sooner or later – yes, of course. But before that, we've got to fight the war we've just finished all over again.'

'That's what Lord Lake said.'

'Well, he's right. Thank you for telling me about your

brother. I'll arrange for you to meet the Hindu Rao. And let's keep hoping that Lake will work wonders in England.'

'I'm afraid there will be more misfortunes for me. My star is setting – and I am not yet thirty! Thank you for your help, Colonel.'

Some time later there was a reception at the Residency. Though Delhi was the Mughal capital and though everything in India was done in the name of the Mughal Emperor, Delhi for the British was a small station – a frontier town. There were no European troops and very few military officers. There was only the Residency staff, who on such an occasion acted as hosts, a dozen officers of Indian infantry, James, Robert and a Cornet from the Yellow Boys of Skinner's Horse, less than a dozen European merchants, and about as many again of Muslim and Maratha noblemen. There were no ladies; Ochterlony and most of his guests were agreed that the place for wives was the *zanana*. All the same, the scene was lively. It was evening, cool after the heat of the day, and quite still, so that torches burnt steadily. The Residency gardens had smooth lawns and flowering shrubs. Troopers of Skinner's Horse, dismounted, stood sentry, lance in hand. With their long yellow *alkhalaqs*, long black boots and scarlet Muslim turbans, finishing in a great frilled fan above their head, they seemed ten feet high. The guests in bright uniforms, or in gold brocade, or *sherwanis* in pastel colours, pink, primrose, sky-blue or maroon, moved here and there among the shrubs, but they were drifting towards the veranda where there was to be a *nautch*.

James had not been long in Delhi but he had quickly been accepted as one of this small society. It was a circle to which English officers and officials had the entry unless they excluded themselves, and to which merchants or Indian nobles were admitted if they were agreeable to meet – a point settled unofficially and almost without spoken words. In spite of the melancholy which hung about him at this period of his life, James was asked to all parties in Delhi.

Ochterlony caught him by the arm.

'Step aside with me a moment, will you, James? I've bad

news for you. I won't beat about the bush. Lord Lake is dead. Died soon after reaching England. Caught a chill. Turned to fever. Never recovered. I knew you'd feel it.'

He turned and took two steps away. James stood motionless, frozen. Ochterlony came back to him.

'I knew you'd feel it, quite apart from your hopes. I was fond of him too. But I'm afraid your hopes are dashed – at any rate from that source.'

'Yes, I do feel it,' said James. 'He was very kind to me and I felt – oh, as we natives say, he was my father and mother. I know I feel as though I had lost a father. Much more than I felt for my own father. As for my hopes, I have long tried to have none. I did not expect anything.'

'You shouldn't give up hope. Barlow won't last for ever. There's something else I'd like you to know before anyone else. I'm transferred to command at Allahabad. A soldier's job again. I shall like that, but shall be sorry to say goodbye to you. But you'll like Seton who relieves me. I'm sure you will. He has a very high reputation.'

'A civilian?' James asked. 'A man like Barlow?'

'Not a bit like Barlow. You'll see. I tell you, you'll like him.'

'That you should go is one more misfortune for me. But I shall endure it. You must go to your guests.'

When he was alone, James walked away from the torches, the guests, the bright colours, into the dusk in the shadow of the trees. Here he found an ornamental seat and sat down, covering his face with his hands. He had lost not only a father but faith in a just world.

# PART SIX
# FRIENDSHIP

## 26 The Turn of the Tide

As Ochterlony had guessed, James liked Seton and they became friends. One morning, nearly three years after his arrival in Delhi, Seton sent James a message. Could he see him? He had something to tell him.

When James arrived, Seton wasted no time but told his tale at once:

'My dear James, I'm glad to say I have good news for you. *You* will think it good news, at least, though for myself – I'm not so sure. But here it is. There's more than a possibility of war with Ranjit Singh and the Sikhs beyond the Sutlej. The Sikh chiefs on this side of the Sutlej have promised to provide us with a force of ten thousand Sikh horsemen. You are to command this force. An army of regular troops is collecting under Ochterlony at Saharanpur and you are to march at once with my escort – your three hundred Yellow Boys. You will be under Ochterlony's command once again. You won't mind that.'

'No, indeed,' said James. 'I certainly shan't mind that. You're right, it's good news for me – though I wish I could have six months to train them and introduce some discipline. Ten thousand Sikhs! They're a wild lot. I wonder what powers I shall have and what rank. Cavalry without discipline can be a sword that breaks in the hand. And are they to be under chiefs of their own, or directly under me? You don't know? Well, I shall find out.'

James paused and looked thoughtfully at Seton.

'Who knows what the future may hold?' he said. 'To-morrow we shall leave for Saharanpur, perhaps for a war. I may never come back; you may be transferred. Three times in my life, Seton, I have had to start at the bottom. Once when I was first commissioned by de Boigne; I was a boy of seventeen and I knew nothing. Nothing. I fought in battles; I began to win the confidence of my men and my employers. I had command of up to three battalions. And then I had to start again – with the British. I was right back at the beginning. Hardly anyone trusted me at first. Only Lord Lake. But Lord Lake did trust me and I built up my regiment and once again I began to have the confidence of my men and of the army. And then came peace and my regiment was disbanded and my *jagir* disallowed.

'Once again I was back almost where I began. I started to trade. Once again I knew nothing; I had very little. I was bitter and unhappy when I said goodbye to Ochterlony and when you came. Now – I've made a beginning again. This new life is not like a soldier's – but it has its interests. I've had some lucky ventures. And then came your friendship and kindness.'

He remembered the efforts Malcolm had made on his behalf and how at last Malcolm and Seton between them had managed to get him a *jagir* instead of a pension. So at last he had land and a place in the Indian countryside and in the life of the villages. And he had done well there already. He had built an indigo factory; he was growing indigo and buying up the raw crop and selling the finished dye. It was a paying crop. And he was beginning to improve the breed of cattle. His trading too was doing well; the Hindu Rao had found him a good partner.

'Still, I'm glad to go back to soldiering,' he went on. 'That's my true calling. But now – if this war comes to nothing or if I am still alive when it is over and if all irregular forces are disbanded once again – well, there'll be something to come back to. I hope you will still be here. Friendship means more as one gets older – but I'm talking like an old man and I'm thirty-one!'

Suddenly he felt young again. His cares dropped from him. He turned to Seton with all his old enthusiasm.

'Seton,' he cried, 'this is the turn of the tide for me! It means I'm not forgotten – that there are still people at the head of affairs who trust me! I don't put too much confidence in this talk of war. Ranjit Singh may well concede the point if he thinks we mean business. But what makes my heart rejoice is that it looks as though the spirit of Sir George Barlow has altogether disappeared!'

He pictured Sir George Barlow, heard his cold grating voice and remembered what he had said about Skinner's *jagir*.

'Rules are rules and are meant to be obeyed. I will not be a party to making exceptions of any kind for the favourite of a Commander-in-Chief.'

And he remembered too Barlow's reply when Malcolm had tried to get Skinner a commission in the British army.

'Do not let us deceive ourselves. The natives of India are utterly different from Europeans and are never to be trusted. Nor should we admit to positions of responsibility the offspring of native women, who are likely to inherit the weaknesses and vices of their mothers.'

Everything he had ever heard of Sir George Barlow he had disliked. Most of it came from Malcolm and to Malcolm the man's whole outlook was anathema. He had said to Malcolm:

'Trade is our sole interest in India. If native princes despoil and oppress their subjects, it is nothing to us. We are responsible only for what occurs in our own territories.'

Seton smiled at him. He felt just the same himself about Barlow. He said:

'Goodbye and good luck – bring my escort back if you can. I shan't find another as good!'

It did not disturb James at all that he was leaving his business, his farms and his factory. Each of his enterprises was in the hands of a capable partner or assistant, someone quite capable of running it for six months on his own. The master would only be needed if a crisis arose or if the results showed that a change of policy must be made. He left the next day without a qualm on that score.

But in fact it was not for long. James was quite right in thinking that Ranjit Singh would give way. He did not want war with the British but he was prepared to go to the last step short of war to resist anything which would help the British if war did come. The dispute was about posting troops at Ludhiana, which was on the British side of the frontier but nearer than Ranjit Singh liked. So it was not long before James was back in Delhi, and once again he was sitting in the great vaulted room in the upper floor of the Residency, where he had watched Ochterlony's wives and where he had said goodbye to Seton.

'Well, here I am, back again after only three months and you've more news for me?'

'This time it's absolutely official. Skinner's Horse is to be raised from 3 squadrons to 8. Here's the letter.'

'That's the best news you could give me. And what are we to do?'

'Oh, there's work to be done all right. Did you know George Thomas?'

'Indeed I did. A fine soldier but unstable. In the end it was the bottle that undid him – that and his temperament.'

'Well, you will remember then that he had a big property for which he had a grant from the Emperor. He lived there like a prince – minted his own rupees, founded his own cannon.'

'I remember very well. He never spoke to anyone five minutes without telling them he minted his own rupees. He offered me service once.'

'Well, he ruled that country of Haryana like a prince. It's fine country. Fine cattle. Dry of course if the rains are bad – it's not far from the desert – but that's only about one year in five. Revenue must be remitted then. But it's a lawless country. It's been no-man's-land too long. The Emperor's had no control over it for years and if a gang of robbers has made Jaipur or Bikanir too hot to hold them – they'll run for Haryana. They had short shrift from Thomas.

He wanted the land revenue himself – to pay his army with. He improved the country; kept the peace and fixed rents that were regular and moderate. He really did keep that country in order. They've never had such good rule for centuries.'

Seton saw the Haryana country from the point of view of the Company's government. Much of what he said James knew already. When Thomas was defeated, Haryana had been added to Perron's vast principality – but Perron had fled to France and Haryana had been no-man's-land again. Seton continued:

'When peace was made with Scindia, Haryana was given to a Muslim noble – Abdul Sanad Khan his name was – but he never really took charge; he never lived there and I don't believe he collected a rupee of revenue. It's in absolute chaos. Now he's resigned it into the hands of the Company. It's full of robber gangs fighting each other and looting everyone else. It's got to be cleaned up and it won't be done without a good deal of fighting. There's a fort every ten miles with a robber chief in it and all the country in between devastated. They'll have to be reduced one by one and then the people will come back and start cultivating. William Fraser is the Deputy Commissioner; you and Skinner's Horse will be the main force at his disposal.'

'Military police as much as cavalry. Still, by the time we've cleaned up Haryana, there'll be that war with the Marathas which we have still to do all over again. Where's the headquarters?'

'Thomas's old capital of Hansi. Fraser will be there too.'

'It'll take me no time at all to raise another five hundred men. All of them old Yellow Boys or the sons of Yellow Boys – so they won't need a long period of training. Oh, this is good news!'

James paused and looked at Seton.

'There is one thing. I suppose – ? No, you'd have told me.'

'I know what you have in mind. I'm afraid there's nothing about rank. You're still a local captain.'

James said no more.

Years later, talking over his life with Baillie Fraser, dictating his memoirs to a scribe and then discussing them again, James found this a difficult part of his working life to describe. Sitting on the veranda of his house at Hansi, he said:

'I don't remember much of the day-to-day detail of those five years at Hansi when we were settling Haryana. We were very active; there were few days when I didn't go out somewhere into the district, perhaps to get information, perhaps to make an arrest. There was always work at headquarters – training the men and horses, looking after stores and food, all that kind of thing. There was no adjutant, no quartermaster. Only Robert and myself and the risaldars. Eight hundred men. Quite a lot of business. Then I would be questioning my *harkaras* and seeing all those visitors from the district who came to give news or to pay their respects or to keep on the right side of the administration. You have to listen. You never know when a grain of wheat may not be slipped in among the chaff. And I would go on tour in the district, with one of the squadrons, for a week or a fortnight at a time. And of course I was always sending out the risaldars to tour the district and I used to hear their reports. It was like the very first days of Skinner's Horse, when we were guarding the road from Delhi to Agra and settling with Madhu Rao.

'Now and then, we would have a little war; there would be some chief who was terrorizing the villages all round, who wouldn't pay revenue or come out of his fort and we should have to bring him to heel. But one such affair was very like another. My men always showed the greatest gallantry and determination – and when this was known, such affairs became less and less frequent. People came back to the villages and began to cultivate again. They were very pleased. I was young and well and vigorous; it was hard work but interesting and I enjoyed it. What more can I say? Five years went by – it seems now that it went by in a flash.'

He remembered those years as a succession of adventures;

one of his *harkaras* would come in with news of the hiding-place of some well-known robber band and a squadron must be off at once to try to catch him. A gallop across country – the village surrounded – a night attack; faces, torches, sudden shots; hasty justice without any delay, punishment accepted by all as just, robbers hanged. But the scenes and faces flashed by quickly, one after another; one day was not to be distinguished from the next, but gradually the impression grew of peace restored, villages happy and contented, a smiling, fruitful countryside.

Something else was happening at the same time, a friendship that grew closer and closer with William Fraser, whose brother, Baillie Fraser, was later to write the account of James's life.

William Fraser, though a civilian by profession, was a fighting man by nature. Like James himself, he was a Rajput at heart. Danger was the breath of life to him; he could not be happy without danger. He volunteered for military service whenever there was a war and came back to district life in peace. The chief employment of his leisure was hunting lions, which in those days were very numerous round Hansi and a great nuisance too, killing cattle as well as blackbuck. Many a time James went with him on such hunting trips, always on foot. They would follow the tracks and walk up to the lion's hiding place by day, rouse him, face him and shoot him as he charged, usually killing him with a single shot. It was a sport that demanded the greatest courage and unflinching coolness. It was the danger William enjoyed, but the villagers were delighted whenever he shot a lion and would do anything to help him. He shot more than eighty.

James spoke of this friendship to Baillie Fraser.

'William and I got on well from the start. He saw as well as I did the need to be prompt. It was a lawless turbulent district and a quick blow at anyone who defied authority was worth ten later. That was the secret. We saw eye to eye – and that grew to friendship. He learnt to ride as my men rode, to fire at the gallop, to take a tent-peg from the ground at the gallop – all those things. He was my pupil in such things but I was his in running the district. And we would have long long talks. It was not like a life where there are European ladies who come to meals. The women stayed in the *zanana*; his and mine. He and I would dine together and talk, just the two of us. Or sometimes with Robert. It was a good life – but there is not much to say about it.'

'A good life – but it came to an end?' Baillie Fraser ventured.

Yes, that life, in just that form, James explained meditatively, had come to an end with a new Governor-General. Lord Hastings – so James always spoke of him, though he was not Lord Hastings when he first came to India – saw as clearly as Lord Lake had done that the work of the Second Maratha War would have to be done again if India was to have peace. But before that there had to be another war, with the Gurkhas of Nepal, who had built up an Empire in the mountains and were spilling over aggressively into the plains. These two wars ended the first close partnership of James Skinner and William Fraser in Hansi and the surrounding country of Haryana.

War was coming – that was clear enough – and Lord Hastings decided to raise the strength of Skinner's Horse from eight hundred to three thousand. There were to be three corps, virtually three regiments, of which only one would be needed at Hansi. Raising the two new regiments took much of Skinner's time and made an end of the old close co-operation in district work. And then William Fraser succeeded in getting himself seconded to the military and went away to the Gurkha War. He never failed to be there, whenever there was a war.

But though James Skinner was commanding three thousand men, he was still only a local captain.

'When Lord Hastings was Governor-General,' James continued, 'he came to see us here at Hansi. He was very kind about the regiment and asked if I would accept the honorary rank of lieutenant colonel. Well, of course, I said I was pleased. I *was* pleased. It is better to be called a colonel than a captain. But honorary rank carries no command with it. With local rank you only have command in your own corps. This added nothing practical. If there was a company of regular infantry at Hansi commanded by a boy of twenty he would command the station. He was over my head. I could not help feeling that. And you see it is only because of my birth. That is what makes it hard to bear. He saw in my face what I was thinking. He told me he had to carry his council with him, but he was going to propose that a colonel of irregular horse should command captains in the regular line. And they would make sure no one but captains would serve alongside me, in Hansi. Even that never came to anything. They said in Calcutta that men in the regular line would object. In Calcutta, they must have rules for everything. However, I knew Lord Hastings wished me well and I said no more.

'But Robert was not promoted – not even honorary rank. He grew more and more bitter and at last he put in his resignation. I sent it on. There was nothing I could say. As his commanding officer I sent it on without comment. Lord Hastings wrote to me himself and begged me to get him to withdraw his resignation. They made him a major. Honorary major of course. He withdrew his resignation but – he still felt it. You see, birth is not important. Being legitimate makes no difference when you go to storm a fort. It is courage that counts and zeal for the service. Birth doesn't count when there is service to be done – but it becomes very important when there are rewards to be given. It was about this time that Worseley wrote to me – from the Isle of Wight. Wight? Like White? Is that how you say it? Do you remember Worseley? He was in Delhi in Ochterlony's time and a good friend of mine. He told me I had been recommended for the Order of the Bath and the Earl of Buckingham had said, yes, he had often heard of Skinner's Horse but, no, it was impossible because I did not hold a commission from His Majesty. Then I asked if our *jagirs* could be made hereditary – like Amir Khan's, you know, but we didn't ask for a thirteen-gun salute. But no, that was not possible; it was contrary to the principles on which *jagirs* are given. Of course, those principles only apply to faithful servants. Not to enemies. There are different principles for enemies.

'Never mind, I was still young and we had three thousand troopers in Skinner's Horse. The regiment was really a brigade of three cavalry regiments. I commanded the whole regiment and the 1st Corps; Robert had command of the 2nd Corps and your brother William had the 3rd Corps. William, of course, managed to be embodied and became a soldier whenever there was a war. There were never any rules for him. There was the war against the Gurkhas first. Ochterlony distinguished himself in that. There was very little work for cavalry in that war but William took a detachment from the 3rd Corps and made himself useful. It was after that war that he was given the task of settling the hill districts.'

The Gurkha War was hardly finished when the Pindari War began. It is sometimes called the Third Maratha War. This was the war which Lord Lake had foretold. It had to be fought, as he had seen it would, not because the Maratha powers were dangerous – they were too divided among themselves for that – but because they harboured Pindari gangs. The Pindaris were not a race, a clan, a caste or a nation; they included men speaking many different tongues. They were simply robbers – freebooters, ruffians who would band together and sweep across the country, as Amir Khan had done, looting every village they chanced on, slaughtering, burning and raping. Whole districts were devastated; there was hardly a soul to be seen. Everyone went into hiding. There was no cultivation. What was the use of ploughing and sowing for Pindaris to reap? For eleven years the people in Central India paid the price of Sir George Barlow's peace. The villagers remembered those times by another name, not Barlow's peace. They called them the bad times, the years of disaster. They remembered them for three generations.

Lord Hastings decided to destroy these Pindari gangs, or rather armies, for they were often many thousand strong. He made a proclamation that there could be no neutrality. A prince must either be on the British side or he would be counted on the side of the Pindaris. Lord Hastings planned the war with skill and collected considerable strength. Because he had planned so carefully, the war was over very quickly.

Telling Baillie Fraser what had happened, James said:

'We didn't play so big a part as in Lord Lake's war. William and the 3rd Corps stayed here to guard Delhi and Haryana. Robert and the 2nd Corps went south to the Deccan. They did very well. I was with Ochterlony once again; he was Major-General Sir David by this time, but just as kind to me. We went to settle Amir Khan first. He waited as long as he could to see which way the tiger would jump; he didn't want to make terms with us but in the end he had to. They were good terms. He was confirmed in his *jagir*, with his thirteen-gun salute. Both the 1st and 2nd Corps of my regiment did good service and were highly commended by the generals under whom they served – but it was not like Lord Lake's war.'

When at last the war was over, the Peshwa gave up the throne and ceased to be head of the Maratha confederacy. He was given a considerable pension and sent to live on the Ganges near Cawnpore. He was escorted there by a detachment of Infantry, about a hundred men. James Skinner, with the 1st Corps of his regiment, was ordered to accompany them to make sure there were no ambushes or surprise attacks. He stayed near Cawnpore six months altogether, guarding the infantry who were guarding the Peshwa.

That company of infantry was commanded by a captain, one John Low of the East India Company's service. He was some years younger than James Skinner and he had far less experience of war; he was in command of only a hundred men while James had direct command of a thousand, besides being the colonel of two other regiments of cavalry. But Low was the commanding officer – just because he had a regular commission. James Skinner went to him and talked it over. He knew by the look in his eye that Low expected him to resent the situation – and indeed, he found it hard not to resent it. But he told Low frankly that he would not hold it against him personally and he would do his best to carry out his orders.

'He was a very nice fellow, John Low, and he felt it as much as I did. We talked it over together, he and I, and we made it work. We became good friends and he wrote me a kind letter when I left. But you see – it was not just a fancied grievance; it was something quite real. We overcame it, Low and I. I was not always brooding over my grievances, even then. But it was like the sore spot on an elephant's head, the place where the *mahawat* hits it with his iron *ankhas*. You have seen that sore place on an elephant's head? The *mahawat* has to make it feel pain to control it and it is not easy to make an elephant feel pain. I have a fairly thick skin myself – but Robert – Robert would fall into rages.'

So he would talk, sitting on the veranda of his house at Hansi, talking to the brother of William Fraser, his dead friend, remembering the past.

## 27 I Cannot Look

AFTER the Pindari War, James and the 1st Corps of Skinner's Horse came back to Hansi. William Fraser's 3rd Corps was disbanded but William Fraser became Second-in-Command of the regiment. The 2nd Corps under Robert, which had greatly distinguished itself in the war, now had separate headquarters at Mhow, away in the south. Robert of course was there a good deal but he had a bungalow at Hansi, which he thought of as his home. In the course of the twelve years since Skinner's Horse had come to Hansi, the two brothers had built up estates there which were now bigger than the *jagirs* they had in de Boigne's old country of Aligarh, the other side of Delhi.

It was 1821 and James was now forty-three, rather lame

from an old wound, a little heavier than he had been, but still an active vigorous man who would compete with any of his men in feats of horsemanship or in managing his weapons. He was sitting on the veranda one evening in February when he heard the voice of his head *khidmatgar*, the principal personal servant of his household. Nagendra Singh still put out his clothes but he was too old to travel and of course as a Hindu had never had anything to do with James's food.

'Sahib,' Ilahi Bakhsh began, 'the Major Sahib has come.'

James thought he meant William Fraser and looked in the direction from which he might have been expected. Ilahi Bakhsh understood the movement at once and said:

'No, no, not the Deputy Commissioner, the young Major Sahib.'

He meant Robert and James turned his head the other way.

'He has only just ridden up the lane from the road,' Ilahi Bakhsh went on. 'No one was expecting him.'

'If they aren't expecting him, he may want dinner,' said James. 'Send someone over with my salaams and say he may come to dinner if he would like to. But he may be tired if he has ridden far. Say he is to do just as he wishes.'

Ilahi Bakhsh disappeared. Ten minutes later he was back. All his usual dignity had disappeared; he was breathless as though he had been running.

'Sahib! A great disaster! A great horror! You must come at once!'

'What is it?' James asked.

'I cannot tell you. I cannot speak. My heart is too full. You must see.'

James caught up his sword and went across to his brother's bungalow. He did not run. Something in Ilahi Bakhsh's manner told him it was too late for running. But he walked fast, full of apprehension, expecting disaster. There was a huddle of servants on the veranda, as though afraid to go inside. They were quite silent.

'Nabi Bakhsh!' James called out as he reached the

veranda. His brother's head *khidmatgar* was first cousin of his own, Muslims of a landowning family from near Meerut.

Nabi Bakhsh came forward. He was stony-faced, grey of skin, his hands trembling, but upright and unweeping.

'What kind of trouble is this?' James said sternly.

'Be pleased to look, Sahib. Be pleased to come with me. Only be pleased to look.'

No one else came with them into the bungalow. Nabi Bakhsh led the way through the *gol-kamra* to the corridor that led to the women's quarters.

'The first room,' he said. 'The young Begam's. I cannot look again.'

There was a curtain over the doorway; the two doors, meeting in the middle, were open. James slowly drew the curtain. There was blood everywhere. The woman on the bed had perhaps been crouched with her hands over her face; she was still crouched but her neck and wrists had been severed as though by one tremendous sword-cut. At the foot of the bed lay the body of a young man, his head too almost separated from the body by a stroke which seemed to have caught him as he turned to fly. Both bodies were fully clothed.

James had not gone into the room. He withdrew his head and let the curtain fall.

'And the Sahib?' he said to Nabi Bakhsh. 'He too?'

Nabi Bakhsh bowed. 'Yes, Sahib, he too,' he said. 'In the office.'

James strode back into the *gol-kamra*. The office opened out of that big central room. He went straight there. Inside he saw his brother sitting in his office chair. There was a pistol on the desk. He had shot himself in the head. There was not much left of the top part of his head and the room was covered with blood and brains. But there could be no doubt it was Robert. He had brought his sword from that other dreadful room and dropped it on the floor before he sat down and pulled out his pistol. James came back to the *gol-kamra*.

'Tell me,' he said.

'The Sahib came back. No one expected him. He rode to the front of the bungalow. He gave his horse to the boy who was watering the plants on the veranda. The boy took the horse to the stables and called me as he went past my quarters. I snatched my turban and put it on and came out. As I came out I heard a scream, a woman's scream. I ran round to the front of the bungalow and into the *gol-kamra*. As I went in I heard a shot in the office. I went there and saw – what the Presence saw. I went on to the front veranda and called for my brother. He did not answer. Other servants came running. They said there had been women sitting on the little veranda outside the young Begam's room. They had heard shouts and a scream and they had run away. I went to look in that room.' He shuddered. 'Then Ilahi Bakhsh came. And then, Sahib, you were pleased to come.'

'And who was that young man?'

'Sahib, he was my younger brother. My true brother.' He meant that he was not a cousin but of the same parents. 'He came three months ago to learn the work.'

'And what was he doing in the young Begam's room?'

'Sahib, I cannot say. I do not know. He had no work there. How could he have? Her own women took her what she needed. They were on the back veranda, outside her room, when it happened.'

'And did you know that there was – anything? Anything between those two?'

'No, Sahib, no. How could I know such a thing and keep quiet? It would be a matter of the greatest dishonour – to the Sahib, to my family. I knew nothing.'

'Did you suspect anything?'

He hesitated. 'Not till yesterday, Sahib. Yesterday he was here in the *gol-kamra* about this time of day and he had no business to be here. I asked what he was doing and he said he had left a cloth for cleaning the silver. I did not think it was true. So then I did suspect that he might be doing some mischief – perhaps planning to steal something – perhaps some other evil – but I did not know. There was nothing

I could do. I decided to watch. I would have come to you if I had been sure.'

'The two older Begams? Where are they?'

'They went out in the phaeton and are not yet back.'

'Where are the women who were on the back veranda? How did he get in?'

The older of the two women who had been on the veranda could not be found. The other seemed dull and unobservant. But she did remember that not long before the scream Rupni, the older of the two, had sent her away to fetch something. So Rupni had been alone when the young man came.

That evening James talked it over with William Fraser.

'There can't be any doubt about what happened,' he said. 'I don't think anyone knew about what was going on except the woman Rupni – and it cannot have been going on long. Perhaps it was only their second meeting, though Nabi Bakhsh may have had suspicions longer than he admits. But there can be no doubt about what happened when Robert came. He caught them together. His arrival was a surprise to everyone – and I was on the spot within fifteen minutes. There was no time for the servants to arrange anything.'

'I agree; there's nothing to be done, officially. I shall write a report and send it in, but there's nothing to be done. James, I'm sad for you. This is a blow – for me, too, but a much harder one for you.'

'Yes. We had been through a great deal together, he and I. He was always quick-tempered – but lately I think he had been more on edge. This injustice about rank – I begin now to feel that it matters less. Less than it did. Everyone knows who I am and what I have done. But Robert took it very hard. He chafed and fretted. It preyed on him. And this – he would feel it as another blow to his honour and he would not stop to think; he would feel he must make it clean at once – and completely.'

James stopped and wiped a tear from his eye.

'The men of the regiment will not blame him,' he said. 'They will think he did right. But, William, what do you think? What would you do if you found a servant with one of your women, in your own house? I don't mean a casual woman you took home for the night, but a companion, a wife. What would you do?'

'I should not be so unwise as to leave a young girl – and a pretty one they tell me – so long uncared-for. But that is a flippant answer. I don't know, James, I really don't know. My first instinct would be to act like Robert – but I don't think I *should* do as he did. I should stop to think. You can't fight a duel with a servant. But you couldn't ignore it. No one in the district would respect me if I ignored what the man did. The girl – I should want just to send her away. I shouldn't want to kill her. But the man – I couldn't kill him and face a charge of murder. I could quite easily arrange for someone else to kill him – but I shouldn't respect myself if I did that. I don't know what I should do, James.'

'You couldn't ignore it because of what the district would think.' James said that, half as a question. For William, or for himself, or for Robert, who were like kings in that district, it would have meant dishonour and contempt. 'For yourself, you would rather send them both away than kill him and shoot yourself?'

'For myself, yes, I think so. You see, frankly, James, there is not one of these girls I would think worth shooting myself for. You feel differently?'

'I feel differently about many things. Yes, we are different in the end. We are all different – every man that God made from every other – but I am more Indian than English. All the same, I begin to wonder, as I grow older, about this idea of honour. Not the honour of a soldier. I have no doubts about that. I could not respect myself – or be content to live – if I had changed sides in a battle. That would mean I had betrayed myself. But I mean the honour of a husband. If a woman is faithless – she is the worse but I am still the same man. Why should I kill myself? I too do not know what I should do. But I cannot blame Robert.'

'Nor can I blame Robert.'

And with that the matter ended. They did not press hard the search for the woman Rupni. She was never found and

James was glad. What could he have done to her? Sewn her up in a bag and dropped her in the river? Of course not. Yet she was the cause of his brother's death. Of that he was sure.

Someone else, a Major Baddeley, who held a regular commission, was appointed to command the 2nd Corps of Skinner's Horse in Robert's place and it became Baddeley's Horse. A hundred years later, in 1922, it was joined once more to Skinner's Horse. As for James, something went out of his life with Robert – but something came in too. He seemed to grow a little older, a little more reflective. Now there was only William Fraser left to whom he could talk of what was nearest to his heart.

## 28 The Battered Old Spoon

A YEAR after the death of Robert, James was invited to Calcutta to say goodbye to Lord Hastings, who spoke to him very kindly and praised his regiment. He had now only one corps, but it was 1,200 strong; he begged Lord Hastings to leave it at that strength and was assured that it should not be reduced again. But scarcely had Lord Hastings left India than orders came reducing his strength to eight hundred. This however was not for long. New orders arrived a year later telling him to raise once again a second corps of eight hundred. Not long after that, each of the two corps was raised to a thousand. With each of those fresh instructions he was able to comply with very little delay; there were always men eager to come to his colours of the griffin and bloody hand.

The 2nd Corps was raised in good time for the operations against Bharatpur* which began in 1825. Bharatpur had been Lord Lake's one failure. He had believed he could take this formidable fortress without a battering train of heavy

* To rhyme, more or less, with turret-poor.

guns, by the impact of his name and the courage of his troops. It had been an error that had cost many lives at the time and for twenty years afterwards the first siege of Bharatpur was remembered throughout India as proof that the British could be beaten. Now Bharatpur, relying on its reputation as impregnable, had defied the British again and it had been decided to prepare a force to take it.

The newly raised 2nd Corps of Skinner's Horse stayed behind; the 1st Corps went to join Lord Combermere's army before Bharatpur. For most of the siege the regiment was divided, five squadrons operating under James and five under William Fraser. William Fraser's detachment distinguished themselves by carrying out the first brush with the enemy, pursuing a party of cavalry almost to the gates of the fort and retiring under fire with exemplary courage and discipline. Most of the work was that proper for light cavalry, scouring the country for information and supplies, escorting convoys of grain, chasing back any foraging parties who ventured out for the enemy. In all this work, they maintained their reputation, which was already so high that nobody could ask for higher praise than that.

James, however, was sometimes detached from his corps to act as an adviser, a part he was reluctant to play. He never volunteered advice and, even when directly asked his opinion, was diffident about giving it. Lord Combermere had already inspected Skinner's Horse and had been pleased with them but James did not yet feel he had won his full confidence.

On one occasion, the heavy guns had for three days been throwing iron shot weighing eighteen and twenty-four pounds at a section of the immense outer wall. Much of this was dried mud, embedded in which were entire tree-trunks. It was many yards thick and dried mud was a material with which not many British engineers were familiar. At first, the shot simply buried itself in the thickness of the wall. But in the end – after long pounding – the wall began to crumble. That morning the engineer officer who was the technical adviser for the siege had pronounced that enough damage had been done. The breach could now be taken by assault. Lord Combermere turned to James.

'And what is your opinion, Colonel Skinner?' he asked.

'I am hardly competent to advise when a qualified engineer has given an opinion, least of all to your lordship, who has seen sieges in Spain and in Madras.'

'But we had no mud forts in Spain or Madras and you have Indian experience wider than any of us,' said Combermere. 'Come, tell us what you think.'

'If your lordship insists, then, I will say what I think. Bombarding a mud wall like this with shot seems at first to have little effect. And then at last it begins to crumble and you seem to have made a breach, but there is so much debris that it is very deceptive. That breach will be over a man's shoulders in dust and splinters. I do not think any soldiers in the world could get through it under fire. You will have to mine it. The more you bombard the worse it will get.'

'I don't agree,' said the engineer officer. 'But I will go and make a closer inspection.'

And very gallantly he did, under the eyes of the Commander-in-Chief's party, and under a spattering of fire from the sentries on the ramparts, who did not however think it worth turning out the guard. When he came back, he clapped James on the shoulder.

'You are right,' he said, 'and I am wrong. It is not practicable. We must mine it.'

From that moment Lord Combermere listened very carefully to anything James said and confidence grew between them. As Sir Stapleton Cotton, he had commanded Wellington's cavalry in Spain and he understood the value of cavalry.

There was another incident of the siege on which James used to look back with pleasure and emotion. The infantry had been worked hard and one battalion of infantry that was expected had failed to turn up. Each cavalry unit was asked to provide a detachment of dismounted volunteers for an assault; the Yellow Boys were to find two hundred men commanded by a risaldar. But a difficulty at once arose. Every man in the regiment volunteered and the risaldars told James that if he picked those he thought best the others would feel slighted. It would be better to take two squadrons as luck dictated; since all the squadrons were good – true Yellow Boys – they would be better than the picked men of any corps. So it was decided to send the two squadrons whose duty to provide guards fell on the day of the assault and the day following. James could not go himself, but he chose to lead them his old friend and comrade Shadul Khan. He felt sad that he could not go with them. He spoke to them.

'This is the first time,' he said, 'that I have sent you off to a task of danger without leading you myself. You know that you are all my children and that I feel a father's affection for all of you. I cannot let you go without something of mine to go with you. Here is my son – bearing my name, James Skinner – newly arrived. Take him with you – and earn for him such glory as you have earned for his father.'

James the younger was only seventeen. The order increasing both corps to a thousand had for the first time provided for an adjutant – and James the younger was the first adjutant.

Shadul Khan stepped forward and took young James by the arm.

'God be your protector, Sahib,' he said. 'And may he protect us, and help us to do our duty and maintain the honour of the regiment.' And with that he marched them away to the volunteer camp in readiness for the next day's assault. But the missing infantry regiment turned up and the cavalry volunteers were not used.

Bharatpur fell in one cataclysmic day; the great mine – at that time the biggest ever used by British engineers – went up on 17 January 1826 and the next day, at eight o'clock in the morning, three subsidiary mines were exploded. By four in the evening the whole fort was in Lord Combermere's hands. He reviewed Skinner's Horse again after the siege; this time his compliments were based not only on what he had heard, as had been the case before, but on what he knew. By now, James could count on his friendship and he invited the Commander-in-Chief and his personal staff to an entertainment at his house at Belaspur, where his *jagir* lay.

Lord Combermere's tents were pitched in a grove of mango trees, nearly a mile from the site of the entertainment, which had been arranged in a similar grove near James's house. The mango is a handsome tree with glossy dark green leaves, giving a thick shade by day; the trees are usually planted in rows and the lowest branches spring from the stem at such a height that there is ample room for tents beneath them. At night, by the light of fires and torches, the trunks of the trees appear as architectural columns – round Roman columns – and the boughs as a vaulted roof. The guests rode from their camp to the entertainment, dismounting at the entrance to the grove. Here the torches had been placed at regular intervals between the trees, heightening the effect of columns and vaulting. The aisles of the cathedral nave thus formed were lined with troopers, lance in hand; the long yellow tunics, high black boots and scarlet turbans glowed in the orange light. In the spaces between the last four trees on either side appeared the heads of elephants, massive, motionless as though carved in stone from the walls of a gigantic temple. The Commander-in-Chief, with a Military Secretary and two ADCs, advanced on foot, to be greeted by James Skinner and his officers who stood in a blaze of light in a marquee at the far end of the nave. A fanfare of trumpets soared out as they reached the marquee and a ruffle of kettle-drums. The elephants threw up their trunks and uttered a tearing, ear-splitting call.

Here on his own territory, as a feudal lord, James felt much more Indian than in a camp where everything went according to British military custom. He found himself speaking to Lord Combermere phrases more natural in Persian or Hindi than in English and sometimes used words from these languages.

'It is a great honour that your lordship does my humble home.'

'It's very good of you to ask us. What splendid arrangements you've made, Skinner. A most picturesque scene. Ah, Major Fraser, good evening.'

James introduced his son and then one by one his ten risaldars. Then he said: 'Everything is in the Hindostani manner and not really suitable for your lordship except as a curiosity. We should count it a further favour if your lordship would look at a little *atishbazi*.'

This baffled Lord Combermere but Fraser quickly said: 'Fireworks, my lord.'

'Ah, yes, fireworks. Delighted, of course. Nothing prettier than fireworks – except of course a pretty girl, eh, Skinner?'

'They will come later. Will you be pleased to come this way, my lord.'

They went to one flank of the marquee. Here a curtain was dropped and they saw a great crimson fort with towers and battlements, that clearly represented Bharatpur. A dozen guns outlined in silver fire began to discharge balls of green and scarlet flame at the fort, which eventually blew up in a cascade of brilliant fireballs. Rockets streamed up to heaven and burst into scintillations of emerald and sapphire stars. It was all much prettier than the real siege and no one was hurt.

Dinner was in the Persian style, with great mounds of golden rice, kids roasted whole, with quails, snipe, partridges, wild duck and the fat little hog-deer, the most esteemed of all Indian venison. The service was less formal than it would have been in an English mess and from time to time the guests moved round, exchanging places. The risaldars joined in the feast, though they were not placed near Lord Combermere since they had no English. At one stage, James made excuses and left Lord Combermere; William Fraser took his place.

'Our host has disappeared altogether,' said Lord Combermere. 'You have a very unusual man as commandant, Major Fraser.'

'I have indeed. He's a very close friend of mine. There are sides to his character that most people don't suspect. Now that he has an estate here and another at Hansi, and business interests too, he's quite well off, but he once had nothing, literally nothing. His father tried to apprentice him to some tradesman in Calcutta but he ran away with only the clothes he stood up in. That was all he had except for one thing. It was a spoon, a silver spoon given him when he was a baby by his godfather, old and battered now. His mother – who was a Rajput lady, as I think you know, my lord – used to tell him he must use that for his meals because he was an English sahib as well as a Rajput. And – do you know, my lord? – he has that spoon placed on the breakfast table every day, to remind him that once he owned nothing but that.'

'You mean, he doesn't want to become proud and take his good fortune for granted?'

'Exactly. And I suspect, though I don't know for certain, that he has slipped away now with a similar purpose.'

'To do – what exactly? You interest me very much.'

'There is something he has done before when he has given a feast for the men. They are all eating now, you know, behind the scenes, except the sentries, who will be relieved in a few minutes, so that they can eat too. And on such occasions – more than once – he has made a point of himself carrying his dinner to the latest joined drummer-boy. It's not what a British colonel would do – but the men understand. They respect him for it. They know he's their father and cares for the least of them.'

'It would be no bad thing if some British commanders did do something of the kind – but I must say I can't picture the Duke in such a part! Fraser, let us see if we can watch him. I won't speak to him or let him know – it would embarrass him. We will just watch.'

They rose from the table, Combermere signing to his aides-de-camp to sit still. Fraser led the way from the back of the marquee towards the house. Men were sitting on the ground in rows. Cooks were ladling out piles of rice and meat on to banana leaves and the men were taking their helpings to their places and eating. Combermere and Fraser were in time to see James approach the cooks and take a platter of food which he carried carefully to the end of the line where the drummer-boys were sitting. They were waiting their turn to go and fetch their own food but James came with his plateful to the last and youngest. The boy scrambled to his feet, protesting.

'No, Sahib, no; you mustn't serve me.'

'Yes, I must. And you must sit and eat. Yes, you must sit and eat. I shall not go till you begin.'

A duffedar, who had been tactfully hovering near by, spoke to the boy, not unkindly.

'Go on, boy, do as you're told.'

So the boy sat and began, shyly, to eat. James watched for a moment, smiling, and then turned away. He did not see the two watching figures in the shadows. Combermere and Fraser slipped back to the dining table, where James soon rejoined them.

After dinner, dancing girls came to sing and dance; the officers sat in the centre to watch while the men crowded behind and on either side. It was an entertainment in which all could share.

Nearly a year after this, when they were back at Hansi, Lord Combermere came to inspect the Yellow Boys for the third time, and to say his farewell to the regiment. By this stage of his life, James had come to feel that friendship was more important than anything else. He had done whatever he had been asked and the reward he had won was the friendship of such men as Lord Lake and Malcolm, Ochterlony and now Lord Combermere. Compared with this the rank he had once coveted seemed of little importance. He looked every morning at that battered old spoon which had once been the only thing he possessed and thought how fortunate he had been, how easy his life had now become. He was only fifty years old but it seemed to him as though he had already achieved something of the serenity of old age. But, though he still had friends, he was lonely at heart. He pondered often on the unassailable walls that divide every man from every other, so that no one can ever know for certain what it is like to be anyone else.

None the less, when recognition came at last, it gave him great pleasure. His memory of that morning was mixed with much else that gave him pleasure too and it was not easy to remember in what order events had come. The day had ended with an entertainment like that he had given at Belaspur for the Commander-in-Chief – but here at Hansi there were no mango groves to compare with those of the Doab. Once again he had served the youngest drummer-boy, once again there had been a *nautch*. And before that there had been the tent-pegging and shooting at the gallop, horse after horse galloping past and the men leaning over to snatch a coin from the ground or to show their mastery of sword and lance and James Skinner the Second showing he was as good as any man in the regiment. And then in the morning, after the formal part of the inspection, how splendid had been the Rahtor charge, when the whole regiment advanced in line towards the review point, first at the walk, then at the trot, then at the canter, quickening to a hand-gallop, then to a full gallop, yellow and scarlet, every man yelling, turbans flying, lances level, to pull up with a flourish, horses back on their quarters, foaming and snorting, only a dozen yards from the Commander-in-Chief!

Yet all those memories had been coloured with gold by one short scene before the parade began.

'My dear Sikandar,' Lord Combermere began, 'I can't tell you how pleased I am at the news I bring you. His Majesty has been pleased to confer on you the Order of the Bath. It's the third time you've been recommended – by Lord Lake, by Lord Hastings and by me – and of course the old objection was raised that it was impossible because you didn't hold a commission in His Majesty's Forces. They said that to John Malcolm, who was in London. "Then why doesn't he hold a commission?" said he. "Who has deserved it more? Who has done better service? Why not put two wrongs right at the same time?"

'And His Majesty agreed to that – and I'm told he was very pleased – so now you have a commission of lieutenant-colonel in His Majesty's Forces – and the Ribbon of the Bath. I shall have the great pleasure of announcing it on parade after the inspection.'

That scene too had been made even more pleasant to remember because of another. After Lord Combermere had said goodbye to the regiment, James Skinner and his son went to Calcutta to see him off and there spent four nights on board the frigate *Pallas* which was to take Combermere home. Neither had seen a warship before and they were delighted by a demonstration of the manoeuvres of which she was capable and of the power of the fire she could deploy from her guns on to a moving target. But all that pleasure was forgotten when the time came for the last farewell.

'I have long looked forward,' said Lord Combermere, 'to having the privilege of decorating you myself with the Badge and Ribbon of the Bath. But your own insignia have not arrived and since I cannot deny myself this pleasure, I propose to give you mine.'

And with those words he took off his own decoration and put the ribbon round James's neck. James tried to answer but could say nothing. He was in tears. He wrung the General's hand and fled.

## 29 He Was a King

'After the fall of Bharatpur and Lord Combermere's departure,' said James, talking over his life with Baillie Fraser, 'my fighting days were done. I always hoped that one day I might be called on again and that I might die in a charge at the head of my Yellow Boys. For a few weeks it looked as though perhaps it might happen. There was to be a war with the Afghans and I was to command a cavalry brigade – my own two regiments and Robert's old regiment. I was a Brigadier General for a few days. But the force was reduced and my brigade was broken up. Some of my men went to Kabul and did very well. I was proud of them.

'I stayed on at Hansi and saw my friends and had letters from friends. It is the great happiness of age. I had a letter from Sir John Malcolm that pleased me very much. Here it is.'

He read it again before handing it to his friend and as he read it, Sikandar saw Malcolm clearly and seemed to hear him speaking:

'You are as good an Englishman as any I know – but you are also a Rajput, half by birth and more than half by upbringing. There are great advantages in this for a leader of irregular cavalry. You armed your men yourself; you trained them, you understand their characters, you enter into their prejudices. . . . Your risaldars are men not only of character but of family; those under them are not only their military but their natural dependants. Your personal kindness and generosity have also done much to build up the excellence of your corps. It is a family, united by family spirit and affection for yourself and I have found in the districts I have known that every horseman of yours considers, whatever he has to do, that he has the reputation of Sikandar Sahib in his personal keeping.'

'That was gratifying, was it not?' said James. 'And then, I made a new friend in Lord William Bentinck. He was a man of very wide views. I went with him to visit Ranjit Singh, the Maharaja of the Sikhs. Two of my squadrons came; they were chosen from all the cavalry of India to impress the Sikhs with our quality. And then I went with Lord William on a tour of Rajputana and advised him on matters of etiquette – the proper attentions that he ought to pay to each of those Rajput princes. You know they are as jealous as – oh, there is nothing to compare them with. They are more jealous of each other than peacocks in the breeding season when there is only one hen. Lord William gave me a splendid vase with a very kind inscription; but he said the same things himself, even more kindly.'

And once again he saw Lord William shaking him by the hand and saying goodbye and remembered the words of his farewell speech:

'In a long and varied service, it has been my good fortune to make the acquaintance of many of the most distinguished officers of the armies of Europe, as well as those serving under the British flag. But I do not remember meeting anyone who engaged so general an esteem as Lieutenant-Colonel Skinner. Everyone likes and admires him. Again and again he was commended to the Supreme Government by that distinguished commander Lord Lake – and since then every single Commander-in-Chief has praised him just as highly. He has won their private friendship as well as their public respect.'

But James had not heard how the sisters of another Governor-General wrote and spoke of him. Miss Fanny Eden, the sister of Lord Auckland, said:

'Forty-two officers to dinner! And not one I have ever heard of before – except that dear, brown, delightful Colonel Skinner – and I'm sure I shan't be lucky enough to sit next him.'

And Miss Emily replied: 'He is certainly much better company than any of the white colonels I have met so far.'

Everyone liked his company. Talking over his life with him, helping to put his memories in order, Baillie Fraser reminded him of many occasions when he had invited friends to meet him at some place of interest near Delhi – by the river at the tomb of the Emperor Humayun perhaps – or beyond the tomb of Safdar Jang at the beautiful ruined buildings round the Hauz-i-Khas, the Private Lake – or near the tombs of the Lodi Sultans. The Lodi Sultans were Afghan invaders and their tombs were plain and strong like forts, good tombs for soldier kings, he thought, like great rocks in the desert. One evening in particular he remembered when he had invited his friends to join him for dinner in a spot near the lofty tower known as the Qutb Minar, and from which they could also see the vast ruined city of Tughlakabad. He had sent tents there and servants and when his guests had seen the mosque and the well and strolled among the buildings that surround the Qutb, they sat down to a lavish dinner. When the hookahs were lighted, James talked, there among his friends, of the ruins that surrounded them and the passage of time.

'He would be a strange man,' he said, 'who could wander in the countryside near Delhi without thinking of the past. Look at Tughlakabad, spread out before our eyes. When the great Emperor Tughlak built it, he meant it to be a monument that would preserve his name for ever! A whole city he planned and built. The walls surrounding it, with towers and gates and gatehouses; palaces and temples and mosques; streets of shops, streets of houses, processional ways. But a holy man prophesied that within one man's lifetime the owls and the hyenas would live within its walls and no man would come by but the wandering Gujar with his cattle. And he was right. And wherever you go near Delhi it is the same. The tombs of Kings and Emperors!'

Then their talk turned to other things and Fraser would perhaps tell them of his latest lion-hunt or a poet would recite Persian verses or a dancing girl sing to them. Or they would persuade James to tell them how Lord Lake kissed the wicked Begam Somru.

Everyone knew that she was wicked. Everyone knew that after her husband's death she had kept and managed his grant of land and his private army, defending herself by skilful changes of side so that she had survived through all the turmoil of half a century. Everyone knew about her liking for handsome young soldiers of fortune and about George Thomas and the slave-girl she had given him as a wife. Everyone knew also about another slave-girl who had roused her jealousy and whom she had first flogged and then had buried alive. And on that girl's grave while she still lived she had smoked her hookah. But Lord Lake's kiss! Only Sikandar could tell that.

The wicked Begam had lately decided that she would be a Christian, which would give her more freedom than had been possible as a Muslim. But of course that did not go so far as kissing a man in public – something quite unknown in India where the least public caress, even between husband and wife, is regarded as most improper.

'Well,' James would tell them, 'Lord Lake had won his great victory over Bourquien near Delhi. It was the decisive victory of the war with Scindia, and Lord Lake hoped that all the smaller chiefs would come over. Of course the Begam was the first to make up her mind; she was always a weather-cock to show how the wind was blowing. She started at once for Lord Lake's camp – but she was delayed and arrived in her litter after dinner, when he was still in his headquarters mess and had been drinking a good deal of wine. He was very cheerful. They had been betting on who would be the first to sign a treaty. Someone came and whispered to him and he understood that some independent chief had come and wanted to make a treaty. He didn't catch the name. No matter which, he thought, they will tell me that in the morning. Whoever it is, I must make him welcome. So out he went at once – overjoyed – eager to welcome good news – just as I remember him so often – just as when I first met him – just as when I came back with the bullocks. He came straight from the lighted tent – and there in the dark were torches and a litter and a small person advancing – whom he greeted, in the French or Hindostani fashion, with an embrace. But imagine his astonishment when he found that he held a woman in his arms! And it did not need daylight to tell him that this was a woman – how shall I put it – not unaccustomed to caresses and certainly still worthy of caresses. Oh, in those days, a delightful armful. It was Lord Lake's maxim in war to attack when he was surprised – and he acted on it now. No half measures! Since he had her in his arms – make the most of it! Not that it was a prolonged encounter. She kept her head and, having met his assault in a spirit like his own, she withdrew and turning to her escort – whose mouths and eyes were very wide open indeed – remarked: "Among the English the Commander-in-Chief is a kind of padre and this is a padre's salute to his daughter!" '

'And when they met next morning?' someone asked.

'A twinkle in the eye, I suppose, just a twinkle,' said James.

All that had been when William was alive. William Fraser became Resident in Delhi and sat where Ochterlony had once sat. Among all those friends, who came to dinner and sat talking far into the night, William was by far the closest, the one to whom James opened his heart. When William was alive, and those other friends surrounded him, his life had been full and happy.

For James as well as for most of his friends, customs were in many ways as much Mughal as European. They all smoked the hookah or hubble-bubble; most of them kept a *zanana* from which their women did not come into public without a veil. James had a Persian title from the Emperor; he was Nasir-ud-Dauleh Colonel James Skinner Bahadar, Ghālib Jang – Defender of the Realm Colonel James Skinner, the Courageous, Victorious in War. He spent some of his time dictating in Persian to a scribe, not only his memoirs, but a treatise on the castes and tribes of Hindostan, which he caused to be beautifully illustrated, another on the Princes of India, their history and customs and relative precedence, and a third on cavalry manoeuvres with a manual of rules for Skinner's Horse.

It did not disturb him now that he belonged to two worlds. He looked every morning at that battered old spoon and thought of his mother, her hands ruffling his hair, telling him to eat his rice with a spoon because he was English but never to forget that he was a Rajput too and that, for a Rajput warrior, honour came before everything and death was not important. To be an Englishman had meant for him doing things properly, setting sentries every night and inspecting them every night, keeping line in a charge and riding knee to knee, pulling up after a charge when you heard the trumpet. But discipline was no use without the Rajput virtues – dash and chivalry and utter devotion. Lord Lake had had both and Skinner's Yellow Boys had both. He thought of Shadul Khan, whom of all his risaldars he had loved best; he had had both. His eyes filled with tears; Shadul Khan was dead too.

When so many old friends were dead, it was strange that he should be alive, sitting at the breakfast table, remembering the dead, looking at his old spoon, which had once been all he possessed. Now he had two hundred villages and he had not forgotten the vow he had made long ago, when he was talking to the Raja of Uniyara. He said he would build a temple, a mosque and a church, and now he had built all three. He pictured himself, lying on his bed in the Raja's tent, talking to the Raja.

'If I live to a good age and am in comfort and have money, I will build a church for the worship of my father's God and a temple for my mother's gods, and a mosque for the God of those who follow Mohammad and have fought by my side. I swear it.'

There had been no difficulty about the mosque and the temple; he had simply chosen a site, found a holy man acceptable in the neighbourhood, given him the money and told him to build. The church had been more difficult. He had to get the permission of the civil authorities. William Fraser had helped in that of course and at last he had been given permission to build near the Kashmir Gate. He had found an architect – and the Bishop had approved the plans – and the building had begun and week by week it had gone forward till at last it was finished. And the Bishop had consecrated it as the Church of St James. The Resident and everyone who was anyone in Delhi had come to the consecration, and afterwards they had all come to his house. Later, he and three of his sons had knelt before the altar to be confirmed. He had a feeling that it was important to be committed to whatever faith you professed and that the commitment to that faith counted more with God than what faith you chose. He did not say that to the Bishop, but the Bishop perhaps guessed at something of the kind and did not press him on his theological views.

'My sons and I are Christians,' he explained to the Bishop. 'My wife – and no man had a better wife than she has been to me for thirty years – remains a Muslim.' Here there was some reticence – but the Bishop did not press him on his marital affairs either. It was at this interview that James expressed a wish that was never gratified.

'I should like,' he said, 'to be buried in my church. Would there be any objection?'

'I can see none whatever.'

'But not,' James went on earnestly, 'in a place of honour. I should like to be buried under the sill of the door, at the principal entrance, so that the feet of everyone who came to church should trample on me. I say this because I know I am the chief of sinners.'

But after his death no one paid any attention to that part of his wish.

From the day of confirmation till his death, he read the gospels every day and those who stayed with him discovered that he rose early every morning and set aside for prayer part of the early stillness before the day began.

He said little about such matters even to William. But after William's death, when Baillie Fraser came to settle William's affairs and, in the end, took his brother's place as the confidant to whom James would rehearse his memories, he fell into a way of talking aloud, almost as though to himself, on subjects that puzzled him deeply.

'I do not know why I was spared,' he would say. 'So many died! Men killed in battle! Men hanged to bring order to the countryside! Why was I preserved? When I was young and did these things, I never stopped to think. I made up my mind at once. I would make up my mind that here was something I must do. And – I do not know how often – but – oh, several times – I determined that if I could not do what I had set my heart on doing I would die. I made up my mind to die. It did not matter, one way or the other, who won some of those battles. But it would have mattered if I had run away. Do you understand? I was preserved – but I do not know why, any more than I know why I fought. Why was I preserved when so many died?

'I did not stop to think in those days. But I do think now. I think often of that time when I lay two days and a night on the battlefield among the dead. I thought I should be dead soon and I almost vowed never to fight again. But I was too tired, too weak, to make that vow. Then the Raja, the man we had been fighting, told me that it is written in the Hindu scriptures that a man must do what it is his nature to do. And there are some whose nature it is to fight. It is their task, their function. He thought I was such a man. You know that my mother was a Rajput. It is no sin for such a man to kill. I thought often of that. Perhaps it is true. That must be why I was so sure I must be a soldier. Or was it because of the stories my mother told me about Rajput warriors who vowed themselves to death?

'I have been the friend of great men, governors, the Governor-General, Commanders-in-Chief. I have made my regiment and it is famous. I have built my church, and a mosque and a temple, and here I have my farms and villages. Here I am a kind of prince. All I once wished to be. But it does not mean a great deal now. I wonder now why I was so *sure* in the past. I was the friend of Lord Lake. He too was a man whose nature it was to fight. Nothing stood in his way when his mind was made up. He sent men to die. Yet he wept when he saw the dead. It was his nature to fight, like mine.

'Sometimes I get a Brahman to read me that Hindu scripture about the prince in a chariot whom Krishna advised to fight. I never mastered the Hindi script, only the Persian writing and the English. It is not true that all religions are alike. The Hindu scriptures tell us that each man must do what is the right act for that man. They seem also sometimes to say that in the end it does not matter what you do and I find that puzzling. The Christian padres tell us it does matter very much - but they also tell us to love our enemies and none of us do that. But they all tell us - Brahman, padre, maulvi - to trust in God. And that I try to do. I know I have done much wrong. But the Christians say God will forgive me. And that I believe. He knows all and surely he will.'

In those years before the death of William, James did not spend so long with the regiment as he had done once. Young James was the adjutant and did a great deal that in the past Sikandar would have done himself. He still loved to watch the men at their exercises and talk to them about their homes; he still held every month his regimental durbar, when any man might put forward a suggestion or a grievance. But now he had other children to care for as well – nearly two hundred villages. He went to them all. There too he held court, listening to what they told him about the idleness of this official or the corruption of that, sifting out so far as he could the truth that usually underlaid these stories, hearing the disputes about division of the crop and payment of rent, remitting rent where there had been hail or drought or locusts, postponing it sometimes when there was a daughter to be married. He saw to it that they observed the customs of the village, that they cut thatching grass at the right time and were provident about the cutting down of trees, that they repaired the roads and put right the damage done by flood-water in the rains. He would sit among them by the hour, sometimes on the floor, sometimes on a bedstead under a *pipal* tree, patiently hearing all and in the end giving a decision which they would always accept.

That was when he went on tour among his villages. But at home too, at Hansi, they would come with disputes and requests and crowd round him for decisions. And wherever he was they would come for medicine and advice about health. Sometimes there would be as many as a hundred. There was an assistant surgeon, Mr Staig, and two Indian doctors, on the strength of the regiment, and since in peace there was not always a great deal for them to do, James did not hesitate to send them the worst cases among his patients from the villages. But for a great many, he prescribed simple remedies himself, knowing that often it is not so much the medicine as the doctor's assuring presence that works the cure.

It was a life in which he was constantly trying to act for the good of these people whom he felt were his children. But he could not afford to relax. The times had so recently and for so long been turbulent that there was still tension in the air. James was widely beloved – but he had restored order where there had been robber bands, he had often struck hard and quickly. He had hanged men who had left sons. He had enemies. He was never out of touch with Mangat

Das and his network of *harkaras*. He took care never to sleep in the same bed two nights running.

That was the background to the warning he gave William Fraser about the young Nawab Shams-ud-Din. The boy had been a minor when his father died and it had been some time before he had full control of his property. Fraser had been his guardian and had thought of him as almost a son. He had been fond of the boy and was sadly disappointed when, soon after he came of age, he started a law-suit with some cousins. It was a quarrel in which Fraser thought he was unjust to his cousins; furthermore, it was greedy and unnecessary. He had remonstrated with the boy and when he persisted had told his servants that the Nawab of Firozpur must be publicly turned away if he came to visit him. James advised him against this.

'It's a public rebuff; he will never forgive you.'

'But he's only a boy, James, and practically my son. I must show him that I am angry and teach him to behave properly. He has an affection for me and will be sorry when he has time to think.'

'He's of age, William, and newly come into his own. Surrounded by flatterers. He would have taken anything you said in private – but a public insult he will never forgive. It would not surprise me if he tried to murder you. You must not go about at night unguarded. You know how careful I am.'

For weeks, William Fraser had taken precautions. But it was not his nature to be careful and little by little he relaxed. One night he went to dine with the Raja of Kishangarh, riding from his house with only an armed trooper. He was shot, coming back late at night, near the gate of his house, by a man on a good horse who easily got away from the trooper.

Sikandar guessed at once who was behind the crime. He went straight from the scene of the murder to the Nawab's house in Delhi. There were tracks of a galloping horse; they pointed the wrong way – towards the crime not away – but that was an old trick. There, in the Nawab's house, he could smell the unforgettable smell of hot iron and singed hoof that means farrier's work done recently; there was the horse and there were nail-holes in its hooves where there should have been none. It was easy to see that the shoes had been turned and turned back again. He soon knew who had fired the shot. He soon learnt that the assassin and an accomplice had been at the Nawab's town house for months, waiting for a chance. Proof was not so easy. The accomplice disappeared and it became a question of who would find him first – James or the Nawab. The Nawab wanted him so that he might be put out of the way before he could tell what he knew. James wanted him so that he should tell. In the end, it was James and his *harkara* network under Mangat Das who found him first. He confessed and told the whole story. Both the man who fired the shot and the Nawab were hanged. But there was no satisfaction in that; it did not bring William Fraser back.

William was buried in the churchyard of James's new church of St James. James saw that the tomb was a fine one, in handsome white marble. He stood by it soon afterwards and said to Baillie Fraser:

'In him I have lost the best friend I ever had in this world and my friendship with the world ends with him. I only wish I were lying with him.'

He reproached himself. He had warned him – but warning was not enough.

'I ought to have fasted on his doorstep until he took my advice,' he said. 'I ought to have had the Nawab's house watched. It is too late now. Too late.'

Time softened the loss but he was alone now. Shadul Khan was dead and his old retainer Nagendra Singh; Robert was dead and now William. He was not physically alone; his family surrounded him. They were numerous and they were devoted. They cared for him and observed his least wish. But his wives were all *zanana* wives and, though he loved them with tenderness and affection, there had never been much to talk about. As for his sons and daughters, they belonged to another world than his. None of them drew directly on either the Scottish or the Rajput traditions; they took for granted the world of the country-born, of their schoolfellows and friends. The battles and sieges, the forced marches, the wary night-long adventure of following up a wounded but formidable enemy, the resolve he had made so often that he would die if he did not bring off this enterprise – all this that had stirred his blood meant nothing to them. To none of them but James the younger. He alone understood such things but even with him there remained – in the father's mind at least – the faint shadow of reproach because the boy's mother was one of those *zanana* wives, dear to him but never an equal, never a companion. They never mentioned her but talked of the farms or the regiment. There were silences between them but they were friends.

James lived five more years. He died after a short illness of only a few days in December 1841, when he was sixty-three.

When his coffin went to Delhi, with his sword and helmet laid upon it, his favourite charger led behind, and his Yellow Boys following him for the last time, there came out to see him go by so many people from the villages around and from the city of Delhi that the oldest of those then living said:

'Never was one of the Emperors of Delhi brought to his tomb with such a following as that.'

In the villages where he had been a father to his people, they spoke of him and of his life and of his justice with drawn breath.

'He was a King indeed,' they said.

They buried him in the church he had built, not, as he had wished, beneath the threshold, where everyone who entered might trample on him, but in the chancel before the altar. There he lies. One monument to his memory still stands above his burial-place. The other is the regiment he founded and that too still remembers Sikandar.

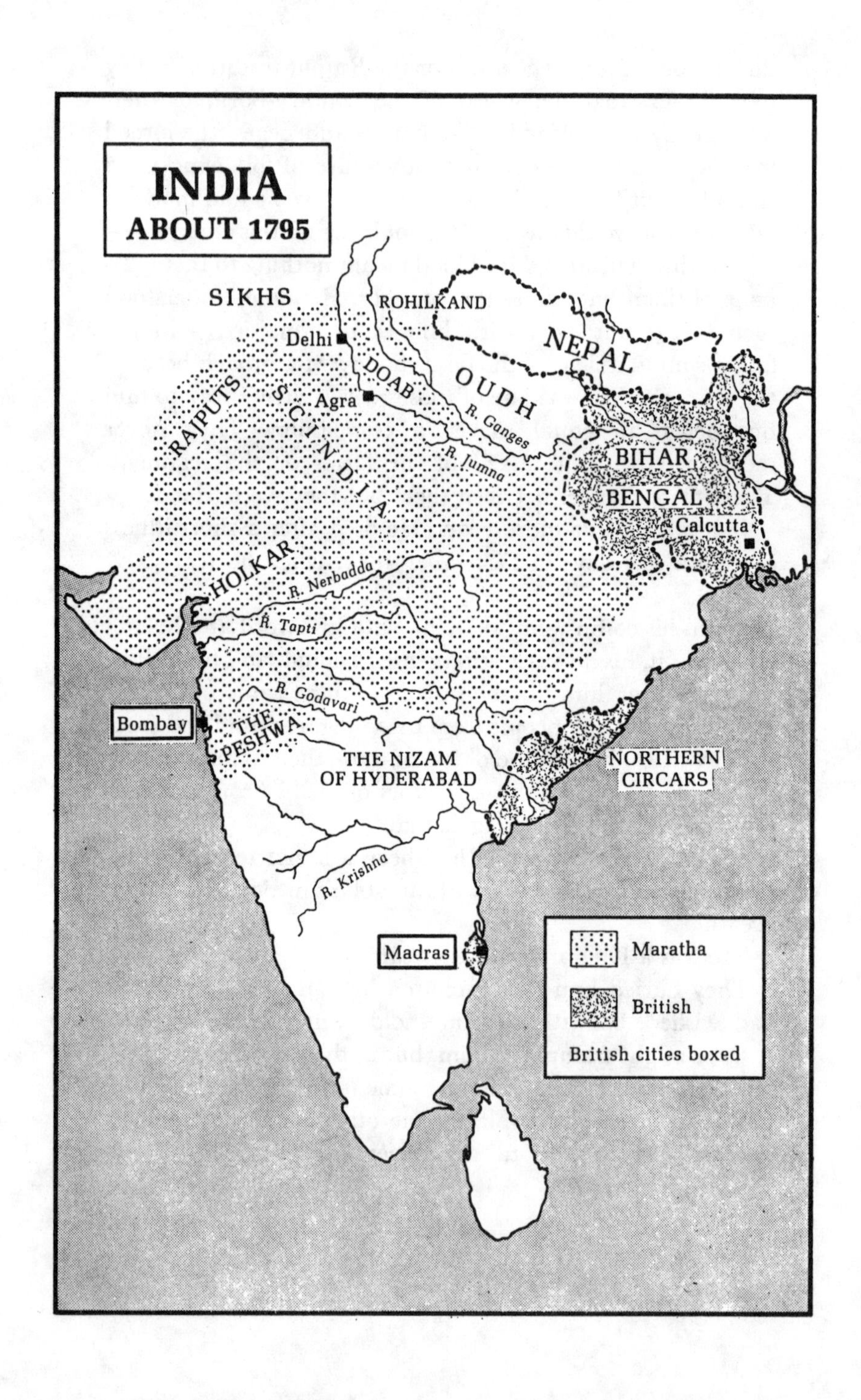
INDIA
ABOUT 1795
SIKHS
ROHILKAND
Delhi
NEPAL
DOAB
OUDH
RAJPUTS
SCINDIA
Agra
R. Ganges
R. Jumna
BIHAR
BENGAL
Calcutta
HOLKAR
R. Nerbadda
R. Tapti
R. Godavari
Bombay
THE PESHWA
THE NIZAM
OF HYDERABAD
NORTHERN
CIRCARS
R. Krishna
Madras
Maratha
British
British cities boxed

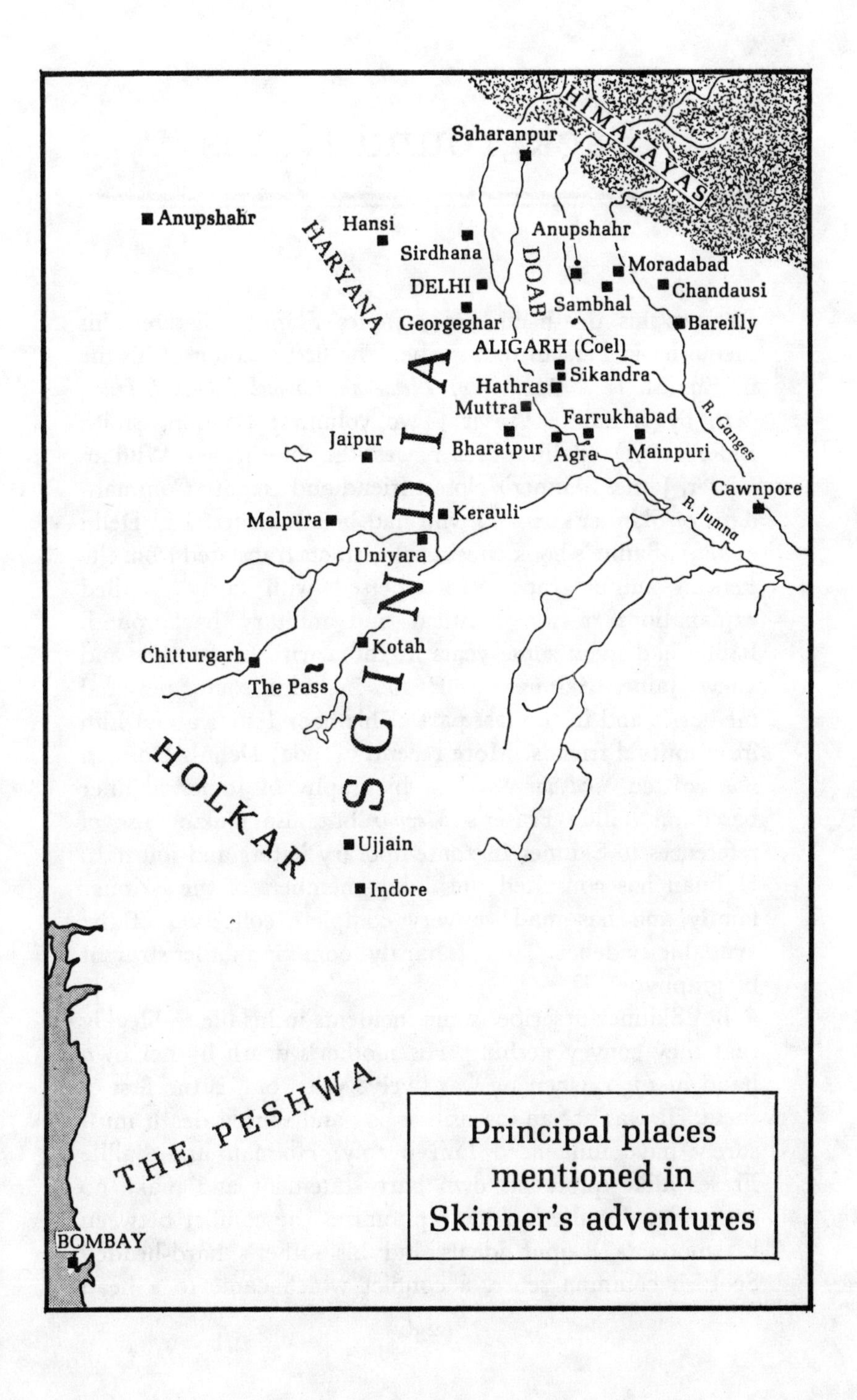


Principal places mentioned in Skinner's adventures

# Background Notes

BEFORE his death in 1841, James Skinner dictated his memories in Persian to a scribe. The first account of his life in English is *A Memoir of Lieutenant-Colonel James Skinner, C.B.* by J. Baillie Fraser (Two volumes: London, Smith Elder, 1851). Baillie Fraser was the brother of William Fraser, James Skinner's closest friend and Deputy Commandant of Skinner's Horse, who had been murdered in Delhi in 1835. Baillie's book consists of extracts translated from the Persian autobiography, interspersed with fairly detailed explanations of the political and military background. Baillie had spent some years in India with his brother and knew James Skinner well; he includes some personal memories and in the last part of his book letters about him from mutual friends. More recently (1962) Dennis Holman has written *Sikandar Sahib*, a biography of James Skinner based on Baillie Fraser's *Memoir* but also making use of references to Skinner in contemporary letters and journals. Holman has consulted the living members of the Skinner family and has made a very complete collection of the available evidence. There is hardly room for another straight biography.

But Skinner describes some incidents in his life so bleakly that they convey nothing. His mother's death by her own hand in 1790, when he was twelve years old, is the first o these. He was not an insensitive boy and such a death must surely have influenced him deeply. Holman and Baillie Fraser alike quote his own bare statement and make no comment. But the incident epitomizes the conflict between his mother's Rajput ideals and his father's hard-headed Scottish common sense, a conflict which came to a head again five years later when his father apprenticed him to a printer. His father and mother had six children and had lived together for more than fifteen years. There must have been physical attraction between them; there was kindness; but it appears, from the few hints we have, that there was not the least understanding of how the other felt. The barriers of early teaching were too strong. They belonged to different cultures.

That is to me the first point of interest in James Skinner's life. The second is the readiness of himself, and the men under his command, to die for the sake of honour, conceived as a naked, unadorned abstraction, even when the cause in which they were fighting was a bad one, as it was in the battle with the Raja of Uniyara. And surely his consciousness of belonging to two distinct peoples combined with his fantastic concept of fidelity to determine his attitude when war came between the British and the Maharaja Scindia. He wanted to stay with Scindia and would have fought the British. This was not because he was an Indian nationalist; such an idea would be an anachronism and there is not the faintest hint of it in anything he wrote or said. But he was fanatically faithful to the salt he had eaten and he was afraid of being snubbed on account of his birth by Englishmen he did not respect. Circumstances forced him to go to Lord Lake, who perceived his rare qualities and persevered in pressing him to found his regiment. Not many Commanders-in-Chief would have had the patience to persist in the face of the stubborn fidelity to Scindia which James displayed. It was personal affection for Lord Lake rather than 'patriotism' that brought him to the British side and led to the founding of his famous regiment. It was personal allegiance that he understood and for him 'patriotism' could mean little.

The need for union with something beyond the self as a means of realizing the self is perhaps universal, though often unconscious. Many men find confidence and a sense of security in identifying themselves with a church, a nation, a cause, a regiment, a college, or perhaps with another person in a happy marriage or a close friendship.

Such an identification may be a substitute for religious conviction or a personal philosophy; it may supplement and enrich such a faith. To me the evidence suggests that James Skinner – a man instant and positive in physical action – felt this need more deeply than most and, because of his dual inheritance from two cultures, found it most difficult to satisfy. From the day of his mother's death, he was always in search of some such centre for his life; again and again he was disappointed or betrayed. That seems to me the key to his behaviour and more than anything else is what makes him interesting.

None of this has come out in previous accounts. It seemed therefore worth attempting a fictional or dramatized portrait, which would attempt to reconstruct the most important episodes of his life and emphasize these points. I have followed his own account of his life in the main, simply trying to put flesh on the often very bare bones he has himself provided. Sometimes I have had to depart from his account and I have indicated this in the notes which follow. For example, the adventure of bringing in the sixty thousand bullock-loads of grain which enabled Lord Lake to march for Delhi cannot have happened exactly as he tells it. He allows no time at all for the information to travel twenty-seven miles. I had to work out how it could have been done. Where possible, I have told the story by visual pictures and conversations; this is what I mean by a fictional portrait. The conversations of course are imaginary. Some incidents are changed but nothing important and I hope I have drawn a true portrait of James Skinner's character. I have tried to simplify without falsifying the political background, which is extremely confusing and in which James Skinner was not much interested.

### Chapter One: The Dagger

Skinner does not say that his mother told him stories of Rajput chivalry and honour. But he always speaks of Rajputs with a regard which suggests that she did. The story in this chapter is to be found in Tod's *Annals and Antiquities of Rajastan*, first published in 1829.

### Chapter Four: The River

I have made a change here. James says that Captain Burn followed him up the river three weeks later. But I wanted them to get to know each other, so sent them in the same boat.

### Chapter Five: General de Boigne

There are many references to de Boigne in the memoirs of the period, and a long account in H. Compton, *European Military Adventurers of Hindustan*, Fisher Unwin: London, 1893. See also: Desmond Young, *Fountain of the Elephants*, Collins: London, 1959, a life of de Boigne.

### Chapter Eight: The Ambush

Sutherland was later re-employed by Scindia and was always Perron's enemy. But he does not come into James Skinner's story again.

### Chapter Thirteen: War with the English

There is some confusion about the order of events after the destruction of George Thomas. James Skinner says he went on leave in 1802 and after eleven months' absence returned to duty in January 1803, when he accompanied Perron to Ujjain and was present at the dramatic scene when Perron confronted five hundred Afghans. But according to Compton, in *European Military Adventurers*, the Afghan episode took place a year earlier in 1802. Compton is certainly right. James Skinner must have been confused by Perron's two resignations, one in April 1802 and one in February 1803. He must have gone on leave immediately *after* the Afghan episode. But dramatically, the order in which he remembered the events is better – a period of uncertainty followed by a vivid event which puts it in focus. I have kept the events in Skinner's order.

### Chapter Fourteen: Neither Fish nor Flesh

Carnegie and Stewart were right to fear that they might be not only distrusted but murdered. Later, when Holkar entered the war, he put to death several officers of British origin who had been entirely faithful to him.

Lord Lake: I have ennobled Lord Lake earlier than the King did for the sake of simplicity.

### Chapter Fifteen: The Thirteen Rajputs

The tale of the thirteen Rajputs is not told by Skinner in his memoirs; Baillie Fraser recounts it to illustrate Skinner's respect for Rajput traditions. It must be a story Skinner had told him over the dinner-table.

### Chapter Seventeen: A Very Near Thing

'. . . line of messengers . . .' This was called 'laying a dak'. It was an old Indian custom widely in use till the coming of the petrol engine. Ponies or tongas would be waiting at intervals of about eight miles and would gallop the whole stage.

### Chapter Twenty: The Duck Are Flying

Mangat Das. His was a romantic story but it would hold up the main action. He was the son of a young widow, a woman of the Chamars, the leather-workers and skinners, who are outside caste. His mother had been widowed more than a year when he was born, and it was rumoured that his father was a Nat, one of a tribe of wandering gipsies. This was scandalous even among Chamars and he grew up an outcast among outcasts, living on scraps of food thrown away by others. Since he was hardly a person at all, people often talked as though he were not there. He stored up this information and found he could sell it and became the regular spy for a group of robbers and burglars. They suspected him of giving news of their movements to another gang and were on the point of putting him to death when James Skinner surprised them. James recognized that he had a genius for spying and made him his own man.

James tells us nothing about the private life of his spies. But he had to trust them and, as I pondered on the relationship, I pictured someone like Mangat Das with some such story behind him.

### Chapter Twenty-two: Lord Lake is Coming

'Lord Lake's terrible dragoons' were King's troops, not Company's; that is, they were English. But I am a little puzzled by this story. Skinner's primary object was to keep Lord Lake informed about Holkar's movements. But Lake's object was to bring Holkar to battle. One would expect Skinner therefore to have orders to convey the impression that Lake was far behind. Can he have been told that the first thing was to get Holkar out of British territory? He does not say so but there would be no revenue for some time from a district where Holkar had had time to linger, so humanity may have coincided with policy.

### Chapter Twenty-three: Hired to Die

Pathans. Most of these men were not Pushtu-speaking Pathans from the Afghan frontier but the sons or grandsons of such men, now settled in Hindostan.

### Chapter Twenty-four: These Are Sad Times

'. . . Moments when every tiny thing seemed beautiful . . .' Here James is anticipating Julian Grenfell's poem 'Into Battle'. But I think he did go into battle in the same spirit as the young men of 1914.

### Chapter Twenty-nine: He Was a King

(i) The most serious departure I have made from the written evidence concerned Baillie Fraser, not Skinner. Baillie Fraser stayed with his brother William in the course of various visits to India between 1815 and 1835, during which time he also travelled extensively in Persia. He was in England when James died. But he was pressed to write a memoir of him, which he did, ten years later, on the basis of the Persian manuscript, many letters from friends, and his own memories of stories James had told him. I felt, however, that James must speak for himself in the last scenes of his life and his biographer was the best audience I could give him, so I have made Fraser stay in India longer than he did and talk over the Persian manuscript with James while he was writing it. He seems to have been in England when his brother was murdered and I have no evidence that he was in India again.

(ii) 'He was a King indeed!' This is quoted in the Dictionary of National Biography, as having been said by a villager near Hansi. (But the D.N.B. has a mistake in its Hindostani!)